Razor Burn

To order additional copies, please contact us.
BookSurge, LLC
www.booksurge.com
1-866-308-6235
orders@booksurge.com

SCOTT&SCOTT

RAZOR
BURN
A ROMENTICS NOVEL

2003

Razor Burn

ROMENTICS

A Novel Approach To Gay Romance

***

Introducing a line of romance novels written just for gay men. It's all the steamy passion, crazy excitement and gay drama you'd expect when two men fall for each other—maybe even more. And they're all written with love by Scott&Scott.

***

www.Romentics.com
Log on and fall in love with Romentics.

***

Cover design by Jamie Allison / Authors' photo by Blakely Crawford

CHAPTER 1

I think you have the wrong idea," Blayne said to the stranger.

"I just asked if I could buy you some coffee."

Blayne looked down at his full cup and back up at the blue-eyed man without stating the obvious aloud. There was something much more obvious than his brimming mug going on here.

"Well then, I guess we have some time to kill before you're ready for a refill," he said as he sat in the leather armchair across the table from Blayne. "I'm Ben."

Ben wasn't usually this forward. But he figured he may as well press his luck today. It was bound to start improving sooner or later. Trying his odds at the coffee shop in the early afternoon was a new technique he was testing since he'd been laid off.

"Look," Blayne began to be straightforward and then changed tactics, "I've got everything I need."

"Everything?" Ben crossed his legs, ran a hand through dark bangs and settled back into the worn leather. He was almost ashamed of himself for being so blatant and obnoxious. Maybe he was just sick of rejection. Unemployment will do that to a guy.

But there was something else. Ben wasn't totally indiscriminate. The man across from him was beautiful. Ben happened to be a sucker for blonde hair and brown eyes. There was something about the combination that was so much more rugged and masculine that the Arian blonde-blue cliché.

His skin looked tanner. His hair was sandier. Ben was also fond of the suit and tie, but he really wanted to see this man in a swimsuit after a few days on the beach. He could just tell the top of his hair would lighten, even his eyebrows. His skin would bronze, and he'd absolutely glow. Ben smiled at the thought. He smiled at this man.

"I'm straight," Blayne just came out and said it.

Ben didn't even blink.

"That's an odd name for this part of town," Ben had his sights set, and he wasn't about to be distracted by such a pathetic excuse.

Blayne looked around at the few lone men scattered amongst the tables and couches. He knew what part of town he was in. He knew what went on in places like this on slow afternoons. But couldn't a heterosexual man relax with cup of coffee if he wanted one? He looked down at his untouched cup and forced himself to take a sip.

This wasn't a gay bar, for crying out loud. It wasn't even sleazy. It was quaint and comfortable, and the coffee wasn't half bad. After all, most things were nice in the gay section of the city.

"My name is Blayne," he said. He kept an edge of annoyance in his voice to show he wasn't impressed by Ben's joke or his company.

"And you're straight with a name like Blayne?" Ben scoffed.

Blayne got up to leave. That was it. He wasn't going to put up with this shit all afternoon.

"I'm kidding," Ben protested, but he wasn't. There were just certain names. Come on... *Blayne?* What were his parents thinking? "Sit down and relax."

Ben reached out and tugged at the knee of Blayne's pants until he sat. He let his hand rest there just long enough to feel the heat of his thigh through the summer fabric.

Blayne glanced at the hand on his leg, fine dark hairs creeping from the wrist, long slender fingers. But he didn't say anything. Before he could, Ben took it away.

"Look, I'm starving," Ben said. "Let's get out of here and grab a bite. I know this great sandwich place down the street."

Blayne didn't respond. He just stared across at Ben's raised eyebrows—two quirked dark lines above blue eyes.

"Come on," Ben nagged, "you wouldn't let me buy you coffee. It's just a sandwich."

"I guess I should eat something quick before I head back to the office."

Ben was halfway out the door before Blayne was halfway through his sentence.

There's nothing wrong with getting lunch with this guy, Blayne told himself as he followed after him. He only glanced slightly at the snug way Ben's jeans fit as he approached from behind.

By the time Blayne caught up, he found himself walking down a nearly empty street of brick buildings warmed by midday sun. He also found himself walking next to a complete stranger for no obvious reason, or no reason he wanted to admit.

He put his hands in his pockets awkwardly and jangled his change. It was a less obvious display of masculinity than rearranging his package through a thousand-dollar suit.

"It's right down on the corner," Ben said. He obviously didn't enjoy the silence either. Blayne's tinkling coins weren't holding up their end of the conversation.

"Huh?"

"The sandwich place," Ben reminded him. "They make the best chicken pesto wrap."

"One of my favorites," Blayne tried to focus on lunch. He tried not to focus on Ben's smile or eyes or tight little tee-shirt.

"How did I know you were going to say that?" He didn't point out that anything resembling pesto was just about a gay as the name Blayne. He just turned into the next doorway and put his key into the door.

"I thought you said it was on the corner?"

"It is. This is my place," Ben opened the door and laughed at the horrified look on Blayne's face. "Don't worry. I just need to grab some more cash."

"That's all right," Blayne insisted. "I'll pay."

"I told you, I'm buying you a sandwich," Ben stood in the hall looking out at him. "Come on in. I'm not going to bite you."

Blayne walked into the narrow hall and shut the door behind him. True to his word, Ben did not bite.

He kissed him instead.

Blayne didn't know what to do. So, for the moment, he did nothing. He wasn't kissing another man. He was being kissed. There is a distinct difference, he told himself.

He felt the foreign scrape of stubble against his face. He felt Ben's hands, the long fingers of one on his waist, the other holding the back of his head. He felt soft lips and the strength of insistent desire. He felt a man's kiss, and he felt his own body respond whether his mind had made itself up or not.

Ben leaned up into their kiss. Blayne was taller and wider, but Ben didn't mind taking the upper hand. He could feel every inch of the man's bigger body through the thin, expensive material of his fancy suit. Every inch. Ben felt Blayne's immediate reaction pressing against him before the rest of that solid body budged.

Ben took that as a good sign. So he just kept kissing those scared, motionless lips. He kept holding that rigid jaw and that narrow waist, and he waited for the rest of Blayne's body to catch up with the erection that pressed against Ben's belly.

He felt Blayne's hand at the small of his back at the same moment he felt lips soften and relax. Blayne kissed him back.

Now that the hard part was over, desire picked up the pace where surrender left off. Ben wriggled out of jeans. Blayne's jacket and tie fell to the floor. The weight of his silver belt buckle brought the fancy pants to the ground as soon as it was unfastened. There were much harder parts to tackle now.

Ben stood there in white briefs looking down at this man on his bed. What to do now? He tried not to look into Blayne's nervous brown eyes. He didn't want to spook him. He didn't want to scare this gorgeous closet case away before he was done with him.

He even left him in his starched white shirt and boxers, emphasizing the exposed portions of smooth tan stomach and thighs. Ben let him have his modesty as protection. Not to mention the businessman fantasy that drove Ben crazy and made him leave Blayne's navy dress socks on as well.

Blayne avoided eye contact with Ben, too. But in doing so, he

4

was forced to look down at the rest of him: the pale skin; the thinly muscled runner's frame; the oddly attractive and isolated stripe of dark hair that drew itself from his bare chest down his flat stomach to the waistband of his briefs; the hard, diagonal line of his penis that pushed defiantly at that same band.

I can't believe you're doing this, Blayne thought to himself in the second person, as if it weren't really him, as if doubting the reality of the moment would erase this mistake. His own erection throbbed and bounced noticeably under his boxers to distract him from the thought. Ben crawled on top of him to block out any doubt completely.

Their mouths met again, and this time Blayne didn't hesitate. This time their kiss was almost familiar. He grabbed Ben's head and back. He pulled him against him. The sheer force of gravity was not enough to press the taboo weight of a man onto him.

He felt the solid rub of their erections through cloth, and an electric tickle ran up his spine to his gut. He was breaking the rules, crossing the line, sneaking over the fence into forbidden territory. The grass was greener. He was indulging himself in a way he swore he never would.

Ben ran his hands under the crisp shirt, over smooth skin and onto ample pecs. He could tell this man worked out hard, and he'd bet his unemployment check that no one ever got to enjoy the fruits of his labor. He let his thumb find a dark brown nipple and circle it lightly. He would have given it a little pinch, but he could tell this guy needed to be treated tenderly.

That's why it surprised him so much when Blayne rolled them over and pressed Ben into his own mattress. It was a soft fluid movement that never separated their lips, but it had the strength of neglected hunger behind it.

When Blayne pulled back, Ben was certain he was having second thoughts. He had reassuring words on the tip of his tongue. He placed a lightly restraining hand on the muscled mound of Blayne's shoulder. But it was all unnecessary.

Blayne dragged the tip of his own tongue down Ben's chest and found that long, dark trail. He followed it with wet, voracious kisses to the elastic edge of Ben's briefs where the bulge of his erection had oozed a darker spot of precum into the cotton.

Blayne must have been operating on instinct. His logical mind never would have allowed any of this to happen. But somewhere in his subconscious, he knew exactly what to do. He peeled back the waistband with one hand and devoured the salty sweetness at the head of Ben's cock. He felt the firm ridge against his lips and slid that long shaft in and out of his mouth slowly, savoring each inch.

Blayne worked up and down firmly, burying his nose at the musky base and lingering with his lips and the tip of his tongue at the top. He was taking his time. He was obviously enjoying himself. And he was driving Ben crazy.

Ben wasn't a braggart, and he wasn't going to break any records, but he also knew that he wasn't lacking at all in the size department. He was a bit surprised at how Blayne took over and submitted so readily. He was even more impressed at how he took the entire length in long slow swallows. It was hard to believe that this guy hadn't done this before. Right this second, Ben didn't give a shit one way or the other.

Blayne's fingers moved up Ben's stomach as his mouth increased its pace. His thumb and forefinger traced that thick line of fur up and down the median of Ben's abdomen in rhythm with the motion of his mouth.

Ben looked down, and he could see that Blayne's eyes were closed in rapt concentration. He watched the length of his own cock disappear again and again into Blayne's warm mouth. He saw the wrinkles they had worked into the starched dress shirt around its collar, and he could feel the shaft of Blayne's cock pressed against his calf.

It was more than he could take. Ben's thighs tensed, and his stomach tightened. If this poor straight guy didn't know the signs, it was his own damn fault. He shouldn't give such great head.

In that breathless moment, pleasure didn't leave any room for regret or second thoughts. Ben didn't really think about what he was doing to this guy or what would happen afterwards. Blayne didn't think about work or guilt or denial.

And then Ben came. He came in one long shuddering breath as he heard Blayne's own gasping breath echo from his newly emptied mouth.

For one orgasmic moment, Ben thought Blayne had surrendered the lip-lock on his cock to avoid the surprising mouthful. But then Ben realized Blayne's breathless, gaping mouth was a symptom of his own climax.

Halfway through his quivering, Ben felt the warm, wet burst of Blayne's orgasm spill through boxers and against his leg. He felt his own wetness land on his stomach and chest in warm strands.

Then things changed. Of course. Ben knew they would. He just hadn't let himself think about it before now. He knew he was going to have to break the silence with breath. He knew they were both going to have to open their eyes and untangle themselves.

But it had been worth it. He reminded himself of that before he opened his eyes to face the awkward music of the moment.

At least he thought it had been worth it. Blayne was off the bed as it were on fire. He was buckling his pants over his stained boxers. Ben knew that wet spot must be the most uncomfortable feeling imaginable. But then again, the expression on Blayne's face looked even more uncomfortable.

Ben decided against politely offering him a dry pair of underwear. It would only emphasize the fact that this 'straight' guy had blown his load giving head.

"You don't have to go, you know," it was a stupid thing for Ben to say. It was the middle of the afternoon, not the middle of the night. And by the way Blayne was focusing on his belt buckle and the buttons on his shirts, it was obvious he couldn't get fastened and out of there fast enough. Ben figured grabbing that sandwich was out of the question now.

Blayne was looking for his tie. It was in the hall, and he stepped uneasily back into the bedroom as he tried to knot it.

"I have to get back to work," he looked at his watch halfway through his half-Windsor. The knot fell apart. "I can't believe how late it is."

"Well, I guess unemployment makes my day a little more leisurely," he was trying to lighten the mood. But it was a little late for ice-breakers at this point.

Blayne didn't answer. He tied his tie and tucked the uneven ends under his jacket. Ben guessed that the disheveled look was very unlike him. Despite his apparent expertise, this couldn't be something Blayne did every day.

"Well, thanks," Ben said. He knew it was trite, but what the hell was he supposed to say? "I had a great time."

Damn, it sounded like a first date in junior high. Ben could actually see Blayne's jaw clench from where he propped himself on the bed.

"Look," Blayne said—if he said he was straight again, Ben was going to smack him—"I'm married."

The look on Ben's face must have rivaled the embarrassment on Blayne's. He was shocked and horrified and caught completely off guard.

He was supposed to have the upper hand here. He was out of the closet. He was gay. He was comfortable with himself and blowjobs and everything else that came with the territory. He was not comfortable with married men who gave head.

"You're full of shit," he said.

"No. I'm married."

Blayne stood there fully dressed and obviously ready to leave. And Ben sat there completely naked. But that's not what made him feel so vulnerable. He swung his legs over the edge of the bed and pulled the sheet over his lap.

He was too angry to speak. He couldn't think of a single thing that would piss him off more. There weren't many things Ben wasn't willing to try once or twice, but this was one he'd sworn he'd never do. He knew some guys really got off on sneaking around with married men as if they were sexier for leading a confirmed hetero astray. But Ben wasn't so impressed by their confirmation.

All he could think about was the poor clueless wife and kids sitting down to the dinner table and wondering why daddy was late again. It wasn't fair to the innocent and unknowing participants. It sure as hell wasn't sexy to betray a family he didn't even know. Right now Ben just felt used. He hadn't known he was committing any betrayal. He was an unknowing participant as well.

"It's pieces of shit like you," Ben spoke slowly through his anger, "who give gay guys and straight guys and married guys and every fucking guy on the planet a bad name."

Blayne actually looked relieved by Ben's anger. He almost looked smug. He stood there in his power suit and seemed to relish the power shift. The focus was no longer on his shame. This guy had crossed his own lines, broken his own rules. And for the moment, Blayne was glad to be able to share his guilt.

"I suppose picking strangers up in coffee shops earns a lot of respect for mankind?" Blayne just had to rub it in. He'd feel just as bad about the whole thing later, but right this second it took a little of the weight off his chest where it pressed heavy and painful.

And there was another reason, almost an instinct, a business sense. If he stood there and acted like a complete asshole, it made things less personal. No one would like him. They may not even respect him. But business was business. And the more this exchange seemed like an awkward board meeting, the better.

"Get out of my apartment and back into your closet," Ben yelled toward the door, "It must get awfully crowded with the wife in there, too."

Blayne gritted his teeth and took the jab like a man. A few moments ago there was nothing he wanted more than to get out of that cramped apartment and away from the summer stench of men and sweat. But now he hesitated. He couldn't let Ben win. He couldn't let him have the last word.

"If you're so fired up and full of energy, why don't you get off your ass, stop picking up married men and go find a job?" Being unemployed was not as shocking as being married, but Blayne used the material he had.

"If I'm not mistaken, I think you just gave me a job."

That was it. Blayne wasn't putting up with anymore of this. He'd have to cut his losses and hope to God he never saw this guy again. He moved one foot out into the hall to leave. Then he paused.

There was something in his competitive nature that wouldn't let him lose. And there was something in Ben's voice that said Blayne could still win. Ben was ashamed. He was scared. He was just as guilty and angry and embarrassed by his actions as Blayne was. Even if their paths happened to cross again, there was no way he would make trouble for Blayne.

So for all those reasons, and maybe a few he couldn't justify, Blayne decided to press his luck. He decided to tempt fate.

"Well if you decide you want a job with a few less benefits, why don't you send me your resume," Blayne could tell Ben thought he was joking. "My father happens to own Mandatory."

"Oh, a men's cosmetic company, how fitting. Which blush do you prefer?"

"Personal care line," Blayne corrected, "and I bet ten bucks you have at least one of our products in your medicine cabinet, shaving cream, deodorant…"

"Of course I do. I'm gay, remember?"

"I'm trying to forget."

Blayne left. He left his words hanging in the air and left Ben sitting there on the bed. He hadn't exactly lost or won. And he certainly couldn't forget.

Ben didn't move. He listened to the door slam and waited for the moment to retreat into his memory just as Blayne retreated back to the lie that was his life. There went one more thing Ben wished he could forget. But he knew he wouldn't be able to.

With all the things he had forgotten in the past, why was he left with these unwanted memories?

Ben ran his finger over the diagonal scar that cut through his left eyebrow. He didn't mind it really. It looked rough and tough.

It was the bad-boy element that offset his thin frame and sharp features.

It never seemed fair that he was stuck with all this pain and useless information: grocery lists; deaths; sitcom plots; an afternoon like this. It didn't seem fair that his wounded mind would hold on to all this when there was a giant hole in his memory that let important parts of his past leak out.

CHAPTER 2

Tires squealed. Glass shattered. A thousand sounds of metal and machinery rolled together like screams and punches and fingernails on chalkboards. The world was upside-down and dark and red. Then everything, every sight and sound, turned black.

The phone rang.

Somehow Ben had fallen asleep in the afternoon heat. He had let his anger and the exhaustion of his orgasm drag him down into those sheets where Blayne had left him. Ben could still smell him there. The scent clung there like the dream.

The phone rang again.

It was the same dream Ben always had. The accident. A flashback. His therapist was not impressed. She said it probably was not a real memory at all. A recreation, she called it, an interpretation of known facts. Supposedly his mind was just filling in the blank spots left by the amnesia.

The phone rang. Ben grabbed it before the answering machine did.

"Hi, Em."

It was that time of day again. Ben could tell from the way the sun was shining along the horizon outside his window.

"Of course I'm here," he said into the receiver, "I was just napping. Rough day. I think you'd better come over here for this one."

He hung up and wiped at his lazy face.

Blank spots. Whatever. There were a lot of things during those lost months that Ben wished he could remember or even recreate.

He wished his mind would invent some nice memories of spring break or a couple wild orgies.

Senior year was foggy. The last semester was completely gone. Just a dark spot as if the film ran out and someone forgot to change the reels for a while. Intermission lasted a little too long for his taste.

But what was there to remember, really? That's what he asked himself. But any answer he could imagine never satisfied him.

A few drunken parties? A few boring classes? He'd spent graduation in the hospital, or so he'd been told. He had also been told that those drunken parties had everything to do with the accident that put him there.

Aside from drinking and driving, he must have accomplished something during those dark months. He'd done well enough to get a diploma. It had arrived in the mail just a few weeks after Ben had been sent home. He'd been shipped back before he even knew what was happening. Obviously, scandal warranted faster delivery than good grades.

Opening his diploma was one of the first new memories Ben had. When his mind started recording memories again, he had found himself back at home with his booze-bag father and a weekly therapy session compliments of, and prescribed by, the good ol' alma mater.

Living with Pete Abrahms was therapy enough. Ben couldn't remember what he had to drink that night or why he had gotten in a car, but having his father's alcoholism rubbed in his face certainly reminded Ben not to do it again.

He hadn't even seen his father since his mother's funeral after his freshman year. Her cancer and life insurance seemed to be a good enough excuse for Pete to quit his day job and make a career out of drinking beer. It also seemed to be reason enough for Ben to wait until liver disease and his father's own funeral brought them together again.

So that dank little apartment, with the sound of sportscasters and the stink of stale hops floating through it, was the last place Ben expected to wake up. After he did, he grabbed his diploma, threw together a resume and took the first job he could find.

When Ben told his father he was leaving, Pete asked him to pick up a case of beer on the way back. Ben was fairly confident he managed to find one on his own.

Ben shook off the last of the dream and grabbed a pair of sweatpants from a pile in the corner. He found his tee-shirt on the floor of the hall and tugged it on as he headed for the kitchen.

He tried not to think about how the shirt had ended up there. He put a pot of coffee on and tried to force the thought out of his head. He knew it was pointless. Aside from the obvious gap that started near his scarred eyebrow and reached deep inside his mind, Ben actually had an excellent memory.

Coffee spattered into the pot, and Ben tried to smooth the rooster tails of his nap out of his dark hair. Emily would be here any minute, and he wanted a chance to ease her into the conversation before the inevitable breakdown and tongue lashing. It didn't need to be obvious immediately that he had spent the afternoon rolling around in bed—by himself or with a gorgeous, closeted, married freak of a man.

The tiny living room was sunny at this time of day. And with the windows open and his lack of curtains, Ben could almost pretend his apartment was nice enough to have a porch. So he sat with a magazine and prepared himself to look nonchalant when Emily arrived.

In fact, his apartment was not nice enough to have a porch. But it was neat and small and only blocks from work. Well, his previous place of employment, as the saying went. And that's where Emily was coming from.

She'd survived the layoffs. She'd managed to keep her job and her relationship with Ben. Good graphic designers and fag hags were harder to come by than mediocre creative guys and plain old fags.

He focused on the running magazine. Even the sweaty torsos weren't enough to distract Ben from his anxious thoughts. He kept thinking that if only these men were a little better looking, they'd look like Blayne. Then the buzzer rang.

Ben didn't need to get up. This was part of their routine. She'd just let herself in. He rearranged himself into some position of false contentment and furrowed his brow as he peered down at an article about protein shakes.

The door buzzed again.

Ben had barely turned the lock before Emily busted into the apartment.

"Holy mother of God, what took you so long?" she asked as she breezed by him and headed down the hall. "You never lock the door when you're home."

It was true, but Ben wasn't about to explain the situation. He just smiled to himself and watched the Emily's ponytail bob into the kitchen. Blayne was so neat and controlled that he'd actually locked the door on his way out, despite his temper tantrum. Someone needed to loosen that guy up. Ben smiled to himself again at the thought.

"I smell coffee," she shouted from the other room, "I'm guessing this is a sit-at-home-and-whine conversation instead of a friendly beer at the pub talk. Too bad, I could use a beer after a day like this. You are one lucky bastard to get laid off."

"Hello, Emily," he said. He figured he should stop her before she went and had an entire conversation all by herself.

"Hi," she poked her head around the kitchen door and smiled.

Emily was not your typical fag hag. She didn't wear make-up or like to go shopping. However, there was no question that she was a beautiful girl, tall and thin with her pale features poking into the hall as she peered at Ben. But it was just as obvious that she'd rather have a beer out of the bottle than get her hair done.

Ben had been trying to train her properly for years, but she was a stubborn one. She'd follow him to clubs and listen to his troubles. She was wonderful company for misery. However, she was absolutely no help in picking up men.

People often mistook their slender builds and dark hair

as family resemblance, but even that trick didn't work to his advantage.

"Are you two sisters?" a guy asked at a club once.

Emily had just looked up with her eyebrows cocked and said, "Are you asking if I'm a drag queen, mister? Because it's obvious my tits aren't nearly big enough."

That about summed up the situation. Not that Ben had wanted to meet a man who referred to him as a 'sister,' but no man stood a chance with Emily. That went for her own love life as well, but she didn't seem to give a shit.

"Hey, are you going to join the world of the living, or the awake?" she called down the hall to Ben. "Have you been dressed like that all day?"

She had meant it as a simple insult. But then she saw the blush rise into his face, and there was no need for Ben to answer. He just followed her into the living room as she set two cups of coffee down.

Ben tried to force the blush from his cheeks, but the color held tight to that damn pale skin. He tried to look as if he wasn't embarrassed, as if he hadn't been caught red handed and red faced.

So he sat down and crinkled the running magazine loudly under his sweatpants. Emily just smiled smugly and waited for him to fish the crushed pages out.

"So you got laid," she stated the obvious, "So what's the big deal? I mean, it's rare, but it's not a friggin' miracle."

Emily crossed her long legs, sipped her coffee and batted her long eyelashes. It was as close to feminine and demure as she came, if she weren't being such a bitch.

"He's married," Ben came right out with it.

Now it was his turn to catch her off guard. She uncrossed her legs and opened her eyes wide.

"What the fuck?" So much for demure.

"That's just about how I reacted," Ben answered.

"So why didn't you toss his cheating ass out?"

"He was already on his way," he explained. "That bit of information came a little after we did."

"Charming," she leaned back in her chair. Vulgarity was a bit more comfortable for her. She slurped at her mug and shook her head in confusion or disapproval or dizzy surprise.

"Until then I just thought he was straight."

"Oh, well that explains it then." Emily just waited. She wasn't a big one on lecturing, but if that's what she was here for she wanted to make sure she had as much ammunition as possible.

"I should have known better," Ben mused.

"Well thanks for pointing out the moral of the story for me," she snapped sarcastically, waiting for more.

"There was just something about him." Ben stared off.

"What, he had a nice smile or really pretty eyes or a dick? Something irresistible like that?" she scolded more than she asked. This was why Ben wanted her here. He wanted misery and punishment. It was a sick relationship, really. But Emily didn't mind playing the dominatrix to a gay man. "I'll tell you what it was about him. He's a freak. He probably goes to the opera and has a hatchet collection. You sure know how to pick 'em."

Ben didn't seem to appreciate her act. He didn't seem to notice at all. The nervous lines of Blayne's face floated into his memory. That image overshadowed Emily's best bitchy scowl. It was quite impressive really. Her eyebrows were raised instead of knitted low along her forehead, but the expression seemed even more judgmental and disapproving. She played her part well.

"So," she tried to snap him back to the present, "now you're the other woman."

"Shut up, Em," he glared back at her and returned to reality .

"I'm sorry," she feigned dramatically, one hand to her chest like a apologetic maiden. "This all sounds lovely. Really promising. Can't wait for the wedding... or divorce... or whatever. Did you get his number? Maybe you and the missus can trade recipes... or sex tips. Although I doubt he gives the little wife head."

"What?" Ben shrieked. Then he blushed again. "How the hell did you know?"

"I didn't for sure," she said, "but all men have that same expression when they get blown."

"Really?" Ben laughed. He couldn't wait to hear this one. And he was more than happy to have the spotlight taken over by Emily's sex theories, even if they were based on his own most recent sexploits.

"Yup, gay, straight, it doesn't matter," she rearranged herself in her seat authoritatively. "It's this triumphant, indignant, smug little bratty grin, like a kid who got his way."

"Oh, you mean like the look women have when they get jewelry?"

"Exactly," she said, "So how was Mr. Twenty-four-carat ?"

"Disturbingly talented. One might even say polished."

They laughed, and the sun crept along the hardwood floor as they sipped coffee that was a little too warm for the summer evening. Ben had ingested far too much caffeine today.

"So, is there going to be a second date? Or is this forgive and forget?"

"Easier said than done," Ben answered.

He stared off again, as if he was trying to hold onto the memory of Blayne's face and the shape of his body. He was being overly dramatic, he knew. But screw it, he was gay, and he was entitled to such indulgences. And there was just something about that guy, something more than his hot mouth and his annoying marital status. Forgetting just wasn't an option.

"Well then, resent and pretend it never happened," Emily filled in the pause. "That usually works for me.

Her mug was empty, and she was tapping the one long fingernail she had against the hollow ceramic. She stopped to tuck a stray, dark strand behind her ear. She didn't like the way Ben gazed off like that. She couldn't help wonder if it had something to do with head trauma and his car accident. More than that though, she hated to see him hurt, even in some small way by some mindless jerk.

"Men suck," she said.

"Only the good ones," Ben answered.

It wasn't a new joke or a new response. She wouldn't even have spoken it aloud if Ben hadn't seemed so distracted. She just wanted to reengage him in the conversation. But it didn't seem to be working.

"We could stalk him," she suggested. She was only kind of kidding. It was a valid option, and it could sure spice up the summer. "Where's he hang out?"

"Mandatory."

"What?" she asked. Out of context the word didn't make much sense. Was stalking this guy mandatory? Was Ben completely off his rocker? "You mean the company?"

"Yeah," Ben answered and finally looked back to meet her eye. "In fact, his father owns it."

"Really?"

"The prick actually told me to send him a resume."

"Really?" This time the word was high-pitched and longer. It suddenly had too many syllables.

"Really," Ben said flatly as he looked at the way Emily's eyebrow lifted in a much more curious way. "Don't get any smart ideas, missy."

"A resume," she pondered aloud. "You were that good, huh?"

"Whatever. So he's rich and successful and rubbing my unemployment in my face, not to mention his matrimony." Ben tapped his foot anxiously and put down his half-full cup. He'd really had way too much caffeine or he was simply annoyed beyond belief.

"Sounds to me like he's calling your bluff."

"What are you talking about?" Ben looked suspicious. "Don't give me that look. The last thing I need is for you to complicate this disaster. I am not sending that man my resume."

"If you don't, I will," she threatened defiantly. "And I'll send him mine, too. Mandatory is a great company, Ben. I'd love to work there. Their package design alone is better than any stupid ad I'm going to be able to design at the agency."

"Emily, this is not about the fucking company, and you know it," Ben said. He sat back and pulled at his sweatpants absently. He just couldn't get comfortable. And Emily just couldn't wipe that smile from her face or the scheme from her mind. Ben could see the twisted ideas forming behind her eyes. "I don't even want a job. I'd planned on taking the summer off, living on unemployment and being the laziest fag in town. And that's saying a lot. If there are any interviews in my futures, they're going to be the one I hold right there in my bed for Mr. Right."

"Yeah, well just imagine the look on Mr. Wrong's face when he opens your resume," Emily encouraged. "That thought alone is worth it."

"He doesn't even deserve that much effort," he argued, but he didn't really sound all that resolute in his position.

"Not only does he deserve it," she smiled, "he wants it."

This time, Ben didn't answer. He didn't argue. Emily could see the temptation reflected back at her in Ben's blue eyes.

"What the hell is his name anyway?" she asked.

"Blayne," Ben snorted.

He didn't have to explain the humor to Emily. She knew. And they howled in laughter together. It was almost agreement, a handshake to seal the deal, and they were still laughing about it when they addressed the envelope.

Blayne. No last name.

Emily left after dark with the letter safely in her clutches. She wasn't going to let Ben change his mind and ruin all her fun.

CHAPTER 3

What a view. At least that's what people always told him when they came into his office. Blayne didn't really pay attention. For the most part, he sat with his back to the two glass walls of his corner office. He had enough to look at right there on his desk.

He didn't need to gaze out of the temperature-controlled office tower onto the city that he never really took part in. He was a stranger to all those streets and buildings out there.

The metaphor was too trite for consideration. He was trapped in the glass tower. How very Rapunzel. But Blayne was too busy and business-minded to entertain such flamboyant fantasies.

He picked up another folder of first-quarter sales figures and ignored the sunrise behind him. Long days start early.

They started even earlier when he couldn't keep his mind focused on that facts and stats in front of him. It was very unlike Blayne, but for days he had been unable to concentrate as completely as usual.

Getting lost in his work was the norm for Blayne. It kept his mind off... well, he didn't have to think about those things. That was the point.

But it was different now, and he knew damn well why. But he squinted at the numbers anyway. It was stupid to let himself feel guilty about something he couldn't change. It was done and over, in the past. It didn't change a thing.

It didn't matter what he thought about when he jerked off. It didn't matter what caught his eye in the gym or the locker room or the shower. It didn't matter that he had allowed a brief lapse in judgement with some smart-ass he was never going to see again.

He remembered the crooked expressions Ben made with his eyebrows, his deep blue eyes. He remembered the line of hair along that tight stomach that heaved and clenched right in front of his eyes as he...

He looked back down at rows of numbers. Men definitely used more deodorant in the spring. Sales were up. It was getting hotter. And Blayne wasn't going to be able to loosen his tie for another twelve hours.

Fortunately by nine the phone was ringing and he was several pages deep into a dense analysis of market trends and projections for the next cycle. He opened a fresh chart on his computer and started filling in the blank spots.

Everything was complicated by last year's economy, this year's buying trends, the introduction of a new line of products, competitive spending, and the sweaty thoughts that still managed to creep into Blayne's mind from time to time.

But if anything could help him avoid the fruitless cycle of fantasy and guilt, it was going to be work. And there was plenty of it piled right there on his desk to distance him from that coffee shop and that man.

And Blayne loved his work. He had built his life around this business. Not that he'd had much choice. It was his father's company, after all.

But Blayne could have played the spoiled rich kid without learning a thing about statistics. He was sure many sons could have fulfilled the role much better than himself. He could have bought expensive cars and taken elaborate 'business trips.' He could have become a loafer figurehead for some invented segment of Daddy's company— 'entertainment' or 'internal promotions' perhaps.

But Blayne did a much better job playing the successful business man. Because that's what he was. He loved fitting the fractions and percentages into those neat rows of numbers that made sense to so few people.

Of course, marketing wasn't accounting. It took more than

math. It took intuition and understanding to make sense of it all. It added logic and reason to the equation.

And Blayne knew for a fact that there was nothing logical or reasonable about feeling guilty now. Hindsight didn't do much good unless he was using it to make sure next year's figures compensated for last year's mistakes. And Blayne had no intention of repeating any mistakes, professional or personal.

"Just when you thought you were getting ahead."

Blayne jumped at the voice that came from his office door. The man standing there was nearly obscured by the piles of binders and envelopes he carried. They must have muffled his words too, because Blayne could have sworn he said 'getting head.'

"Good morning, Todd," Blayne said to the skinny redhead. "Just put them down anywhere."

"You know, when Garret said he wanted the new product launch in time for the holidays, he meant Christmas, not Labor Day, Blayne." Todd refilled the empty spot Blayne had created on his desk and plopped himself down in the large office's one other chair.

The chair was straight and metal and uncomfortable. Blayne didn't encourage anyone to hang around and distract him, but he didn't mind Todd's presence. And Todd didn't seem to mind the thin padding and sharp angles of the chair. They matched his gangly form and disheveled attire.

Todd's clothes never seemed to lose all their wrinkles, and his swatch of bright hair could never quite lie flat against his head. His tie was too thin for this decade and his smile was too wide for this business. He was the exact opposite of Blayne—scrawny and goofy and always on the edge of a punch line. And that dramatic difference was probably why Blayne liked him.

Blayne swiveled around to face Todd. He smoothed his charcoal suit. He tucked his yellow tie. He even ran a hand through his blonde pile of neatly tousled hair. Facing Todd was like looking into a funhouse mirror, or a reflection of every grooming taboo there was.

"Well, I'm sure Garret will find plenty more work for us all,"

Blayne answered, "and find plenty of things wrong with what I've already done."

Blayne didn't think twice about referring to his own father by first name. No one ever pointed it out. No one ever corrected him. People didn't make a habit of making complaints or suggestions when it came to Garret Brandon.

Todd laughed silently with his mouth wide open. Blayne could never tell if this was an intrinsic trait or a survival technique Todd had developed at Mandatory. He adapted well to his environment. No matter how he stood out, Todd was a hard worker and he valued his job.

In fact, no one could exactly remember what Todd's job title was or why he had been hired originally. He had assumed so many responsibilities and filled so many gaps, no one ever bothered to ask what exactly he did. But Todd knew every assignment, phone call and piece of mail that came through Mandatory. He knew people's schedules and pet peeves, and he knew when they weren't doing their jobs. He was somewhere between an assistant and a manager, but a little bit more than either. Filling gaps kept things from falling through the cracks.

"Speaking of work," Todd started in a way that was part business and part comedic transition, "Jeanette called the other day while you were out."

Blayne looked up at Todd sharply. The mingled expression of surprise and worry wasn't the kind of reaction most men had when their wives called. But then again, most men weren't married to Jeanette.

"She called for me?" Blayne didn't know how else to respond.

"She wanted to schedule a brainstorming session," Todd raised an orange eyebrow, "So I guess 'brainstorming' is almost like thinking of you."

"Right," Blayne thought aloud. It was about work. That made more sense. It also made it easier to think of her as a coworker. "That's always difficult with the time difference."

"Yeah, but it must be easier having the ol' ball and chain across the Atlantic," Todd laughed silently. "That way you get a longer chain."

Todd tapped a pen against a pad that had appeared from his breast pocket. Blayne had missed the humor in his joke and in the nerdy little pad that always jutted its spiral spine out of Todd's skinny chest. Todd was a funny guy. But suddenly Blayne just wasn't in the mood.

"By the way," Todd continued, "She was not happy to miss you. In fact, she wouldn't believe me when I told her you weren't in. She insisted you only left the office for meetings. There wasn't a meeting, was there?"

Todd flipped a few pages in his pad. He scowled at the possibility that he'd missed something.

"No," Blayne said it too fast. He'd remembered too fast. He'd just made the connection, and he'd made a huge mistake.

Todd just looked relieved.

"Well, good," Todd stood to leave now that he was reminded of all the things that could go wrong if he didn't pay attention. But before he left, he pointed a pale finger at the pile on Blayne's desk, "Estimates from R and D. Sales from the Midwest. Mail with the junk weeded out. There was just that one letter on top I couldn't decipher, so I left it in there."

Todd hustled out the door before Blayne even looked up to acknowledge his departure.

There hadn't been a meeting. Not that kind of meeting anyway. It had been the middle of the day. What the hell was he thinking? How many people had stopped by his empty office that afternoon? How many people had called?

Todd noticed. Even his wife had noticed all the way from London. And if they knew, his father knew. Nothing went on in this company without Garret Brandon knowing about it. And nothing went on in Blayne Brandon's life without Garret Brandon knowing about it. No matter how Blayne tried to forget it, Mandatory was Garret's first baby but not his only one.

Idiot.

Blayne's regret turned almost immediately to anger. He was angry with his father and his wife and himself. How could he have allowed himself to be so stupid? That wasn't like him at all. He was smart and levelheaded and married. He wasn't...

He spun around in his chair and slammed a silent fist onto the paperwork covering his desk. He was even mad at Ben. He was mad at his smug little smile and his snide comments. He was mad at the how Ben had flirted and tempted and tricked him into bed. He was mad at the way those blue eyes burned into his memory and wouldn't leave his thoughts.

Blayne looked down at his desk and the fresh pile Todd has just delivered. On top, there was a yellow note stuck to a piece of paper.

"You asked for it," was written across the note.

Underneath was Ben's resume.

***

The weather changed, but that was about it. The following day was gray and bleak, but at least the weather outside matched the somber mood inside Blayne's glass walls. Paperwork still covered his desk. Deadlines still loomed. He was still in the office before everyone else, including the sun.

Ben's resume still sat on top of a pile of folders.

Blayne kept staring over at it, his hands idling above the keyboard unproductively. It was as if he was trying to catch someone's eye from across the room. His head faced straight ahead at the glaring monitor, but his attention kept darting to the corner of his eye and catching sight of that little yellow note stuck to the neatly typed resume.

With every glance, he became alternately angry and guilty and confused and curious.

He looked at the large sloping letters—"You asked for it"—he wondered if it was a threat or a joke. He wondered if that was the way Ben's handwriting always looked. Did he write every casual letter and formal application is such bold script? Was his penmanship always as boisterous as loud laughter? Or was this a special design for the occasion, a funny postscript, an inside joke?

Blayne looked back to the charts on his computer. He was being ridiculous. There was no inside joke. There was no special communication. There was just one big mistake, and that was the only reason Blayne kept fixating on it.

He was only thinking about it, about Ben, because it was such a stupid thing to do. He was only keeping that resume around as a reminder of his oversight. It was like a scar that reminded you running with scissors was dangerous. You should have known it before, but now you really believed it. Stupid. Never again.

It was regret, plain and simple. Nothing else.

He looked at the note again, this time with contempt. Of course his handwriting looked like that. It figured. Obnoxious and pushy. This guy just wouldn't give up. Just like the way he had approached Blayne in the coffee shop, with arrogance and smart-ass remarks.

If Ben thought he was going to get his way again, he was sorely mistaken. If he thought he was going to be able to intimidate Blayne with a sheet of paper and a sticky note, he took Blayne for an even bigger fool than he had proven himself to be the other day. There was no way in hell Blayne was going to put up with this.

"Blayne."

Blayne looked up at Garret Brandon and away from that resume as quickly as possible. He really had to stop being so jumpy. His nerves were ragged.

"Good morning," Blayne regained a little composure, "I thought you were in Dallas."

"I was," Garret said, never sitting, standing straight and authoritatively over his son. "In and out meeting. Got to stay on top of things. Back this morning on the red-eye."

Garret Brandon couldn't have looked less like someone who had just spent the wee hours on a plane. He was crisp and clean from head to toe. He looked just like the owner of a men's personal care company should. He was all starch and polish, with crisp dark lines and a tightly knotted tie. Even his temples were grayed to

29

perfection, like the steel of his eyes. This man was meant to be a successful and shrewd businessman. He was born to be a boss.

"Got to stay on top of things," Garret repeated. He wasn't one to waste time repeating himself for no reason. Blayne got the point. "Speaking of, how are those projections coming?"

"Coming?" Blayne asked curiously, "They're already here." He handed him several stacks bound together.

His father may have been able to catch him off guard, but he wasn't going to defeat Blayne with a surprise attack. Business was in his blood.

"Good." It wasn't praise or joy. It was expected. Garret flipped through pages with manicured fingers. Things seemed to pass initial inspection. "Can't be too ahead of the game this time around. New products don't launch themselves. Not investments this hefty."

He didn't have to tell Blayne. After digesting the numbers and markets and every cent spent on development, Blayne knew how much of their profit and success was riding on this. In his opinion, it was a little risky. But when Garret Brandon set his mind on something, it was going to happen. Blayne had learned a long time ago not to question his father or his business instincts.

So he didn't. He kept his mouth shut and waited. He knew his father wouldn't waste the early morning hours stopping by for a visit. There was news.

"I'm flying Jeanette in," Garret stated.

It must have been Garret's morning goal to catch Blayne off guard, because he had just done it again. This time, Blayne couldn't keep his mouth shut. It practically fell open.

"What does Jeanette have to do with an American product launch?" Ben asked against his better judgement. Asking questions was too much like questioning Garret's decision.

"Don't you want to see your wife, Blayne?" Garret asked a question he knew would annoy his son just as much. He stood there solidly. This must have been the conversation he wanted to have.

"That has absolutely nothing to do with it," Blayne asserted.

"We need her in London right now. They have projections and planning to do over there, too."

Blayne swiveled his chair to follow his father's movement across the office. Garret put one foot in front of the other determinedly and approached the rain-slicked wall of glass. He gazed out onto the city and the miserable day. Blayne just gazed back and waited.

Absently, almost as if it wasn't a calculated movement, Garret reached down to a low row of filing cabinets and touched one of the photos there.

Jeanette even looked like a business woman on her wedding day. Beautiful, but business through and through. Sharp, bright eyes and dark blonde hair pulled back meticulously. Blayne knew people called her a bitch, but he respected her and hoped that under all the gloss and attitude she returned the favor. They had a professional relationship. There wasn't much else they could have given their respective lives. This company was their lives, their life. It only seemed natural that they should get married and share that obsession. They were in love with Mandatory. And, perhaps because of that, they truly did love one another.

Garret ran his finger along the top of the silver frame, as if checking for dust.

"I need my best people on this," he said. "You know what a gamble it is. Whatever I have to to make this work."

"And so will I," Blayne said. "You know that."

"Of course. And so will Jeanette."

Blayne just watched his father's back. He watched as Garret lifted his finger from the frame and let it hang momentarily in front of the picture of Blayne's mother. Blayne looked just like her—blonde hair and brown eyes—not the dark and pale, black and blue of his father. He wished he could remember her.

"Women make choices, Blayne. I shouldn't have to remind you of that," Garret took his hand away from the photos and turned to face his son. "Some women are strong. Like Jeanette. Intelligent. Leaders. You need women like that. Jeanette has chosen to become invaluable to this company and this family. If you both didn't work for the same company, I don't know when you would ever see each other. I think it's the only way the two of you could be married to anyone. You're lucky."

If he had used a different tone of voice, the statement could have almost been sad. It could have said that he could never make it work, he could never find love, he could never grow a relationship. But that's not how it sounded, and that is not what it meant. He said 'lucky' like a bully, like the kid on the playground after school who releases the collar of your shirt when your mother's station wagon pulls up in the nick of time. Somehow it sounded like a threat.

It must have been the kind of voice he'd used with Blayne's mother. It must have been just one of the things that made her leave her son and her life. Blayne didn't know. He couldn't remember. But he knew his father, and that was enough. The eyes in that photo Blayne kept couldn't have held the hatred it took to end everything. That could have only come from one place.

"Jeanette is vital to this project. This launch. The success of this company," Garret concluded. He headed for the door. That was all he had come here to say.

"You're right," Blayne conceded.

He swiveled his chair back, following the dramatic exit. He gritted his teeth. Garret knew exactly what to say and exactly what not to say. He liked to tread the line between those two subjects very precariously.

As Blayne turned to face the door, he caught sight of that resume once again. And that was it. It was the thing that pushed him over his own line. If he had been angry before, now he was absolutely infuriated. He couldn't articulate why—his father, his mother, his wife, himself, Ben? But he wanted to so something, anything, drastic and vengeful and dangerous.

Some men would have punched a wall or driven too fast or gone for a drink. Blayne decided to play with fire.

"We might need even more help to make this product successful," Blayne grabbed Ben's resume and held it out as Garret turned back surprised. It wasn't like Blayne to talk back. It wasn't like anyone to speak after Garret Brandon was through with a discussion.

"What's this?" Garret asked sharply.

"It's just a resume," Blayne answered innocently. "You never know what you'll find."

"No," Garret held the resume in his hand tightly. "What is *this*?"

Blayne looked up and saw the yellow note stuck across Ben's name. 'You asked for it.'

"Oh, nothing," he stood quickly and peeled it from the paper. "It must have gotten stuck there. It's about something else."

Garret said nothing. He just turned to leave, eyes glued to Ben's resume.

Blayne's heart was beating hard, but he couldn't tell if it was because of his stupid daring or something else—something he had just caught a glimpse of under that note as Garret turned away.

Why hadn't he looked under the note before? Why had he stared at that resume for an entire day without reading it?

Terrington College.

So Ben had graduated from the same college as Blayne. So what?

CHAPTER 4

The sweet smell of earth was very close to his nose. Grass pressed against his face. He could see flowers rising above him, reaching for moonlight. They weren't supposed to be in the gardens at night. Breaking the rules. But that's not what he was thinking about.

He felt strong arms encircle him from behind. He felt soft kisses on the back of his neck. He heard whispers near his ear. The words were so soft, a million miles away. He couldn't understand them, but he knew what they meant.

He moaned back to his lover under his breath in that quiet, familiar language. He felt the warm night air and the cool splash of blue light against his skin. Then he arched his back and pressed against the man's weight above him in a slow, hungry stretch that was not resistance. It was a desperate invitation, almost begging.

One hand on his chest. Another at his hip. He closed his eyes in the dark as he felt the slow, gentle slide of flesh into flesh. The tinge of pain felt more like anticipation. And he held his breath until they were locked fully together, rocking onto and into each other in the closest embrace.

As their movement came faster and easier, he rose onto his knees, leaning on elbows to allow their passion to reach deeper.

He felt the soft, electric trail of fingertips along his torso, from shoulders to the dimples in the small of his back. He felt them retrace their path, grasping his collarbone, circling the hard sensitive point of his nipple. He felt the solid slide of that shaft moving inside him and the sweaty slap of thighs against his ass.

Breath stirred leaves in the windless shadows. Skin heated

dew-chilled grass. The growing desire of their movement disrupted the still of that night.

Suddenly, the man behind him pulled free, panting and unable to take any more. But more was exactly what they needed.

He felt hollow and hot there on his knees in the dirt, and he couldn't wait. But he made himself take a moment to squeeze his painful erection before he stood and grabbed the sweaty man and rolled him onto his back.

Now it's your turn.

There was no time for nice and slow, and neither of them wanted it that way. Nice and slow would be later, back home, exhausted in each other's arms with dirt caked under their toenails.

Now he grabbed the back of thighs, hitched knees over his shoulders. He sank into that sweaty flesh over and over, like quicksand, like love.

He felt muscle tighten and pause. And he watched the man explode onto his own chest in a pool of moonlit blue.

Then the world went black. But first, glass shattered.

The alarm was horrifying. It was the first time in weeks Ben had woken up this early, let alone having to do it to the screeching complaints of that electronic monster. The clock glowed its loud, red numbers at him. 5:30.

For Christ's sake, was that a.m.?

In a moment of brilliant masochism, Ben had placed the clock just beyond arm's reach. He slapped at the nightstand uselessly. Time to get up.

Ben rubbed his face and groaned. He needed a shave. He needed to get up. He needed to wake up first. Despite the summer sun outside, Ben was sweaty and cold. He'd been dreaming again.

It always left him a bit rattled, disoriented and distracted. But this morning the half-memory clung to the hollow parts of his mind stubbornly. It stuck to him like blades of grass or bits of glass.

The dream hangover was a nagging headache that wanted all his attention. There was something new about the memory's persistence, but Ben didn't have the time or energy to indulge it.

He had to get ready for work.

***

It was still too early for the burly security guards to look sexy. Ben just handed over his I.D. and waited for clearance into the glass fortress.

It was still too early for the dizzying elevator ride to seem exciting as it would have in childhood. It just sloshed coffee around in his gut.

It was still too early for a bitter, lazy unemployed guy in his quite-early-thank-you-very-much thirties to be taking a mystery job and trying to be productive when he could be wasting away his summer.

Ben held his empty leather satchel under his arm as he straightened his tie. The brushed brass of the elevator door reflected back a scratchy, foggy image. That's about how he felt.

He was a poor reflection of a businessman. He had tried his best, but his best was a cheap suit steamed in the shower and a joke tie that had tiny naked men in the paisley if you looked too close.

Ben was glad when the doors slid open and whisked away his sleepy reflection. Suddenly, he was wide awake.

He felt like Dorothy or Charlie or any corn-fed bumpkin who stumbled into a Technicolor world.

There was nothing too early or sleepy or foggy about this place. People moved back and forth efficiently in front of chrome walls and black marble. Television screens blinked wide-eyed out of glass block, winking fast images of products and sports and bright colors at wild angles.

Everywhere Ben looked he could see patches of glaring morning sky in the distant glass walls that circled the floor. Everything seemed brighter and flashier up here. Even the sharp silver sign mounted above the reception desk had its own lighting system.

Mandatory

Ben was almost too intimidated to move. He would have let the elevator doors slide shut in front of him and his cheap suit and his empty excuse for a briefcase, but at that moment a disheveled little man jumped into the scene with a smile.

"You must be Ben Abrahms," Todd said, checking a small pad for accuracy and then tucking it efficiently back into his pocket. "I'm Todd."

"Yes, Ben. It's nice to meet you," it wasn't the most eloquent of greetings, but Ben finally exhaled.

He liked Todd right away. He liked the way his shirt came untucked and his hair stuck up. He liked the wild orange-red color of his hair itself.

"Things get moving around here pretty early," Todd continued as he led him down the bustling hallway past cubicles and photocopiers and all the over-productive elements of office life. "That's Mandatory."

Ben liked the way Todd's voice squeaked a bit as he made fun of the company and its name. He liked the fact that this skinny redhead was one big wise ass.

"I'll keep that in mind," Ben answered back in a similar tone. Todd glanced back at him and grinned.

It was a goofy, genuine expression that lasted a brief second as he tossed it over his shoulder to Ben and hustled down the hall. Todd wasn't half bad-looking for a slim, sloppy carrot top. More straight guys should be like him, Ben thought as he followed the crooked creases of Todd's beltless pants. And he was definitely a straight guy, which is more than could be said for half the men in this office.

There were eyes everywhere, and Ben was having trouble telling the curious from the 'curious.' He was the new guy, after all, but a few of the glances he caught from perfectly coifed men made him feel like fresh meat.

Todd made the most of his time-management skills and introduced Ben periodically to passersby and occupied offices along the way.

"Claire, this is Ben Abrahms," Todd would say.

And Claire, or whoever, would smile and inspect and shake his hand.

Everyone looked interested, but no one looked surprised. Apparently, Ben had been the star of an early-office memo. The e-mail with his name on it had circulated hours before Ben followed Todd in a circle around the guts of the office.

And then they stopped.

"Here we are," Todd announced.

But Ben wasn't exactly sure where 'here' was. They stood inside a midsize conference room. A long glass wall faced him across a round oak table. Ben looked out onto the downtown skyline. Everything was so clean and surreal. So this is what it looked like from the top, he thought.

"Where are we?" Ben asked, coming out of his daze a bit.

"It's your office, Benny Boy," Todd answered.

"My office?" It was more disbelief than a question.

"Well, I know it's not an office in the conventional sense," Todd went on while Ben just stared out at the city and the wide-open space inside. This place could rent as a studio apartment for well over a grand, even without the view. "But the television and stereo equipment and all this meeting space should come in handy for you. I mean, it's not exactly a conventional job either."

Ben swallowed awkwardly and looked away from the view for a moment. He looked down at Todd sheepishly and decided this guy was about as trustworthy as they were going to get around here.

"What exactly is that job?" Ben asked in a much lower voice.

Yeah, start the first day off with the dumbest questions. Because today he could be new, but tomorrow he would just be stupid.

The truth of the matter was Ben had been caught off guard completely by the phone call. He had almost been embarrassed when he realized who was on the other end of the line, even though the polite female voice was a complete stranger to him. But the mention of the company name made him feel as if she knew something dirty and secretive. By the time he convinced himself that was impossible, her casual mention of the salary range threw him back into a fog of disbelief.

Ben had done a fairly impressive job of paying slight attention during the short conversation. Thoughts of scandal and wealth and the crease of Blayne's chest that ran from the hollow of his throat were more than enough to distract him from any detailed job description.

Todd just laughed, quietly and politely so no one would hear.

"That's a good question," he answered. "If I knew what my job was, I'd probably never get anything done. Anyway, it's all a big secret really."

"Really?" Ben hoped they were going to let him in on it sometime.

"The secret weapon? The new product?" Todd raised a couple red eyebrows and searched Ben's face for any sign of recognition.

It wasn't there.

"Well, you're the guy who's going to bring it to life," Todd continued. "They build it, and you give it the spark. You're the creative genius supposedly. So you're in charge of 'consumer brand development.' We're calling you the 'Creative Head' for now."

Ben laughed right back. He had no idea what Todd was talking about. But he knew all about secrets and head, creative or otherwise.

"Well, that's about as clear as mud," Ben said.

"You'll get used to it around here," Todd said and slapped him on the back.

They turned to leave, and Ben saw that one thing that was very clear was the glass walls looking out onto the lobby. That was certainly different from a conventional office.

There were thin Venetian blinds that could be employed for discreet meetings or afternoon naps or… whatever.

But everyone would know when those blinds were drawn. Ben wondered absently who wanted to watch him so badly. But he couldn't be that paranoid. Besides, he'd never really been that modest anyway.

"Time to meet the boys," Todd said.

It sounded like fun, but Ben wasn't sure what he meant.

"The boys?"

"The big boys," Todd explained as he stepped back into the hall.

That sounded like even more fun, but it didn't really clarify anything. Ben just followed obediently.

They passed back through the busy lobby, and Ben nodded and smiled at strangers when they looked up from their work. He watched a few seconds of a deodorant commercial as they passed the flashing screen above the reception desk. He wondered what could possibly happen next.

Ben didn't really want to think about the inevitable. But he couldn't help himself. Sooner or later he was going to see *him*, and Ben had no idea how to prepare or react. He had no idea how the hell he ended up here in the first place or what Blayne had to do with it all.

Was he just being set up? Was this some twisted revenge?

Ben could feel himself starting to sweat inside the cheap fabric despite the chilly climate control. All he could do was smile and nod and hope to hell he wasn't on Candid Camera.

Ben couldn't remember being this nervous since he was the one in the closet. What was the worst that could happen? Was he going to be exposed as a homosexual? Was he going to return home tonight unemployed? And how would any of that be different from the way his life was yesterday or last week?

But he still couldn't stop the nervous flutter in his gut or the cool bead of sweat that tickled down his side. He couldn't stop the lingering feeling of regret and shame and anger. At the same time, he couldn't stop replaying the guilty memory of Blayne's sandy head bouncing up and down on his cock.

Ben almost ran into Todd's back when they stopped. And he suddenly found himself in a doorway staring at the back of that same sandy head he couldn't get out of his mind.

There was something so familiar about the curve of Blayne's wide shoulders. It would have stopped Ben in his tracks, even if Todd hadn't been right there to do it for him.

Blayne typed, paused, stared at his screen. He reached for a stack of papers on his desk, and Todd made a slight, polite noise to announce their presence. Blayne jumped.

"Sorry to interrupt," Todd said as Blayne swiveled to face them, "I just wanted to introduce the new guy. Blayne Brandon, this is Ben Abrahms."

Blayne could not have looked more surprised as his brown eyes locked with Ben's blue ones. He didn't move. He didn't speak. He didn't even breathe. The entire room seemed to stand completely still.

This must have been the exact same look Ben gave when Blayne told him he was married.

Ben should have felt vindicated by that silent expression. He should have felt a surge of revenge. But he was mesmerized by it instead. He was fascinated by the wide-eyed gaze and the square cut of Blayne's freshly shaven jaw. From the look on his face, he had almost dropped that pretty jaw when he saw Ben standing there.

And at the same time, Ben was oddly frightened by their mutual recognition and surprise. How could Blayne not know about this? How could he not be a player in whatever game was going on?

"Oh," Todd broke the silence with his realization. It sounded as if he wanted to slap himself in the forehead for being so stupid. "Of course. You two already know each other."

Ben and Blayne could both feel the fear and apprehension tick up a level from opposite sides of the room. But they didn't look at Todd. They kept right on staring as if it were a childhood contest.

"I completely forgot," Todd continued, "You're the one who recommended Ben in the first place. You must already know him."

Blayne took a single moment to breathe. He wasn't stumbling or stuttering or even stalling his answer. He was just taking a breath.

"No, we've never met," Ben stepped forward boldly to shake Blayne's hand and save his ass. He hoped he'd return the favor someday. As it was, he was lucky to get a handshake out of his gracious gesture. Blayne paused, and then he placed the warmth of his hand in Ben's without even standing up. "But I sure do appreciate you sending my resume along... Blayne, was it?"

Normally, Ben would have added a wink to such a smart-ass lie. But there were too many things standing in the way of his sense of humor. There was the strong feeling of Blayne's handshake, the look of gratitude and confusion in his eye, the fact that someone else was playing this game.

"Nice to meet you," Blayne barely managed. The words seemed like a struggle.

Fortunately, Todd seemed preoccupied with his own oversight. He checked his notepad again.

"Well, Ben is the new Creative Head," he added.

"What?" Blayne finally looked away from Ben's gaze. He dropped Ben's hand and snapped his head toward Todd.

Ben smiled. Todd was standing behind him and couldn't see, but Ben wanted to make sure that Blayne saw the oral sex reference hadn't been missed.

"The director of brand development," Todd amended the title, "for the new product launch."

Blayne knitted his brows curiously. He had no idea what was going on, as if that weren't blatantly obvious from his idiotic expression and dumbstruck conversation skills. This must have been a complete mix-up in human resources.

The whole experience was unbelievable. It was halfway between a dream and a nightmare. Maybe this wasn't real at all. Maybe Blayne was going to wake up screaming at any minute. He couldn't tell if he should pinch himself or take advantage of the fantasy and reach over to pinch Ben.

Instead, he continued to look to Todd for answers. He couldn't let himself look back up at Ben in the off chance that this was actually happening. He couldn't look up at his smile, at those bright blue eyes, at the pale cheekbones and jet-black hair. And he certainly couldn't turn and face Ben's belt buckle that was right at eye level.

So Blayne stood up.

"I didn't realize the ad agency was sending someone over," Blayne said.

"Oh, Ben doesn't work for the agency," Todd corrected. "He works for us now."

"But we don't handle branding in house," Blayne explained. He was trying to gain back a little control. He was trying to make this situation make a little bit of sense. This was a mistake, a very very big mistake.

No one in the room seemed to have an answer. The three men stood there with conflicting facts hanging in the air. There was a moment of silence. Then is was broken wide open.

"We do now."

Garret Brandon's voice boomed into the room ahead of him.

Suddenly the office seemed crowded. It was quite a large room with immense windows and plenty of light pouring in. Normally it would have seemed open and spacious. But right this second there were too many people and too much confusion crammed into the area.

Todd and Blayne actually stepped back a bit to make room. Ben stood there completely lost. He had no idea what was going on or who this commanding man in his perfect charcoal suit was.

"As you said, Blayne," Garret continued, "too important to take chances. Our best people and our best efforts to keep it confidential and successful. Everything in house."

The man didn't seem to have the time or patience for complete sentences. His speech was as clipped and efficient as his appearance. He focused his steely gaze on Ben. It was like being caught in searchlights.

"I thought you were in Chicago," Todd checked his pad yet again and actually scratched at the red tuft of his head. He was obviously troubled by his organizational skills today.

"On my way," Garret never took his eyes off Ben. "Had to meet Mr. Abrahms."

"Ben," he said as he extended his hand slowly.

"Garret Brandon."

Ben shouldn't have been surprised. But he was. This was Blayne's father. This was the owner of the Mandatory empire. This seemed to be the only person who knew what the hell was going on.

The corner of Garret's mouth inched up in a way that wasn't quite a smile as his hard, gray gaze drilled into Ben.

Keep the handshake firm, Ben scolded himself. He was suddenly repeating childhood lessons of masculinity.

"Right to the point," Garret turned and shut the office door quickly.

He approached a small round table at one end of the office and waited for the other men to follow the leader and gather around the black enamel circle. Garret spread his hands on the shiny tabletop and leaned forward aggressively. The others sat beneath his domineering stance.

Todd had his pad ready. Blayne sat silently and professionally— the obedient son. Ben tried his best to emulate their devotion, but he couldn't seem to get the pose right. He was sure it just looked like fidgeting, and every time he glanced over at Blayne to compare posture he got distracted by some very unprofessional thoughts.

"Thirty–five years," Garret started. "Mandatory started with a bottle of after shave. I bought the company. Changed the name. Dumped an entire line of failing women's products. Focused on the money. Business men. That's who makes the money. Made them look the part. Today over fifty products."

The history lesson was brief but impressive. Garret had built his empire the same way, with bold and efficient steps. He hadn't wasted a moment, and he had redefined an industry.

Thirty-five years, Ben thought. He did the math. Garret was holding up remarkably well. He was a testament to his own company. He was trim and handsome in a completely different way than his son. His hard features and piercing glare were opposite the wide shoulders and warm skin on his sandy-headed son.

Blayne himself couldn't have been any older than Ben, which would make him just a few years younger than the company. So

Mandatory was his big brother. He must have spent his entire life living in its shadow, and he grew up to serve it. Well-groomed for the position, one could say. And completely neglected.

"Ben, what do you know about Mandatory?" Garret made the question sound like an accusation.

Ben reminded himself to focus. Here he was staring his new boss in the face and he still managed to turn every subject into thoughts of Blayne.

"I use your shaving cream," was all he could come up with.

Idiot. He clenched his jaw, bit down. He should have slammed his head against the table before he got up to return to the world of the unemployed.

"Do you use one of our razors?" Garret asked. He didn't seem thrown by Ben's ignorance and general stupidity.

"No." He almost felt ashamed admitting it, but it was the truth.

"Good," Garret said simply. "We don't make razors."

Ben was glad he hadn't lied, but he still didn't have a clue as to what was going on or where this line of reasoning was headed. That was nothing new. Ben was getting pretty accustomed to being clueless today.

"But we're going to start," Garret stated heavily.

He let the weight of his declaration hang in the air for a moment. That was the big secret. That was why the door was shut and Ben was hired. Frankly, Ben didn't see the big deal, but he figured he should keep his mouth shut. He'd already said enough stupid things today to last well into next week.

"An obvious oversight?" Garret asked rhetorically, "No. Expensive production for a one-time purchase. Cologne. Soap. Shaving cream. Cheap to make and high product turnover."

It made perfect sense. Ben went through shaving cream like a mad man; half of it washed right down the sink without touching his face. But he was fairly certain that he had the same razor he'd started shaving with over fifteen years ago. What didn't make sense was why Garret had decided to go against all that logic.

No one asked. No one interrupted. It seemed that Todd and Blayne had learned their lesson long before Ben had inserted both feet into his mouth.

"So a gamble," Garret answered the unspoken query. "But not unconsidered. Mandatory has a reputation. A solid consumer base. After all this time. A Mandatory razor to go with their Mandatory shaving cream."

Maybe, Ben thought. But he didn't say it. He wasn't sure if he bought the argument. He wasn't sure men would buy it at all.

"Make them want it. If not them, their wives." Garret insisted. He looked right at Ben. "In time to show up in their Christmas stockings."

Garret had never taken his seat. Now, he simply removed his hands from the table and stood up straight.

"That's your job," he stated. "Chicago."

And with that simple end he headed for the door.

"Thank you," Ben called after him. "It was nice to meet you."

But his platitudes were lost in the shuffle. Garret opened the door. Todd reached for the phone. Blayne grabbed some papers and got as far away from Ben as the office would allow.

Wives. Making men want it. Great, Ben thought. This sounded like the mess that got him into this mess to begin with. And he still didn't know exactly how he had gotten into either of them.

As soon as Todd re-reconfirmed that there would be a car waiting for Garret when he stepped out the door, the redhead turned to Ben and exhaled audibly. He lifted his eyebrows in a way that said, 'That was Garret.'

"I guess we should all get to work then," Todd said out loud instead.

Blayne didn't budge. He just stared at his computer monitor intently. For some reason, Ben felt as if he was really watching the reflection in the screen instead of the charts and numbers illuminated there.

Ben watched his back. He tried to catch his eye in the screen's reflection. Ben didn't want to follow Todd back out into the hall and toward whatever responsibilities his new job held. He wanted to ask Blayne how this whole thing had happened. He wanted to get him alone and figure the mystery out. Maybe he just wanted to get him alone. Maybe he should focus on something else.

"It was nice to meet you," Ben said to Blayne's back.

"Yes. Same here."

He didn't turn around. But Ben saw the flicker of his eye shine out of the corner of his monitor.

"I need a drink," Todd said after a few step down the hall.

"What?" Ben asked incredulously as he followed Todd through the Mandatory maze. It couldn't have been much past eleven in the morning on a Wednesday.

"I mean lunch," Todd corrected himself sarcastically as he turned to face Ben, "or coffee... or something."

He winked.

It wasn't the first time a man had winked at Ben. But it was probably the only time it actually got someone a lunch date.

CHAPTER 5

"So, did he call him Blayne just 'cause it's the only name gayer than Garret?"

Todd almost snorted gin out of his nose. It was sometime after noon, but neither knew for sure. They'd been drinking for hours.

They were the only people left in the dimly lit restaurant. Linen napkins that had been folded into crystal wine glasses were now scattered across the table and draped over dishes smudged with the remnants of fine French cuisine.

This place was too fancy to be open this early. But no one seemed to mind their lingering, drunken presence. The Mandatory expense account excused most any behavior.

"Never repeat that unless you want to be put to death," Todd slurred. "Garret would do it... and charge admission."

Ben emptied his glass and nodded his head at the waiter who appeared immediately at the sound of tinkling ice cubes.

That's how drunken communication should happen. Silently. Tongues got a little too loose when lubed with booze. Of course, the last thing Ben had intended to talk about was homosexuality or Blayne Brandon or his queer name.

He should have been more than happy with the free lunch and the reassurances that Garret was 'just that way' and 'not as bad as he seemed.' Instead, Ben had managed to blaspheme his new company, his boss and his boss' son in one sentence. He'd also expressed an extremely unprofessional interest in the latter and his sexual preference.

"But, since you bring it up," Todd continued conspiratorially in a lower voice that sounded downright silly in the empty room, "there have been rumors."

"Really?" Ben prompted. He knew he was going to like Todd.

"Well, I mean," Todd stumbled over his tongue and his outspokenness. "The place is full of them. Hello, 'men's personal care line.' Plenty employees would be happier if we made man-strength eye shadow."

Ben couldn't tell if Todd was changing the subject or staggering drunkenly down the wrong path. 'Full of them'? Was this an infestation? Was Todd going to ruin his so-far flawless record in Ben's book by turning out to be a homophobe?

"Todd," Ben said, "I'm gay."

"Yeah, I know," Todd paused and picked absently at a leftover crust of bread.

Ben looked suddenly surprised. It wasn't that he was trying to hide anything, but he didn't normally stand out of the crowd that much, especially not to nerdy little redheads. And this nerdy little redhead wasn't a homophobe at all. In fact, he seemed so comfortable with the subject that he could pick Ben out of the masses and use phrases like 'full of them' without a second thought, let alone a prejudice one.

"What?" Todd looked up confused. "No offense. But like I said, it's nothing new to me. After working in a place like that, everyone develops a little gay-dar. Not that I needed any the way you kept looking Blayne up and down."

Ben opened his mouth to protest, but he didn't really know how to deny it. Instead, he took it as a mental lesson to watch himself a little more carefully and watch Blayne's ass a little less.

"You're not the only one," Todd said. "I'm pretty safe. They all just want to give me a makeover. But you don't walk around Mandatory looking like Blayne Brandon without turning a few heads, or starting a few rumors."

"Like what?" Ben asked. He wanted to get as much information without giving any away. "I mean, I thought he was married."

"Well, sorta," Todd's slurred response slipped out before he could stop it.

"What does that mean?"

"She's the president of our London office," Todd explained. "Which means she lives in London. And so does her favorite vice president."

"What?"

"Rumors," Todd repeated. "It's all rumors. I have no idea what's true. I have no idea who's sleeping with who. All I know is she can't be sleeping with Blayne much from across the Atlantic."

Or locked in his closet, Ben thought. But this time he had the good sense to keep quiet.

"Wow," he said instead, "Mandatory is just one big happy family."

"Dysfunctional is more like it," Todd added. "And incestuous. I think Garret loves her more than Blayne ever could. She's one hell of a business bitch. The 'Ice Queen' they call her. Garret was really uniting his empire with that arranged marriage. Almost medieval if it wasn't so capitalistic. Great political move. But that's Garret."

"That seems to be the answer for a lot of strange happenings around here," Ben noted aloud.

But of course they weren't around 'here.' Mandatory was miles away, and they hadn't done a lick of work. All the other tables in the restaurant had already been set for the dinner crowd. It must be approaching quitting time, regardless of the fact that they had never started work in the first place.

"The man is a genius," Todd complimented reluctantly, "and a complete control freak. I mean who else could have a men's cosmetic company with more gay employees than a pride parade and a son with a name like Blayne, then put an end to all the rumors by marrying off his two top employees?"

"That's Garret," Ben answered. He was starting to get it now.

"The man loves to tempt fate and then kick its ass," Todd summed up. "That's what you're all about."

Huh?

Ben almost said it out loud. What the hell was Todd talking about? Ben was hired because people thought Blayne was gay? That made even less sense than the rest of Mandatory's twisted story. He wondered how much Todd knew. More important, and more dangerous, he wondered how much Garret knew.

"Huh?" He couldn't help asking aloud.

Todd looked up from the empty plates and drinks. They were both hammered. Ben's confusion didn't really seem that out of place or as suspicious as it should have in this environment.

"The secret project," Todd made blurry shaving motions with his hand. "Risking all this for nothing or everything. That's tempting fate. And you're supposed to help him kick its ass. Go ahead and sell this mystery product that doesn't even exist yet. Garret's put it all in your hands now."

Ben just hoped he didn't botch the project and cut his own throat with that razor. Unless that's what Garret wanted all along.

Todd looked down at the drinks and dinner and then at his watch. Ben did the same, and he saw the hands swimming there on his wrist.

Damn, it was late!

"Want to move this business meeting to a more appropriate boardroom?" Todd asked. "Like a bar?"

Finally Ben focused and his watch stopped spinning around quite so fast.

"Sorry," Ben said as he stood too quickly for his current state, "I'm late."

"For a very important date?" Todd laughed and wobbled to his feet. Mandatory may have picked up the tab, but the littler man was going to pay the price for his small frame and his affinity for gin.

"More like curfew actually," Ben said.

He helped Todd fit all his gangly limbs into a taxi before hailing one for himself.

He wondered how much crazier this new job could get. He wondered how Garret and Blayne and all those other players were going affect his life. But right this second, Ben was wondering how therapy was going to go while he was rip-roaring drunk.

***

Ben wondered if there was such a thing as couch-spins. If not, he was fairly certain he had discovered them.

There was a couch in Melissa's office, but it was not the stereotypical Freudian chaise. The psychiatrist's office was filled with overstuffed leather furniture and bookshelves. It actually looked more like a library, but from Ben's point of view it looked like a nauseating swirl of dark colors above him.

It was not the type of couch meant for lying down. Today, that detail seemed to have escaped Ben. He slouched against the soft leather arm in his rumpled suit. He didn't look any better than his outfit.

"You're drunk," Melissa said as she pinned back her auburn curls with a pencil.

"Yup."

Ben had been seeing Melissa for a decade now. There was no use lying to her at this point. They were pretty straightforward with one another. And if he wasn't honest, she'd know in a second. However, it wouldn't have taken someone with that much intimate knowledge of his life to notice his current state of intoxication.

Melissa was only a few years older than Ben, and after all these years he had trouble thinking of her as a shrink at all. She was more like a friend. He knew every wacko thought of his doctor that way, but Ben also thought he was a pretty unique wacko.

Because just like every other wacko, Ben didn't really think he was crazy. At least he had the folks at Terrington College to back him up on that one. They just thought he should be observed after his trauma. He was medically sound, they said. But dealing with amnesia can be traumatic. They just wanted to make sure he was coping.

Therefore they'd devised this charming alumni relationship. The psychiatrist fresh out of med school got her first wacko. And the fresh wacko got a free shrink. What a deal.

Besides, observing the evolution of an amnesia victim was a unique opportunity for Melissa. Maybe she'd write a book about Ben someday.

But right now, she didn't look that thrilled with her main character and her unique opportunity.

"Do I need to remind you or lecture you?" Melissa started her lecture.

"No," he said as the ceiling spiraled. But he knew she would.

"I don't even know where to begin," she began. "First of all, heredity has been shown to be a strong factor in alcoholism. So you already have one strike against you."

"Strike one!" Ben shouted and slumped deeper into the couch.

"And, I don't think I have to remind you that drinking is what got you into this situation to begin with," she continued.

"Strike two!"

"Twice the legal limit when the ambulance got there," she added. "If you hadn't almost killed yourself, or if anything other than a telephone pole had been involved, the police wouldn't have taken pity and overlooked a thing."

So they kept telling him. Ben couldn't remember a thing about that night or many of the nights before that. However, it had been made crystal clear that he was a very bad boy and everyone was very kind to let him slide. They reminded him of their kindness so often that it sounded more like a threat.

He touched the scar in his eyebrow as he leaned his head back into the padded arm of the couch. He could tell he was going to have a headache right in that spot come morning.

"More importantly at this moment," Melissa went on, "is the fact that you could do some real damage to yourself."

"Strike three!" Ben was lying completely on the couch now.

"You had some serious head trauma, Ben. There's no telling what would happen if you fell and re-injured yourself."

"Maybe it'd knock some sense into me," he suggested. "Or maybe I'd remember something. You know, when I bang on the side of my TV the picture comes in clearer."

"That's a smart medical theory," she scolded. "But as a doctor, I think severe internal hemorrhaging is more likely."

"Ouch. I promise not to fall down, Doc."

"Getting this drunk isn't good for anyone, especially you. I don't even want you passing out in bed," she said, "or in anyone else's bed for that matter."

"Speaking of," Ben started. But then he thought better of revealing too many recent indiscretions. Instead he said, "I had the dream again."

Melissa sighed and leaned back. Ben just stared up at the ceiling, but he could hear the creak of her chair, and he knew exactly which disapproving expression she would be wearing if he turned his head.

"Ben, you know focusing on dreams is counterproductive," she jumped right into her usual speech. "I'm not Freud. And besides, you're just recreating and torturing yourself with false memories of a painful experience. It's called confabulation. There's a technical term for it, Ben. It's not unique, and it's not real."

"But it seems so real, Melissa," he said honestly. "It seems more real every time I have it. And there was something different about it this time."

"Ben, you've been having the same dream for years," she reminded him unnecessarily. "The only thing that's different is you. You want it to change. You want to remember. But chasing your nightmares is not going to help."

"There was something," he said. He paused and tried to focus through his buzz. He tried to articulate something he hadn't even explained to himself. "This time it just felt different."

"Dwelling on the past is the worst thing for you," she asserted. "Even if it was a real memory, what difference would it make? You know you were in an accident. Reclaiming a painful memory can't help you. It's the past. It was a couple months of college. People forget more than that naturally, without a car crash or recurring dreams. Focusing on you future is what matters now."

That was it. That was the end of the speech that was just as familiar to Ben as the dream itself.

Focus on the present. Focus on the future. Ben had heard it all a million times before. Becoming obsessed with his lost memories at the expense of his current life was the most dangerous part of his amnesia.

It had been ten years. Ten years of new memories and trying to remember. If it hadn't happened by now, it wasn't going to. So, focus on the future. Blah. Blah. Blah.

"I have a new job," he said.

There was some current news for her, he thought. He decided to leave out the details surrounding his hire. There was more than enough going on in his present. Ben figured he could omit one insignificant married man. Just because he couldn't get Blayne out of his head didn't mean he had to let the man into this conversation with his head-shrinker.

Besides, he'd gotten one lecture today already. Melissa would have an absolute field day with that bit of information. Promiscuity. Infidelity. Self-hatred. Destructive relationships.

Ben wondered if all psychiatrists were as uptight. He looked over at her inquisitive face and the sloppy pile of copper curls on her head with that pencil eraser pointing straight up. He figured he could have it a lot worse. He leaned back into the couch.

"Well, that's good news," she changed tones. "Where are you working?"

"Mandatory," he said to the ceiling. But he turned his head back toward her when he heard her sharp little breath of surprise.

Was the company that impressive? She hadn't even heard his dirty job title yet.

It wasn't often that Melissa was speechless. She was not one of those psychiatrists who sat and nodded as patients prattled on. In fact, Ben had always found her a little chatty and opinionated for her profession. But that just made things more interesting.

"About your dream," she finally said.

"I thought we were focusing on the present," Ben teased drunkenly.

Melissa didn't seem amused. In fact, she may not have even heard him. Suddenly she was the one who wasn't paying attention to the present.

"What was different about it?" she asked.

Ben replayed the dim memory of the dream, a memory of a memory. But Melissa had never believed it was a real memory before. He wasn't sure why she was so interested now. What had changed?

There had been the same sounds and colors. Shattering glass and fear. But it had been a little different. There had been the slightest variation. He'd even ignored it himself until Melissa had challenged its truth.

He'd had the dream so many times, and each time he had pushed it away. He never really wanted to remember it. It was the one event he was willing to forget.

But this time, something felt different. It was just a moment, a nagging thought, as if the usual dream had lasted just half a second longer. As if he'd kept his dreaming eyes open for an extra breath before his sleeping eyes opened and he woke up.

It was as if someone had reached over and tapped him on the shoulder to remind him, to touch him. A hand beside him.

"There was someone else in the car with me," he said.

CHAPTER 6

S ome mornings the sunlight was absolutely blinding. It seemed to pour into the glass tower from all sides. Every bit of chrome and brass, even the sharp corners of the receptionist's desk, sparkled brightly.

Blayne had found another reason to leave his office. Normally, he came in early, stayed late and rarely left his desk. Today, he couldn't sit still. He was popping up and down like a nervous kangaroo.

"Did those projections get sent to accounting?" he asked intently.

"Yes, Mr. Brandon," the little blonde receptionist answered. "We sent them yesterday afternoon."

The look on her face was absolute politeness as she blinked up at him. But anyone could have guessed that in her head she was wondering why he hadn't just picked up the phone.

"Good. Thank you." Blayne tapped his fingers anxiously on the edge of the desk and rocked back on his heels.

Then he turned his head to the right as casually as he could. It was such a calculated move that it was obviously the only reason he had come out into the lobby at all.

Through the glass wall, he could see Ben sitting there. He had his hand raised to shield his eyes and his headache from the sun as he stared up at the television screen mounted on the wall.

Blayne wondered if he was just kicking back and relaxing, maybe watching the morning news or reruns of classic cartoons. Maybe the habits of unemployment died hard.

But Blayne knew that Ben must actually be reviewing the archives of Mandatory's advertising. He could see stacks of video tapes scattered across the conference table. Piles of folders and ad clippings from magazines took up the rest of the oak surface. They weren't wasting any time familiarizing Ben with the company image. There wasn't any time to waste, on cartoons or hangovers or anything else.

But there just seemed to be something so casual and relaxed about Ben's pose. It was as if he was familiar with his surroundings and Blayne's gaze falling on him. Blayne imagined him sitting there in a robe, kicking his feet up and stretching his arms above his head. He imagined what Ben would look like in the morning with his dark hair in unruly tufts and his lids half closed over bright blue eyes. He imagined that robe falling open and revealing those long runner's legs and the stripe of fur down Ben's perfectly flat stomach.

"Is there anything else I can help you with, Mr. Brandon?"

Blayne snapped his head back toward the receptionist. He tried to bring his thoughts back to the present, too. But that proved to be much more difficult.

"No. No. That's all," he finally managed.

Blayne smoothed his tie and turned to leave. Before he stepped away, however, he couldn't resist sneaking a backwards glance

Ben was staring straight at him through the glass.

It was a smirk. A challenge. But it didn't seem to be an unappreciative look. There was nothing sneaky about Ben's glance. When he wanted to look, he looked, and he didn't care who saw.

Blayne was not that brash. But there was no way he was going to be threatened in his own domain. He couldn't just run back to his office and hide.

He had made a mistake. Plain and simple. But he was not going to let Ben hold guilt over his head forever. He was not going to let him have the upper hand. It was ridiculous for him to be nervous or intimidated by Ben's stare in the first place. If it came down to it, if Ben ever dared make a comment as obvious as his gaze, Blayne would just lie. Plain and simple. Who were people going to believe anyway?

Blayne was going to have to make the balance of power perfectly clear. Blayne was going to have to back up his eye contact with some actual contact.

So he turned and walked straight up to the door. He was almost proud of his professional determination as he stood in the doorway, but he was having trouble finding a nonchalant place to put his hands. He crossed his arms, then uncrossed them and put his hands in his pockets.

"Good morning," he said.

Ben hadn't taken his eyes off Blayne the entire time. He had watched him take that long, awkward walk across the barren lobby. He had watched the way Blayne looked away and found a hundred captivating details to focus on as he approached. And he had noticed how Blayne watched him out of the corner of his eye, no matter where he pretended to look.

"Good morning."

Blayne kept his face blank. It was more than a poker face. It was his business face. The stakes were higher, and he was just waiting for Ben to call his bluff.

"I see you're watching our commercial clips," he noted the obvious as he nodded toward the screen. "What do you think?"

"It's a lot like gay porn."

There it was, calling his bluff.

"Really, is that your professional opinion?" Blayne didn't bat an eye.

"Oh, yeah," Ben answered. He looked back to the screen where a model in a towel was wiping steam off the mirror and splashing a ridiculous amount of after shave onto his face. "Wet, shirtless men. Shower scenes. Close-ups of navels and nipples. Even cheesy background music."

"I hadn't really thought of it that way," Blayne said. Now he did take his hands out of his pockets and cross his arms. It felt more assertive. And it got his hands much farther away from his crotch.

"Really?" Ben asked, and he sounded as if he was truly interested in the answer.

"Really." Blayne kept his arms crossed over his wide chest. He kept his stare solid.

"Well, all they'd have to do to make it hardcore is throw a couple of these guys together and lose the towels," Ben added. "Then they could get down to some real action."

"I'll take your word for it," Blayne interrupted before Ben made him blink, or blush. "Do you really think that would sell more product?"

"Hell, yeah," Ben laughed. Then he actually kicked his feet up on the chair next to him.

It was too close to Blayne's dirty thoughts for comfort. Ben wasn't wearing a robe; he was in a shirt and tie. But he looked absolutely adorable in his rebellious pose. Blayne looked up at the naked torso on the television. Somehow that was less erotic.

"It's the same audience," Ben continued. "You'd just be giving them what they want. I mean, honestly, who do you think your consumers are? Look at these guys up there. Straight men don't look that damn hot."

Blayne had never really thought of it like that before. He knew the demographics of his audience by heart, but some statistical data wasn't as easy to obtain. Certainly a lot of Mandatory users were 'single.' The exact meaning of that status was a little trickier to determine. What if every 'damn hot' single man was gay? Blayne knew it couldn't be that simple. But it was a wonderful theory.

"So," Ben looked back from the screen, "why haven't you been in any of these commercials?"

Blayne blinked.

"Phase two," Garret Brandon burst into the office right past his dumbfounded son.

No one else seemed to have a clue what 'phase two' was.

Blayne was busy worrying about how much his father had overheard.

Ben was taking his feet off the chair and hitting pause on the remote.

Garret was actually lowering the blinds in front of the view of the lobby.

Then Todd came in carrying stacks of folders and binders. He closed the door behind him efficiently with a hip.

Suddenly the intimate morning meeting had turned into a whirlwind of activity. Garret secured the blinds, and Todd plopped his pile onto the table.

"Time to see preliminary designs," Garret stopped at the head of the table and put his hands on his hips.

Ben wondered if this man ever sat down. Supposedly he'd been to Chicago and back in the amount of time it took Ben to sober up. He glanced over, and Todd winked through his slightly green pallor.

Blayne looked over at his father, and he could see it there on his face. Garret had to be in control. He had to make a scene and a production out of absolutely every moment. Power.

That determination and hunger was what had made Garret Brandon a very successful man. It was what had made Mandatory. Blayne didn't feel any contempt for his father's flair and drama. In fact, he respected it. It just wasn't the way he went about business.

Their last name and business were the only things Garret and Blayne Brandon had in common. Garret would boom and control. Blayne would sit silently and crunch numbers. But what it boiled down to was the business in their blood. It fueled this company in two very different ways.

Blayne looked around the room at the top-secret meeting his father had created so flamboyantly. There really was no threat from beyond those blinds. It was a highly confidential project, but there was no one out there who would betray the company or dare cross Garret.

However, the blinds and the silence and the closed door created quite an impressive atmosphere. Everyone just waited for Garret to make the move. Blayne had to respect that kind of control.

He just wondered how Ben was going to fit into this. He wondered if Ben would play his part in Garret's game. Blayne wasn't exactly sure what his father had planned for Ben or why he was there in the first place. But he was fairly certain that Garret hadn't hired Ben to hear about gay porn.

"Designs in development all year," Garret said as he opened the first folder and spread pages across the table. "Brought designers on staff exclusively for this project. Hundreds of designs. These are the finalists."

Blayne knew that the actual number was much lower. At most, there had been one hundred designs, but it didn't really matter. That was Garret. He had to make a big deal even bigger.

They all stepped around the table to view the display Garret had arranged there. There were five designs, glossy printouts of razors from different angles set on bright backgrounds of blue and green.

Blayne had seen them before, and he had no particular opinion of them. Design was not his area of expertise. When he looked at the possible products, he saw profit and loss potential. He had no idea which of these would result in that profit or loss. He just had to make sure it all added up and let everyone else made the aesthetic decisions.

They all looked down at the options, everyone but Blayne. He watched Ben. He told himself he wasn't looking at Ben's jaw or the way his Adam's apple moved when he swallowed. He told himself he was watching Ben's reaction. It was a business decision to focus on Ben's piercing eyes and the long finger he brought to his lips as he considered the designs.

The shape of Ben's face seemed accustomed to this thoughtful pose. Maybe it was just Blayne's imagination, but there seemed to be something about Ben's expression and careful contemplation that was just right. It was as if his face was used to looking like this, or as if Blayne was used to looking at that face.

At the same time there was something so odd about the entire situation. Here Blayne was, standing inches from his biggest mistake, and he felt admiration and familiarity that were opposite the nervousness he expected.

And there was something else: It was the stupidest thing, but for some reason the scar through Ben's eyebrow kept catching Blayne's attention. His eyes kept returning to it over and over. It seemed out of place, as if Blayne hadn't noticed it before, as if it were new.

That's what was so stupid. It couldn't be new. It was thin and white and completely healed, drawing a clean line through Ben's dark eyebrow.

Suddenly, Ben's eyes shot up. Blayne thought he had been caught staring.

Instead, Ben looked beyond Blayne to the door. Someone was breaking into their secret meeting. Blayne had been too distracted to hear the doorknob turning behind him. He had been focusing on the designs, he told himself.

"Jeanette, perfect timing," Garret said, "as always."

"Sorry," she said crisply. It wasn't a British accent. It was pure, polished business. "I would have been sooner, but you know how the airport can be."

Jeanette walked straight up to Ben with her hand extended

"Jeanette, this is Ben. Brand development for the new product," Garret said. "Jeanette is one of our top people."

They shook hands, and Blayne almost winced. Of course, no one else knew it was like having his worlds collide. No one else except Ben.

Jeanette smiled at Blayne as she stepped past. Polite and professional, that was about as intimate as she was going to get. That was all the recognition their relationship needed.

Her suit was perfect, showing off her legs in a business manner that was more dominatrix than pretty innocence. Her dirty blonde hair was pulled into a bun, tight and smooth like the rest of her appearance.

"Nice to meet you," she said along with her handshake. "Don't let me interrupt. Back to business."

It sounded more like an order than an apology. Enough chitchat. Do your job, fancy boy.

"What do you think?" she asked quickly. She wasn't going to let a moment go to waste.

Jeanette didn't even look up at Ben as she spoke. She and

Garret continued to look down at the designs thoughtfully. They really were cut from the same clothe, Blayne thought. Their charcoal suits even matched.

"There's nothing here," Ben said flatly.

Blayne almost gasped. He felt his eyes widen in disbelief. It didn't matter. No one was looking at him. Suddenly all eyes were focused on Ben.

"Nothing?" Jeanette was incredulous. It wasn't a question. It was an attack. "You are looking at six months of work from the top designers in the industry. Any one of these would dominate the market."

"Any one of these would fail in less time than it took those top designers to come up with it." Ben didn't budge. He didn't look back down at the designs. He stared straight at Jeanette.

He's in trouble, Blayne thought. Ben did not know this woman. She used guys like Ben to sharpen her claws. She was going to enjoy this. You could see it on her face. Garret had an identical expression, an expectant glimmer in his eye like a predator about to pounce.

"I don't suppose you have any facts to support your knee-jerk reaction," she continued, "like the exhaustive research that went into this development, for example?"

"I like to call it common sense," he answered. "Every one of these designs looks exactly like something that's already on the market. Something that has been designed and promoted by a company that has been making razors longer, better and cheaper than Mandatory."

"Mandatory has a reputation of quality," Jeanette insisted. "We have a solid customer base with incredible brand loyalty ."

"And every one of them already has a razor," Ben challenged, "a razor that looks just like one of these."

He gestured toward the table for emphasis. Blayne looked at them again. Ben was exaggerating a little. Of course these designs weren't direct knockoffs. But he had a point. Each depiction was slick and shiny, a curvaceous bit of modern design. They weren't exact replicas, but they were certainly in the same vein as everything else on the drugstore shelf.

Maybe he was right, Blayne thought. Then he immediately looked up as if Jeanette and Garret could catch his mutinous thoughts. But maybe.

Maybe men didn't want something so similar. Maybe it would have to be radically different to get them to switch.

Regardless, Blayne had to admire Ben for protesting. He had to admire his balls. Blayne bit his tongue, even though he had absolutely no intention of agreeing with Ben or mentioning the word 'balls' in his presence.

Ben had certainly gotten on Jeanette's bad side. And Blayne wasn't about to join him. It was one thing to pick a fight with a woman who spent most of her time on another continent. But fighting with Jeanette meant he was fighting with Garret, too.

Blayne was amazed, scared and impressed all at the same time. Ben could be a hard ass, and he respected that. But he didn't really expect him to survive against Jeanette. He certainly didn't expect him to survive against Garrett Brandon.

Jeanette was gearing up. She was just getting started. She had a million tactics and a million facts to back them up. She knew the company inside and out. There was no way in hell she was going to let this outsider tell her about Mandatory or blaspheme its name.

Blayne could almost hear the efficient clicking of her business mind formulating its next attack. The rest of the room was so silent, he wouldn't have been surprised to hear it ticking like a bomb.

Todd just kept his mouth shut until it was time to gather the folders and carry them away. He was not choosing a design or a side. He knew enough to stay out of the crossfire.

Blayne was playing even less of a role. He had nothing to carry away when this ended, except perhaps the wounded. He just stared like a horrified and captivated witness to carnage.

Jeanette actually opened her mouth to speak, but Garret stopped her. He raised a slow, steady hand for silence. He was the only person who could have done so without having that hand ripped off at the wrist.

"Fine," was how he forced the truce.

Jeanette shut her mouth without biting, but it was obvious she wanted to open it again in absolute surprise.

"Fix it," Garret continued. He said it directly to Ben, looking beyond Jeanette and her objections.

"I don't know what the answer is," Ben said. He didn't stammer. He was blunt. But he had survived on honesty fairly well today. "I just know what's wrong."

"I need solutions. Not problems," Garret asserted. "Todd, find this boy a designer."

Todd moved suddenly. When Garret spoke, he jumped. He gathered papers and folders and a set himself in motion. The entire room shifted.

The meeting spilled out into the lobby. Suddenly there just wasn't enough room in the large office for that many people or personalities. Even Ben followed the others out of his own office. There just seemed to be more room to breathe out there.

Immediately, the group split up. Ben and Todd drifted to the right of the door, Jeanette and Garret to the left. Blayne found himself standing lost in the middle, not knowing which direction to go.

He felt like an idiot, but no one else seemed to notice. They were all wrapped in their own conversations.

"He fails. We go back to the originals. Nothing lost." Garret was saying. He was reassuring Jeanette. He was trying to calm her down.

"Time," Jeanette pointed out. "Time is lost. Time is money."

"I can spare both," he answered.

Blayne couldn't believe Garret was letting Ben have his way. Garret hadn't lost the battle. He hadn't give in or give up. It almost seemed that this is what he had wanted all along.

But how could that be, Blayne thought. Why would Garret want to throw away all this work and strategy in favor of Ben's opinion?

It couldn't be. Blayne just wasn't used to seeing his father back down. It was an odd strategy, but Blayne was sure Garret would get his way in the end. He always did.

Jeanette obviously didn't agree with the strategy. That was fine. Garret respected her and her opinion enough to allow that. For her part, Jeanette knew that she didn't have to agree, as long as she didn't disagree with Garret Brandon.

She held her tongue for now and turned her attention to the young man that approached her quickly.

The vice president from London saddled up to Jeanette and Garret like the cheap little kiss-ass he was. Blayne knew it was more than ass he was kissing when it came to Jeanette.

Blayne wasn't stupid or deaf. He heard the rumors, and he saw what was right in front of him. He and his wife may not have the best relationship, but Blayne still didn't appreciate being shit on and then having it rubbed in his face.

The VP was younger and blonder and slimier than a pig in shit. He looked just as happy as one too as he prattled senselessly in his annoying English accent. He was nothing but a glorified assistant who was sleeping his way to middle management. He was an idiot. He could have been anyone.

It wasn't this guy shitting on him. It was Jeanette.

"Ms. Brandon, I had all the reports faxed ahead," he was saying. "They're in your office."

Without turning his head, Blayne heard Ben whisper to Todd in disbelief, "Brandon? That's not...?"

Ben didn't finish the question, and Todd didn't answer. He didn't have to. 'Ice Queen.' Blayne knew they were all having very similar thoughts.

Todd switched the topic of conversation efficiently back to work. It appeared he had already asked the receptionist to call one of the head designers, because at that moment the effeminate little man swished his way up to Ben and Todd.

The wispy little designer seemed much more interested in Ben than in his opinion of the designs.

"Did you like what you saw?" he asked in a way that sounded a little too friendly. From the way he put one hand on his hip, Blayne wasn't so sure he was talking about the designs at all.

"Actually," Ben began tactfully, "I was thinking I might try something a little different."

Ben was a charmer, Blayne thought. He was basically telling this man that his work was trash, and the guy was smiling and batting his eyes and falling all over himself to accommodate Ben. Blayne wondered if it had anything to do with Ben's business skill or if it was just his cute ass.

"I'd love to help you out," The man offered.

This was too much for Blayne. He was literally caught in the middle of these two completely offensive scenes.

The last thing he needed was to watch his wife have an affair to his left and then watch his own indiscretion pick up a new lover on his right.

Blayne had to get out of there. He glanced down at his watch awkwardly. And, shit! He was late on top of everything.

He made some mumbled excuse that he barely heard himself and rushed off. He didn't have to glance back to know that both Ben and Jeanette thought he had stormed away because of their individual offense. But they each only knew half of it. In fact, they knew even less than they thought.

That fact annoyed Blayne during his entire trip across town for his midday, midweek therapy session.

The double flirtation and the power Jeanette and Ben presumed they had over him annoyed Blayne so much that he even managed to work the subjects into his conversation with the therapist. Jeanette was not a new topic. But Blayne was a little more cautious when he introduced Ben's role.

He didn't mention his exact involvement with Ben, just his annoyance at this morning's fiasco. It must have seemed like an awfully big deal to make out of a little flirtation, one that Blayne wasn't even a participant in.

"Blayne, not every gay man is a rapist," Dr. Carver said.

Blayne flinched at that ugly word. He didn't want to talk about this again. It didn't even seem real—that the worst thing that could happen to a man had happened to him. It didn't seem real because he couldn't even remember it.

But it was undeniable true. It was the reason he was here in the first place. After Blayne had woken up, his father had told him himself. Matter-of-factly. Just the facts. Like a business report.

They had knocked him out. They had knocked him straight into a coma and knocked out a good portion of his memory with it. The rest was just details.

Repression, the shrink said. Internalizing his pain and fear and even homophobia.

But Blayne didn't remember. He didn't want to. And he sure as hell didn't want to talk about it.

So he just changed the subject. He said that he was going to ask for a divorce.

Dr. Carver didn't look pleased with the subject change or the subject matter.

"Don't you think that's a severe reaction?" she asked as she flipped her reddish curls and pinned them up with a pencil.

CHAPTER 7

I've got someone I want you to meet," Ben said to Todd as they parted ways.

As soon as he was left alone in the office, Ben was ready for a nap. It had taken the rest of his energy to get rid of that slutty little designer and his over-eager cooperation. Ben had no doubt that he was a team player, but Ben also had no desire to play with him.

As for the rest of the team, Ben was absolutely exhausted from the battle of the bitches. No wonder Blayne stood there in silence. With a wife and father like that, there wasn't much he could say. If you can't say something nice, the old saying goes.

Suddenly Ben could understand why Blayne had needed to take a break and run out for 'coffee' the other day. Blayne's fucked-up family dynamic didn't make his behavior excusable, but it sure made it a hell of a lot easier to comprehend. He'd just needed to blow off a little steam. Well, blow something. And Ben had been happy to oblige.

Maybe Ben was just tired, but he felt a little of the guilt and resentment melt away. It was easier to forgive Blayne when there were so many other people to hate around here. And it was even easier when he watched the rear view of Blayne stomping away from their meeting.

Maybe Ben could forgive and forget. Maybe he could overlook what Blayne had done. After all, when it came down to it, all the guy had really done was give Ben a blow job and a new job. That was a hell of a lot more than Ben could say about any other guy he had ever met in that coffee shop.

However, what was a lot more difficult for Ben to admit

to himself was that he didn't want to forgive and forget. He had already forgotten far too much in his life. There was something about this man that made him want to hold tight to the memory. It made him want to seek him out and figure out what was going on in his head.

But that's stupid, Ben told himself. The man was married. The man was the son of his boss. But that man also had the softest mouth and the strongest lips Ben had ever found rolled into one beautiful package.

Ben stopped himself before his thoughts got completely out of control. He rubbed his face and yawned. He let his thumb massage the tight pain that focused around the scar in his brow.

He really was worn out. It could have been the hangover, but Ben preferred to blame it on his new coworkers. Fortunately, the blinds were already drawn in his office. So no one could see how he slumped in his chair and spent the rest of the day on the phone with Emily.

By the end of the day Thursday, she was convinced. And on Friday, Emily called in sick at the agency and followed Ben to work at Mandatory. By quarter past nine, Todd was convinced as well.

"I told you I had someone I wanted you to meet," Ben said smugly.

He hadn't really thought it would be that simple. He knew Todd and Emily would get along. He could tell by the way Emily insisted on wearing her signature ponytail and jeans ensemble to the interview that Todd would appreciate her disheveled determination. But Ben had no idea that Todd could make such sweeping employment decisions.

"Garret told me to find you a designer," Todd said, "I just didn't know you were going to do all the work for me."

"So the day has finally come when I'm working for Ben Abrahms?" Emily asked. "I might need to rethink this."

Todd laughed nervously and patted the pad in his pocket. As he reached to smooth his bright orange hair, Emily laughed right back.

Ben almost thought they were flirting, but he knew better. He knew that the real situation had a lot more to do with job insecurity than physical attraction. Siding with Ben was a pretty risky career move in this company. They were both taking a chance for him, and he appreciated it.

"Well, no time to waste," Todd said as he stood. "We've got deadlines to meet."

"So what are we shooting for?" Emily asked.

"That's the scary part," Todd said, "You never know when Garret will blow the whistle. It's a countdown to whenever."

Ben had watched Todd become an absolute ball of energy over the past couple days. He buzzed about constantly with tasks and papers and cups of coffee. Ben figured there had to be something other than caffeine fueling that bright orange spark. Todd was more than overworked. He was more than nervous. He was scared shitless.

"But what about taking time to find solutions and hire designers?" Ben asked. He didn't really want to know the answer, but he was already in over his head. So he threw in the real question, "What about hiring me?"

Todd smiled widely. For some reason it didn't make Ben feel any better.

"Well, you could have been his yes-man," Todd said through his smile. "You could have figured out which design he really wanted and what he wanted to say about it. You could have ridden his coattails. Then if this ship sinks, as you so gently predicted, you could have held on tight and floated to safety."

"But I didn't," Ben said.

"You certainly did not," Todd shook his red head.

"So, why am I still here?" Ben decided to push his luck. "Why would he give me the chance?"

"He wants you to prove him right," Todd said simply.

"So he's just setting me up to fail," Ben interpreted.

"I didn't say that," Todd answered. But that's what he meant. "He's setting himself up to succeed."

The three of them stood there in silence for a moment. Ben wondered why he was even bothering. He didn't want to work harder just to end up unemployed again. He could be sleeping in his sweatpants at this very second.

He certainly didn't want to bring Emily into this mess if it was all for nothing. Were they just wasting their time? Were they just waiting to fail, to be embarrassed, to boost Garret's ego and make him look all the wiser?

"Well, why the hell are we wasting time?" Emily asked loudly. She slapped the thighs of her jeans and winked. "Let's get to work."

Todd winked right back. And Ben couldn't help but agree. That was Emily for you. Screw it. Maybe they would fail, and maybe Garret would get his way again. But, damn it, they were going to give it their best and have fun doing it.

The worst thing that could happen was he and Emily would have a lot more time to sit around his apartment with coffee and beers and bitch about life. Hell, maybe Todd would be there to help them.

They started pushing around tables and rerouting computer cables. Todd had suggested that Emily set up camp here in Ben's conference room/office. There was plenty of space, and it helped keep the war camps separated.

The last thing they needed was to put her out there where Garret and Jeanette and the rest of Mandatory could look over her shoulder and make suggestions. But Ben knew there wasn't much chance of that influencing her. Emily was a fighter.

When they'd showed her the initial design concepts, Emily had thrown back her ponytail and howled.

"I've see better looking vibrators," she said. "Which reminds me. I've got a suggestion where they can put these things."

But Ben also didn't want her wasting her time coming up with these witty bits of vulgarity and fighting off the rest of the company. He was happy to keep her to himself and protect Emily and Mandatory from each other.

Emily put her back into it and shoved a desk against the far wall.

"No worries, boys," she said through a grunt. "I'm fast and cheap."

Todd glanced down at her tight jeans, and Ben could see him marveling at Emily's random comment. At least, he hoped it was the comment Todd was focusing on. Easy, boy, he thought, you don't want to get bitten. But maybe he did.

"That's my theory on work and men," she explained. "That's how I've stayed employed and single for so many years."

"You're also the best," Ben added. "Otherwise, why in the world would I keep you around? It's certainly not for your ass."

Todd blushed. It was always so obvious on redheads, Ben thought. But it was kind of cute. They couldn't have a single dirty thought without the entire room knowing about it.

"You want a design or a good time, call Emily," she said. "And you don't have to call me in the morning, 'cause the job's already done. Garret doesn't know what he's in for."

She was a spitfire. That's why Ben loved her, and Todd certainly didn't seem to disapprove a bit. He walked right across the room and helped her push. Ben joined forces with them, too.

They were like the three musketeers, except they were not anyone's heroes. They could feel the eyes peering in at them suspiciously through the lobby window. Word spread fast at Mandatory, and they were the official enemy now. Ben was the leader. Todd was the traitor. And Emily was the new hired gun.

Half the people who passed that glass wall probably didn't even know who they were or what they were working on in there. But plenty of people found an opportunity to walk by and glare. All they knew was that someone had dared to defy Garret, and that promised enough wrath to go around the entire company.

Ben turned and looked out at the passersby and smiled. Emily actually waved. Then Blayne walked right in front of their little show. He looked away quickly, but not as quickly as Ben. Ben actually bowed his head like little boy with his hand caught in the cookie jar.

"Is that?" Emily had to ask. She wasn't going to pass up a chance like this. "Well, well, well, a little too hunky for me. But I'm not really into the Ken doll thing."

"Actually, he looks likes hell," Ben said, looking back up.

Todd joined them at the window and watched as Blayne's haggard form disappeared down the hall. He did look worn ragged, and his tie was even a little crooked. Regardless, Ben couldn't help watching until he vanished around a far corner. There was something that made him want to hold on to that vision as long as he could. Emily was right; even on his worst of days, Blayne still looked like a doll.

"What do you expect?" Todd asked, "Jeanette's in town."

They all laughed, even Emily. It didn't escape Todd's notice that she knew too much about Mandatory even before she was hired. But it was a funny joke, and he liked the way she laughed.

They grabbed another table and shoved it into place to form a long L-shaped workstation near the window. The table scraped painfully against the marble floor. The noise was absolutely dreadful, like a long metallic scream.

Todd and Emily squinted their eyes and gritted their teeth, but they continued to push, and the screech continued to reverberate through the hollow office.

Ben had to stop. He grabbed his head. God, could this still be from that hangover? He closed his eyes and felt the sound shoot right into his skull.

Even with his eyes closed, things seemed too bright. It was like a brilliant light shining out of darkness and directly into his face. It was like the hot buzzing of electricity searing through him.

The pain was more than sound and burning brightness. It was fear and helplessness. It was like panic that coursed through his entire body and pulsated around the focal point of his scar.

It felt like it would never end. In reality, the sound had stopped minutes ago, but it still seemed to echo through him. It radiated through him like a memory.

"Ben, are you OK?" Emily asked.

She placed a hand on his shoulder, and he shuddered. Then he opened his eyes.

"Benny boy, you're sweating like there's no AC," Todd noted. "You feeling alright?"

Ben just stared at them. He saw and heard them through a fog, as if he were underwater or under the influence of some hardcore drugs.

"I'm fine," he finally managed, "fine."

"Are you sure?" Emily insisted.

"Yeah, sure," Ben rubbed his head. "I'm just going to take a breather. I'll take a walk and pick you up some supplies."

He left them there looking out at him, as he stepped into the hall. At least it seemed cooler out there. There was space to breathe, even if everyone he passed glowered at him like a freak show.

What the hell was that? It was like waking from a nightmare and finding himself still in it, breathing hard and sweating in fear.

Was that what it was like to have a panic attack? Ben didn't think this job was going to be a cakewalk, but he couldn't believe that the stress had gotten that bad already. And the most frightening thing about the experience was that it seemed so familiar, even though he could swear he'd never had such an episode before. It was like coming face to face with the monster under your bed after years of hearing him stirring around down there.

Ben took a deep breath and focused on the far end of the hall. Luckily, the supply closet was at the other end of the building. So, he would have the perfect excuse to take a nice long break and clear his head.

He stepped into the long, windowless room and stared up at rows of notepads, pen boxes and a rainbow of sticky notes wrapped in cellophane. He had no idea what Emily really needed. A drawing pad? Some pencils?

He grabbed a few items and stepped deeper into the room. He ran smack into Blayne's back.

"Holy shit!" Ben yelled as he managed to drop everything in his arms.

"Shhh," Blayne hissed back at him. "Sorry."

Ben was on his knees trying to gather his things and his thoughts. Normally, he would have taken the unique opportunity of his position to make a pass or an inappropriate joke, but right this second he really wasn't feeling up to it.

Blayne did look scared and exhausted. He also looked beautiful towering over Ben with an askew tie and sandy bangs falling across his forehead. Ben liked the sloppy look on him once in a while. It looked as if he had just done something naughty.

In fact, perhaps Blayne had committed some small offense. He stood there holding nothing but a pen. It hardly seemed worthy of a trip to the supply closet. Ben seemed to have stumbled onto his hooky hideout. He was trying to conjure up some high-school skip-day fantasy, but he had all he could do to pick up the supplies and stand back up.

"Sorry," Blayne repeated.

He really wasn't the most articulate person, Ben thought. It had taken him an hour to mention his marriage, and he hadn't given a peep at that secret meeting yesterday.

"Apology accepted," Ben said. "I didn't know the supply closet was such a popular spot."

"No," Blayne corrected, "I'm sorry about... everything else."

Well, miracles do happen. Ben couldn't believe Blayne had the balls to come right out and say it, but he was more than willing to help him check for them.

"Look," Ben began, "it's the past, right? I'm not thrilled about it, but I can see where you're coming from."

"Well," Blayne stammered a little, "I meant, I'm sorry for yesterday. Garret and my... Jeanette."

"Oh," Ben said.

"They can be a little overbearing. It's just the way they are, the way Mandatory works."

"Well, it's not the way Ben Abrahms works."

It wasn't the apology Ben wanted, but it was something. At least Blayne recognized the mess he was in, even if only from a business point of view. Good for him, but Ben couldn't just roll over and take it, not that way at least.

"And no one is asking you to," Blayne continued. "Go ahead and try it your way."

"Everyone wants to try it my way sooner or later," Ben tried for a joke or a moment or something.

The supply room was so long and narrow that the two of them were forced to stand right next to each other. Ben didn't know when he'd get another chance to make Blayne feel this uncomfortable, or maybe this tempted. But Blayne was a business man on a mission, and he just ignored the innuendo and continued with his own train of thought.

"Look, I'm no designer. I'm a numbers man," he explained. "But I see your point. It makes sense. I'm glad Garret gave you this opportunity to prove it."

"Yeah, but he doesn't want me to succeed, does he?" Ben just came out with it. If he couldn't bully Blayne, he may as well just be honest with him.

"Regardless, you still have a chance to, right?" Blayne pointed out.

Blayne turned his head suddenly. There were voices coming down the hall, right toward the door.

"See it as an opportunity," Garret's voice was unmistakable. "To have an influence. You're here, Jeanette. That's why. A valuable influence."

Blayne pressed Ben flat against the wall, as far from the door as possible. He kept his eyes glued to the entryway.

"I just don't see the point in losing time on nothing," Jeanette responded. "It's wasteful. And pointless."

With his head turned, Blayne's cheek and jaw were just an inch from Ben's face, from his mouth, from his nose. Ben could feel his heat. He could smell it. Blayne smelled warm, like wood or cinnamon or some childhood scent you just can't get out of your head.

"Testing yourself," Garret said from the hall. "Sometimes the only way. Prove yourself right."

Body heat soaked through Blayne's suit. It pressed against Ben. He could feel the force of his chest and the knot of his tie. He felt the shape of his clothing, of him.

The sound of Garret's voice didn't exactly fade, but it boomed less loudly as the pair moved beyond the closet. Ben felt Blayne's body relax a little. He felt him exhale, and the simple action seemed to bring their bodies even closer, squeeze them tighter together.

Blayne didn't step back. He seemed even more exhausted by the short moment of panic, and he leaned against Ben as if he was completely spent.

The close call had the exact opposite effect on Ben. He couldn't be sure if it was the brief danger of discovery or the raw sensation of Blayne against him, but he felt invigorated. His own body was threatening to stir and awaken.

He closed his eyes. He tried no to concentrate on Blayne's breath or body. He tried not to breathe too deeply and press himself harder against this man. What was he supposed to think about? Baseball? Men in tight uniforms. Balls. Massive thighs. That sure as hell wasn't going to work.

When he opened his eyes, Blayne was staring straight at him. He had turned his head back, taken his watchful eye off the door and placed it on Ben's fine features. Their eyes locked, brown on blue. Their lips could only have been closer in a kiss.

No one blinked. Ben lifted his hand and placed it lightly on Blayne's hip. He let his hold grow firmer. He smoothed the material flat against the muscle and bone, the hard plane between thigh and ass.

The space between their lips was palpable. They felt connected by it more than separated from one another. Their noses touched.

What the hell was he doing? Ben had to regain a little composure here. He needed some perspective. This man's father and wife had just passed a few feet away. Even if Blayne insisted on calling them both by name instead of admitting their close relation to him, Ben had to admit the truth to himself.

They were at work for Chrissakes. And Ben was being faced

with the most difficult challenge of his career. Of course, being face to face with Blayne was no simple task either.

He had to resist. He couldn't make the same mistake twice. They had just reached some small resolution on the subject without even mentioning it. Why would he want to repeat it and return to that awkward feeling of guilt and blame?

It was a stupid question. Ben knew exactly why he wanted to. This body. This man. His familiar scent and feel. He wanted to breathe him in and taste him.

It just wasn't possible. And what did he think he was going to do about it here in a supply closet? It would have made a nice setting for a porn, but this set wasn't closed. They'd almost been caught fully clothed. Discovering naked, sweaty flesh amongst the memo pads and file folders would have been even more incriminating.

He pushed against Blayne's hip with his hand and peeled himself from him. Ben could feel the separation. He felt the heat evaporate. It left him cold.

"Thanks," he said, "for the apology. And your support means a lot. Thanks."

Ben took a step toward the door, but he never took his eyes off Blayne. Blayne stood there, strong but dazed. Disappointment and relief spread a confused expression across his handsome face that just tore at Ben's gut.

"I meant it," was what he managed to say.

Ben reveled in the ambiguity of that statement. Meant what? This teasing was almost better than completing the deed. Almost.

"Doesn't Mandatory make antiperspirant?" Ben asked.

"Huh?" The subject changed baffled him. "Yes. Why?"

"You might want to put some on." Ben nodded toward the dark stains that crept from under Blayne arms.

They laughed, and the moment seemed to lighten just enough to step back into the hall. Blayne readjusted his suit coat over his sweat stains and cleared his throat.

They didn't say a word all the way down the hall, but there seemed to be some mutual agreement where the uncomfortable tension had been before. Blayne followed Ben back to his office. It just seemed like the right thing to do, and neither of them questioned the choice.

"Blayne this is Emily," Ben said as they entered the room. "She's the new designer for the project."

"It's nice to meet you," Blayne said.

But she didn't respond. The atmosphere in the office had changed dramatically from the jovial rearranging Ben had left behind. Emily didn't even take the chance to make some smart-ass remark about Blayne and embarrass them all. Something was wrong.

"It's your dad," she said. "I called the office to give my notice. They were trying to get in touch with you."

Ben was baffled. He couldn't remember the last time he had spoken to his father, let alone on the phone, let alone at the office. But the mood in the room was dead-serious. The flat expressions on Emily and Todd's faces couldn't have conveyed more sincerity.

"I haven't spoken to him in years," Ben said. "There's no way he would call."

"He didn't," she said. "The hospital did."

CHAPTER 8

I'll drive," Blayne said.

And no one objected. Emily practically led Ben as they followed Blayne to the car parked in the underground garage. Todd was in charge of making excuses at the office. He called it 'holding down the fort.'

Ben didn't notice any of the arrangements that were being made around him. He was in an absolute stupor.

Pete Abrahms had certainly never won father of the year, and he and Ben had never been close. But hearing that Pete and his liver had finally made it to the point of hospitalization caught Ben off guard no matter how inevitable the situation was.

There was very little traffic at this hour. It wasn't even lunchtime, and the city was eerily still. It made the ride to the hospital quick, but it made it even more surreal and silent.

The silence that had stood between Ben and his father all these years was just as odd. There had been no big fight, no big falling out. There was no bad blood between them. There was just blood, and that was their only connection.

They didn't talk because they had nothing to talk about. Ben didn't watch sports very often. He didn't drink enough beer. That was that.

Pete Abrahms was a drunk and a shut-in, but Ben didn't have to hold that against his father to cut off contact. Pete was like a casual acquaintance from Ben's youth. After he left for college, he just stopped coming in contact, stopped keeping touch.

Ben had heard Pete's voice rooting in the background when he called home to speak to his mother. And they'd both been at her funeral. They mumbled something to each other through their mourning, probably the same thing they mumbled to other far-flung relatives that day.

The next time Ben had seen his father had been in the foggy wake of amnesia. Resuming his memory and finding himself in his father's apartment had been almost as disorienting as the amnesia itself. So he'd left.

Ben was pretty sure that had been the last time he had seen his father, but he honestly couldn't be certain. His uncertainty made him feel guilty.

He felt guilty because he didn't know what else to feel. Ben figured most sons had a relationship with their fathers. It may be good or bad, but they had one. Ben and Pete Abrahms simply did not.

Now Ben was being called on to fulfill some dire duty as son and remaining survivor, and he had no idea what to do. He couldn't play the part of the loving son. He couldn't play the part of the angry, wronged child. It was like asking him to go to the hospital and watch a stranger die.

But there was nothing he could do about it now, sitting silently in this car. He couldn't rewrite his family history. He couldn't change the past. Ben couldn't even remember all of it.

He sat in the backseat with Emily's hand on his knee and stared at Blayne's back. He looked so solid and strong as he gripped the wheel tightly and focused straight ahead.

There was something comforting about his presence. Ben knew it was odd. It was crazy. Of all people to drive him to this awkward scene, Blayne should have been the last choice. His convoluted role in Ben's life should have only complicated matters.

There was just something so reassuring about the simple sight of the back of his head, the way his tawny hair met the collar of his suit. When he had volunteered to drive, it had been the one small moment of relief Ben had experienced since hearing the news. It seemed to be the only thing about the situation that made any sense at all.

Now Ben was just left with the silence. The silence in the car.

The silence of the mid-morning city. The silence inside his head where memories were lost and memories with his father were never made. Most of all, he feared the silence that was waiting for him in a hospital bed, a silence that had been growing for years toward this moment that would soon fall silent forever.

Ben stood looking down at his father as he slept, and the electric sounds of machinery helped him bear the rest of the quiet.

Pete looked old and tired. There was a film of sick sweat on him, and the puffy skin around his eyes quivered in a way that didn't look like dreaming.

Ben sat. He knew that was how these things went, the typical deathbed scene. He pulled a chair from the other side of the room, but he had no idea what he was going to do once he got there.

The chair leg scraped against the floor, as if it were announcing its arrival at Pete's bedside. It wasn't as loud as the painful screech which had shot through Ben's head just an hour before. It was just a low rubbing, almost a honk. But it was enough to wake Pete from his fitful state.

"What the hell?" Pete grumbled. He sounded just as impatient and unhappy as always, but there was an unhealthy fatigue dragging his voice deep inside him. It sounded as if he were talking through mud.

"Sorry," Ben said as he sat, "It's just me. It's Ben, Dad."

Pete flicked his eyes toward his son without turning his head. Ben wasn't sure he could manage the movement, or maybe he just didn't want to waste the energy.

His eyes seemed small and wet, but there was recognition in them. Not only did he recognize Ben, he seemed to understand what his presence meant. He looked resigned to the situation. He would never see another basketball game. He'd never have another cold beer. He'd never even have another warm one.

"You're supposed to be at work," Pete said. It was his way of saying he still knew what time it was, what day it was, who was talking to him. It was his way of saying that Ben shouldn't have bothered.

"It's all right," Ben insisted, "I took the afternoon off. We haven't visited in a while."

"Hmmph," Pete snorted. That was his way of dismissing Ben's pitiful excuse. They both knew what was happening, but he wasn't going to talk about it either. "You still at that advertising place?"

So this was going to be small talk. It was going to be as simple as a conversation in a bar with any old drunk. Ben almost felt relief as he looked down at his father's bloated body, but he knew nothing was going to be simple about it.

"No," he answered, "I work at a bigger company now. It's called Mandatory. Maybe you've heard of them. They make shaving cream and stuff."

Suddenly Pete mustered the energy he had seemed to lack only moments before. He practically bucked in the hospital bed as he turned his head toward his son and knit his brows together angrily.

"Shaving cream is shit!" he yelled. He practically spat the words at Ben's chair.

The explosion of energy was too much for him. Pete coughed and hacked. Ben would have been concerned, but he'd been too caught off guard by his father's sudden hostility to respond promptly. By the time he reached for the nurse's buzzer, Pete's coughing spell was wheezing to an end. By the time Ben thought to ask if he was all right, Pete was picking up where he'd left off.

"Gave it up years ago," Pete said just as spiritedly, "Now I just use soap and water like any normal man."

Ben couldn't believe his father was fighting for breath and using his final gasps of air to start a fight. What the hell did any of this have to do with shaving cream? Ben could have asked the obvious question, but that would have been too easy. Pete wouldn't have given him a normal answer anyway. If it was a fight he wanted, that's exactly what Ben would give him. It was one hell of a dying wish.

"Well, there seem to be millions and millions of men out there who aren't normal then," Ben challenged his father sarcastically, "Because shaving cream is one big business."

"Oh, and big business makes everything OK?" Pete challenged him right back, "Money makes everything just fine?"

Pete sounded just as fiery, but his body was tiring around his spirit. Beads of sweat had popped up along his already slimy brow. He was pale and yellowish where his puffy skin poked from the covers. His head faced forward in exhaustion, but his eyes darted all the way to their corners to fix upon his son. He seemed to be clinging to this pointless argument like a lifeline.

"Giving people what they want makes it all right," Ben said less hotly. "It's something they need. That's why it makes money."

"Snake oil!" Pete insisted. "Lies! Flimflam in a can."

He sounded almost lyrical, poetic. Or completely crazy, Ben thought. It was hard to argue with that. He looked down at his father's desperate eyes. He had to come up with something to keep this going.

"Well, I like it," Ben tried. "I think it gives a great shave."

"Of course," Pete huffed, "it's just soap and water in a can. Slap a different label on it, cover it up with a lie, call it something else, and charge 'em twice as much."

"Well, some people aren't as clever as you, I guess," Ben said less sarcastically. "They haven't figured it out yet."

"True," Pete agreed. "Wouldn't believe me if I told 'em."

He sounded suddenly quiet. Ben didn't like the way Pete seemed to settle down into himself.

They had finally found something to talk about, after all these years. It was almost as if it hadn't been ages, as if they talked daily and could simply waste time on some meaningless subject like the weather or shaving cream.

A lifetime of nothing to say to one another, and now the floodgates were open. They had discovered something to fight about. It was silly and stupid and pitiful, but it was the most wonderful conversation Ben could remember having with his father, and he didn't want it to end.

"Maybe they don't want to figure it out," Ben tried to rekindle the precious fight. "Maybe they like thinking they're getting something better. Maybe they want to be lied to."

"Would you?" was all Pete asked. It didn't sound rhetorical. He actually sounded interested in Ben's specific answer. He was grasping at this ridiculous line of reasoning for no logical reason.

"I like my soap and water in a can," Ben said.

He thought that alone would be enough to get Pete going again. Instead, it seemed to be a completely acceptable answer. Pete closed his eyes, but just briefly, just long enough to let the answer soak in.

"I thought so," he said, and he seemed pleased enough with the conclusion. "Myself, I could sure go for a good old-fashioned soap-and-water shave."

Pete tried to lift his hand to his face. He tried to rub that stubble that clung like moldy gray moss to his drooping cheeks. He didn't have the strength. Ben watched the sheet billow as the hand under it shifted, but it fell motionless again in resignation. Pete couldn't manage the gesture, let alone a shave.

"Coming right up," Ben said as he headed for the bathroom.

It was the least he could do. It was no big deal, and Pete didn't have the energy to refuse the service. It seemed a little intimate, a little close for comfort. But after all, this was his father.

Ben found a razor. He even found a fresh blade. But he had to make do with the bright-pink liquid hospital soap squirted into a little paper cup. Still, it was better than shaving cream, he supposed.

It lathered nicely. Ben had to concede that point. But it did dry out and cling to Pete's face in a thin layer of white scum. Ben had to keep rinsing and re-wetting the razor in the tiny cup.

Pete closed his eyes, but for some reason it didn't worry Ben this time. He seemed to be enjoying himself. He seemed to be relaxing. Someone could almost mistake the contentment on Pete's face for a smile. The corners of his mouth just didn't lift that high any more. And, besides, it would have ruined his shave.

Ben scraped and stroked and rinsed. It was a soothing ritual. It seemed to calm both their nerves. By the time Ben has whisked away the last patch of gray whiskers from Pete's chin, he had fallen into a deep, restful sleep. Clean and comfortable.

Ben sat back down in his bedside seat. He noticed Pete wasn't snoring. If there was one thing Ben remembered about his father, it was the rumbling that came from the recliner or the bedroom or whatever corner of the house Pete had chosen to fall asleep in. But now he was too far away. The storm clouds of their fight and his past had receded, and his breath could no longer thunder out so angrily.

Ben just sat there. Pete didn't die right then. That would have been too dramatic. He just slipped further into sleep, further away. Ben waited peacefully for it to end. He closed his eyes, too, and waited for his father to stop breathing.

And when it happened, that's all it was—silence. There was no drama. There was no weeping. It wasn't like something happening at all. It was more like something that didn't happen. No breath. No tears.

***

Emily was in a tiny waiting room, some quiet place tucked behind potted plants and lit with fluorescent bulbs. She sat there alone with her hands in her lap. When she saw Ben approach, she knew it was over.

The look on her face was blankly accepting and sympathetic. It was so genuine, the way a jokester's expression changes when she's called upon to be suddenly serious. She didn't know Pete. She was there for her friend, and she was prepared for whatever reaction he might have.

"You didn't have to stay so late," he said as he sat next to her.

She answered him by taking her hand out of her lap and placing it on his knee. Of course she didn't have to, her gesture said. She could do whatever the hell she wanted. And she had wanted to be right here for him.

"I can't help it," Ben said. "I can't be sad."

"No one says you have to be," Emily insisted. "Who do you have to answer to?"

"There are just so many reasons," he said. "I could be sad about all the years we lost, or Mom, or all the things we never came close to doing or saying. But I just can't be sad about this. It was the inevitable. I expected it, and I've been prepared for it all my life."

They let the silence hang there. All those possible emotions and reasons floated in the air around them, but none of them felt right.

The hospital was so quiet at this time of night. There weren't nurses bustling or doctors hurrying. Emily and Ben seemed to be tucked into some corner of the building where everyone else was asleep or dead.

"I'm angry," he said finally. He turned his head toward her and looked her straight in the eye. She still had that expression—honest, caring, open.

"That makes perfect sense," she said. She raised her dark eyebrows in complete understanding. He could tell her anything, no matter what.

"But I'm not angry that he died," Ben explained. "I'm not angry that I never got the chance to know him better or spend more time with him or have a better relationship. I'm just angry at myself. I'm angry because I don't know what else to feel. I should have figured that out by now."

"You can't control everything, Ben," she said as she rubbed her thumb across his kneecap reassuringly, "not even how you feel all the time."

"Maybe," he said, "but I don't have to sit back and let something just happen when I could be doing something about it."

He sounded so determined. Somehow his loss had inspired him. It had motivated him to take charge. He may have lost his father, he may have lost his memory, but he didn't have to keep letting things slip through his fingers again and again. He could hold tight and try to make things work.

"So what are you going to do about it?" Emily asked. She was always one to challenge him, even when he was already challenging himself.

"I'm going to make that fucking razor," he declared.

"Not without me you're not," Emily said. She was right there with him, and she'd follow him into unemployment if she had to.

"Count me in."

Ben looked up, and there was Blayne holding a cup of coffee. He handed it to Emily and as he did, his face passed right in front of Ben's. He held Ben's gaze firmly.

Ben hadn't know Blayne was still around. He couldn't understand why he would have waited all these hours, but Ben was glad to see him.

Suddenly, Ben knew how to feel. He felt strong. He felt determined. And he felt glad to have people around him to support him. Strangely, one of those people was Blayne Brandon, but that just made Ben more confident for some reason.

"Good," he said, "because I'm counting on both of you."

***

Blayne was more than willing to drive Emily home. They weren't thrilled about Ben taking a taxi, but it just seemed easier. In the end, they realized he probably just needed to be alone. They'd done everything they could for him.

He was drained. Whatever emotions and energy he had gone through, they'd left him feeling limp.

Ben didn't even turn on the lights when he got home. He just crawled under the covers and left his clothes in a pile next to the bed. A lot had happened. A lot more was coming. For the moment, Ben didn't want to think about any of it.

It would be only a couple hours until the summer sun came up, but Ben fell into a dark, dreamless sleep. It shut out the light better than any blinds could.

When he woke, the absence of dreams was almost unsettling. But aside from the vaguest sensation of someone next to him as he rolled over, his night had been black.

Outside, the bright daylight of a beautiful Saturday beamed at him through the windows. It would have been a great day to do nothing. I also would have been a great day to throw open the windows and clean or paint or do any overly productive project. Ben wanted to do anything but what he had to.

He felt rested and weary at the same time. He knew what tasks lay ahead of him, and he wasn't looking forward to them.

There was no funeral, no graveside ceremony. Pete had been uncharacteristically thorough about those points. It would all be taken care of before the weekend was over. Pete would finally be planted in that hole next to his wife that had been waiting for him for fifteen years.

But Ben still had to deal with the apartment. He wasn't looking forward to facing the dank memories of that place, memories he hadn't shared. He didn't want to paw through his father's existence

The landlord, or building manager, or whoever the hell had that big ring of keys, didn't bat an eye at the news. He didn't ask for proof or ID or last month's rent. He just opened the door.

Ben looked around. It was as if the windows hadn't been opened in years. Nothing had changed since Ben had found himself here after the accident. It was the kind of place with gray carpets and off-white walls, cheap green linoleum and countertops, the kind of place that could go without cleaning for a decade and look exactly the same.

Ben wondered why he had even bothered. There was nothing here worth salvaging. There were piles of clothes, piles of sports magazines, even piles of potato chip bags and beer cans next to the recliner. The TV was on. The sound was off.

Ben walked from room to room, and it was the same sad scene. The refrigerator had nothing but beer and hotdogs in it. Pete's life had really been like a nonstop ballgame. It didn't matter what ball or what season, he was there in his own reclining VIP section with a dog and some suds.

In the bedroom there was one small change that Ben didn't remember from before. It wasn't a drastic alteration, but it seemed out of place in Pete's home. In one corner, tucked among piles of tee-shirts and socks, was a tiny desk. It was more like a collapsible tray or a child's homework table. It would have been more at home next to Pete's chair holding a six pack.

Instead, it was here, inexplicably tidy amid the clutter. There were a couple pens arranged in a row. There was even a little lamp sitting to one side. In the center of the mini desk, there was a fat plastic binder.

Ben sat in the folding chair and opened up the mystery. He stared down at rows and rows of dates and numbers. Pete's penmanship was sloppy and childish, but his bookkeeping was meticulous. There was a checkbook and a decade of withdrawals and deposits.

Ben had never expected his father to be so careful with his finances. Even more surprising was the fact that there were significantly more deposits than withdrawals. Ben could see the repetition of rent checks. He could see the tiny deposits from social security. What surprised him most, however, was the reoccurrence of one number over and over in the deposit column: five-thousand dollars.

Ben squinted and peered even closer. It didn't help him see things any more clearly. Five-thousand every month, for pages and pages, for years and years.

On the final page, two things astonished him.

First, the balance. Pete had very few expenses. Beer and hotdogs weren't going to break the bank, certainly not this one. Those monthly deposits had really added up. In fact, they added up to well over half a million.

Ben certainly had never expected an inheritance. He figured he'd end up with some debt and a wide-screen TV. But the second mystery in the back of that binder was an even bigger shock.

Paper-clipped to the last page was a stack of uncashed checks. There must have been half a dozen of them, and they were all for five-thousand dollars.

Ben spread them out in front of him. There were identical. The same illegible scribble of a signature was in each bottom corner. Along their tops was printed the same senseless name: Choices, inc.

It must have been a company, but Ben had no idea what it meant. Had Pete been working all these years? Had he made some brilliant investment? Was this the clever device of some bookie? Ben had never considered his father to be a gambling man. He certainly never considered him to be this lucky.

Obviously there were a lot of things Ben hadn't known about his father. Ben had no real idea of what the past ten years had been like for him. This was just one more small mystery that he'd never solve.

He walked into the tiny bathroom and ran the cold water. He splashed it on his face and took a deep breath. It was time to clear his head and search for a clean towel.

He opened a cabinet and looked under the sink. True to Pete's word, there was no shaving cream to be found. Ben saw his father's razor resting in a coffee mug next to a thin bar of soap. It was the one sight in this dingy little apartment that seemed to brighten it at all. Ben smiled.

That sight right there was his father. It's what really made it Pete's place to Ben. It's finally what made it all real.

This is where his father had holed himself up through years of baseball, football and basketball seasons. This is where his father had drunk himself to death. This is where his father had truly died, years ago. And this was where Ben finally wept. He let the tears run silently down his already-wet face.

Screw it. Let a cleaning service deal with it.

On his way out, Ben grabbed the checkbook. The maid or some charity was welcome to the wide-screen TV.

CHAPTER 9

He had waited until late Sunday afternoon to drive by the cemetery. He knew that everything had probably been taken care of much earlier, but he didn't want to have to make a return visit.

Ben wasn't a big fan of graveyards and gravestones. He had never understood the pomp and reverence that surrounded these otherwise pleasant parks and gardens. He also knew that Pete would not have appreciated flowers and ribbons and a longwinded sermon.

Ben just stopped the car for a minute and got out. He never even turned off the engine. He just looked down at the fresh soil next to the closely trimmed grass that covered his mother's grave. That was that.

It didn't come close to a final shave or Pete's razor in an old mug. It was just the act that sealed the deal, like a final signature at the bottom of a check.

He was home before dark. He had all intentions of treating himself to pizza and an early bedtime. This weekend had been understandably hectic and tiring. He deserved a little indulgence.

When he reached for the phone though, he noticed a message blinking there on the machine.

It was the cleaning service. Pete's apartment had been broken into. Things were even more of a mess than when Ben had visited. The odd thing was no one had touched the TV.

It must have been drug addicts or someone looking for cash, the maid insisted. He must have left the door open, Ben thought. Maybe it had been that scummy landlord since he knew the place was empty now, Ben thought better.

Was he certain she could have the television, the maid's recorded voice asked for the third time. He'd have to call her in the morning to reassure her. It was weird though. The entire situation was strange. But it was finally over.

Ben stood there with the phone in his hand and tried to focus on what kind of pizza he wanted. Somewhere between thoughts of pepperoni and mushrooms, there was a knock at the front door.

"Hi," was all Ben said when he say Blayne standing on his doorstep.

Blayne looked absolutely perplexed by Ben's greeting. Maybe he'd hoped for some smart-ass remark from Ben to get things started. Maybe he'd wanted Ben to tease him about the tee-shirt and jeans that had taken the place of his shirt and tie.

Blayne didn't really know what he wanted. Maybe he just wanted to stand there and see Ben's face, make sure it was real, figure out what was really happening in his own head.

"I just wanted to make sure you were doing all right," Blayne half-lied. It was true; he just didn't know what the other half of his intentions was. "Do you need anything?"

"Just a date for dinner," Ben smiled.

It wasn't much of a joke. In fact, it seemed completely genuine. But that smile that spread across Ben's long face was certainly one of the reasons Blayne had come here. A mischievous glint flashed through those blue eyes, but he looked truly appreciative. Maybe he was just hungry, Blayne thought, although he wasn't sure for what.

The light was beginning to fade as Blayne walked into Ben's apartment. It was a long, slow summer evening, as if the sun didn't want to let go of the weekend. Blayne could see how moments like this last. He could understand how he could stand in that doorway and look at Ben's smile until the light was drained from the sky.

"Pepperoni or mushroom?" Ben asked as he picked the receiver up from the desk.

"Oh, no pepperoni," Blayne said, "it gives me heart palpitations."

It sounded silly, but it was true. There was too much sodium or something, but it made Ben laugh, and that made it worth it.

"Well, we wouldn't want to get you all excited, now would we?" Ben asked as he dialed. He was talking to the pizza parlor before Blayne had a chance to answer.

There goes the gym, Blayne thought. Pizza. He couldn't remember the last time he'd eaten it. College? Well, he couldn't remember all of that either.

Damn skinny, runner types like Ben could eat whatever they wanted. He probably had pizza every other night and managed to keep his flat stomach and the rest of that tight package.

They sat in the living room to wait for the delivery guy. Blayne had actually never come this far into the apartment. He didn't want to dwell on his previous visit or the way he had treated Ben when he left. He just realized suddenly that he had no idea what Ben's life was like beyond that front bedroom and that sarcastic smile he'd first seen in the coffee shop and every day at work after. That smile seemed so natural to him now, as if it had been burned into his memory, as if it belonged there.

But he had no true understanding of what it meant to be this man, to live here, to go through his life. Blayne hadn't known how gold and orange the light could be as it poured across Ben's living room floor. He didn't know how warm the silence could be between two men, sitting waiting for pizza and the sunset. He couldn't remember a night like this or such a feeling of wonder and ignorance. But he felt that he should.

He needed to understand. He wanted to learn a million things about Ben, and a million more from him. But Blayne didn't know where to begin. Whatever those things were, they were the other half of why he'd shown up here tonight.

How could a man live so openly and freely? How could Ben crack jokes and hang out at coffee shops and then show up at a new job and challenge Jeanette and Garret Brandon? How could he walk into a hospital and talk to a man he hadn't seen in years? How could he watch him die?

Strangely, it had been the death of a stranger that had made Blayne realize Ben's mortality and maybe his own. This was real. Ben was not just a jokester or a threat or a mistake.

Somehow Pete Abrahms' death had made it all seem real and urgent. Blayne hadn't known him. He'd never even laid eyes on the man. It must have been that moment when Ben was stripped of his sarcastic smile. He was no longer just a manipulative smart-ass ready with a joke and a wink. He was just a confused, beautiful man who could be knocked on his ass by fate as fast as the next guy.

"I don't want that to happen to me," Blayne said finally.

"It won't," he assured him. Ben seemed to know instinctively what he meant.

"I don't want to wait years to tell my father the truth."

"It comes out sooner or later," Ben said. "Besides, you talk to your father every day. And he's not a drunk. It's different."

"We have more in common than you think," Blayne admitted. "I speak to him, but we don't talk. And Garret might as well be a drunk. He's drunk on power. I can't take him to a bar and share a glass of that."

"And why would you want to?" Ben asked. "You give him more than enough power by giving him so much credit. He may be Mr. Big Important Business Man, but he's just your father, Blayne. You don't have to tell him anything."

"Of course I do. I can't keep hiding from him" Blayne said. "I can't keep playing along and letting him run my life like he runs that company."

"Fine," Ben said, "but that doesn't have anything to do with talking to him. Maybe you don't talk because you have nothing to say. He's your father, not your best friend. You don't owe him the truth. You owe that to yourself. Telling yourself the truth is the first conversation you need to have."

Ben wasn't angry or lecturing. He was just full of too much experience and realization this weekend. He knew it wasn't about telling your father that you love him or that you're a big homo. Being honest doesn't mean saying the words all the time. It just means living by them. Sometimes it's as simple as a shave, as plain as soap and water.

"Maybe," Blayne conceded, "but I need to stop lying to him. About everything. And that includes you."

Ben looked up from the sun-streaked floor. He met Blayne's soft, brown eyes and honest gaze. He didn't know where this was going, but it was quite a start.

"First of all," Blayne continued, "that means being honest about this project. I support you, Ben. I really do. It might seem like a small thing but trust me, it's the biggest betrayal Garret Brandon could imagine. I won't let him sabotage your efforts and the entire company because of his own pride. If I can't even make a mature business decision, I'm never going to grow up."

Ben was a little taken off guard. It wasn't the typical, tearful coming-out speech. It wasn't 'any weepy personal revelation. But somehow, Ben understood that this was the most intimate and dangerous decision Blayne could make right now. It might seem strange, but it was probably the most touching gesture Blayne could have made.

Ben had spent the entire weekend dealing with emotional trauma and support. He didn't need another shoulder to cry on. He needed people to stand strong beside him. The surprising fact that it was going to be Blayne almost managed to bring tears to Ben's eyes.

He was glad when the delivery man knocked and gave him an excuse to leave the room for a moment.

He couldn't help it. Blayne's words, the deep sound of his serious voice, absolutely thrilled Ben. He also couldn't help it when, halfway through mushroom pizza, he leaned over and kissed Blayne's greasy lips.

Blayne was never a big pizza fan. So he wasn't terribly upset that he'd just finished his first slice when Ben interrupted dinner. However, he was surprised how much better cheese and mushrooms could taste when the flavors were lingering on Ben's lips.

This isn't why he had come here, he told himself. He still wasn't exactly sure why he had made the trip. It was just a evening walk that had taken him across town and deposited him at Ben's door.

Blayne knew there must have been a reason. He thought it had something to do with showing his remorse and support and trying to articulate all the nonsense and confusion that swirled inside his head.

He was definite that he had not come here to be kissed.

That fact didn't make it any less wonderful. Ben's kiss was soft and slow, not hesitant or shy. It was more like a thank you.

There was something beautiful about the moment's simplicity. Shadows were falling across the room. The pizza box was shoved to the side. It hadn't been a spectacularly romantic sunset. There had been no roses or wine.

It was just the two of them, stripping away layers of misunderstanding and miscommunication. It was just two men trying to be honest with one another. They may not have uncovered every secret or truth, but it was one of the most authentic moments Blayne could remember.

He kissed Ben right back.

It seemed like the simplest and most natural thing in the world as their bodies slid across the floor to meet, to join their kiss. They wrapped their arms around each other in a wide, gentle embrace.

Their passion was slow and warm, like the moment and the setting sun. It wasn't the frantic fumbling of desire. It was about touch and taste and the softest brush of lips against lips.

Blayne lowered Ben back onto the floor. He paused, propping himself on an elbow, and brushed Ben's dark bangs from his forehead. He looked down at those fine features and soft lips, and he smiled.

He ran his thumb over the straight, white scar through Ben's eyebrow and cradled his jaw in his hand. Blayne kissed him tenderly with his eyes open.

Slowly, Ben unbuttoned his own shirt. He revealed flesh, button by button, and Blayne's hand followed that path. He touched the smooth white skin of Ben's chest. He grazed the dark circle of his nipple with fingertips as gently as he had traced the scar.

Blayne followed the trail of hair along Ben's stomach to the waist of his jeans and wrapped a big hand around his taut side.

Ben lifted the tee-shirt over Blayne's sandy head and drew slow, wet rings around those tan nipples with his mouth. His hunger was determined yet restrained. And as the firm kisses against Blayne's chest pressed even closer, his low moan was almost a whisper.

Blayne rolled onto Ben and held his head in both hands. The tender points of his nipples pushed wet against Ben's smooth skin. Their kiss became deeper without losing the softness of its beginning. And they struggled out of jeans without breaking their embrace.

They found themselves entwined and naked on Ben's living room floor. And they found each other warm and ready as their breath came harder like hushed urgings near ears.

Blayne couldn't believe he was here. But it was a completely different disbelief than he had felt the first time he'd been in this apartment. This was not shame or regret or self-hatred. This was ecstasy. Blayne couldn't believe he was in the arms of this beautiful man. He was in awe of the electric touch of skin against skin, the scratch of stubbled kisses, the rub of two erections pressed against one another.

Their bodies found a common motion that rocked gently between their kisses and breaths. Blayne felt Ben's long runner's legs wrap around his own muscular thighs. The strong embrace of tangled limbs brought them even closer, and Blayne suddenly found himself pressed against the warmth of Ben's crotch and the undulating flex of his ass.

Blayne placed his hands in hair and his lips on neck. He could taste the slight hint of salt behind Ben's jaw as their heat and intensity grew.

Ben's mouth flew open in a nearly silent gasp as Blayne let his tongue trace the shape of his ear. He nibbled the lobe. He let the exhalation of warm breath express his rapture.

Ben stood. He lifted Blayne from him urgently and took him by the hand. Together, they walked silent and naked down the darkened hall to Ben's room.

They almost seemed too hurried in their passion, and Ben paused next to his bed to recapture the moment's tenderness.

He looked up at Blayne and smiled before kissing him. He ran his hand over the swell of Blayne's chest and down the curve of his arm. He held his fingers on the mound of Blayne's rump as their lips met again. He pressed the dripping head of Blayne's erection against the firmness of his stomach. He wetted that dark line of hair with Blayne's oozing desire. And he pushed him back onto the bed.

Blayne looked up in wonder as Ben climbed on top of him. He watched Ben's body twist and flex as he positioned himself on his knees just inches above Blayne's own quivering flesh.

Blayne reached for him. He grabbed the tops of his thighs. He felt the peppering of short, dark hairs there as he pulled Ben's body to him. Ben fell onto him in complete abandon. Their mouth crashed into each other hungrily.

The slowness was over. The waiting was through. They could deny their desires no longer. They groped and pulled at one another frantically.

Ben ground his hips against Blayne's pelvis, and Blayne returned the pressure with his own upward thrusts. Those two shafts of hard desire crashed against each other over and over. They dueled and challenged one another. It was like a sword fight. Blayne would have laughed at the comparison, but the heat of the battle was too real and consuming to deny it for a silly joke.

Blayne felt the rub of hair and sweat between them. He felt the incredible weight of another man on him, and the simple fact of that reality made him want it even more. He clenched his stomach and lifted Ben's body roughly with a ripple of muscle and passion.

Ben broke the seal of their sweaty skin for a moment, and Blayne worried that he had done too much, gone too far. Had his need and insistence been more than the sweet consolation Ben had desired? Had he crossed the line with his hurried inexperience?

Before he could ask another ridiculous question of himself, Ben was back. And before Blayne could grasp the significance of Ben's brief absence, he felt the slick of Ben's hand and the tight unrolling of a condom around the thickness of his shaft. He felt the sudden delicious coldness of lube dribbling around latex and the hard knot of warmth as Ben lowered himself onto Blayne's waiting rod.

Blayne didn't know what to do, and he didn't have to. He just held his breath as Ben dangled there in silent anticipation on the top of his straight, hard cock. Then he exhaled slowly as he felt Ben's gradual decent and the delicious squeeze and heat of the inside of this man's body.

Blayne felt a shudder, deep and staggered like a sob, as Ben sat fully onto him. But Blayne could do nothing but look up at this beauty. He was paralyzed by the incredible sensation that surrounded him. It felt so new, but so right and familiar. It was as if joining with this man's body was something he was supposed to do, something his body had learned and forgotten. Something he had been searching to reclaim.

Ben's eyes had been closed as he had taken Blayne into him. He had been focused on adjusting to the size and pleasure of Blayne inside him. But now, his eyes opened. He looked down at Blayne's motionless expression of disbelief and bliss.

Slowly, he began to rock back and forth. It was the slightest movement. In half-darkness, Blayne couldn't even see it. But he could feel it. The push and pull of Ben's body around his cock was sheer, electrifying joy.

Ben took both Blayne's hands and placed them on his hips. He let him feel the motion grow, the sway intensify. Blayne gripped the muscle and bone like an eager dance partner as Ben raised and lowered himself longer and harder.

Ben paused at the top of his fluid arc, holding just the swollen head of Blayne's hard-on inside him. Then he came down fast and hard. His body swallowed the entire length and girth of Blayne, and bounced off the mound of matted pubes at the base to start again.

The room was full of the breath and steam and echoes of their pleasure. Ben rode him hard, and Blayne pulled Ben onto him again and again by the tops of his thighs.

Sweat pooled in the hollow of Blayne's chest, but he couldn't be certain whose it was. Ben's dark, sweaty bangs dangled above as he braced his hands against Blayne's solid pecs. Drops fell as he worked his hips up and down and stoked the heat of friction inside him.

Blayne felt the wet slap of Ben's hardness against his stomach, and he bucked upwards and into him as he felt his own cock surge.

Ben leaned back. He took one hand from Blayne's chest and pumped his own erection in long, firm strokes. Blayne groaned at the sight and feel of Ben on him. He arched his back and reached up inside Ben's warmth as far as he could.

In what felt like one long geyser of relief and pressure that had been building for years, Blayne gushed into Ben and filled that condom. Before he had even finished the long breath of exhaustion and ecstasy that accompanied his climax, he felt Ben splash and splatter onto his torso. Droplets of semen fell across his stomach and chest. The musk of Ben's come seeped into those pools of sweat, and Ben himself fell forward into Blayne's warm, wet embrace.

"Stay with me tonight," he whispered.

Ben didn't have the strength or energy to resist his instincts. And there was nothing strong enough to pull Blayne away from him at that moment.

Even the dark clutches of fatigue and sleep couldn't untangle their arms or loosen their grip on one another.

CHAPTER 10

Blayne Brandon," the loud speaker of Mandatory's paging system screeched through the Monday morning, "please call Garret's office as soon as possible."

Ben could hear the page from his own office. He knew that everyone on this entire floor could hear it, too. That was the point of paging someone. However, Ben felt especially intruded upon by the static beep and click of the speaker. It was as if his most precious secret had been broadcast to an office full of strangers.

Perhaps it all felt more disturbing since Ben had not heard a single page in his week of employment at Mandatory. This wasn't the kind of place that allowed such unprofessional intrusions. Ben hadn't even know there was a paging system.

He didn't know why it was suddenly acceptable to page Blayne before nine on a Monday. He supposed any means necessary could be employed when Garret wanted someone at his beck and call. But even if Ben had wanted to, he couldn't have been any help to the man. He didn't know where Blayne was either.

He understood. It made sense. And Ben was trying his best to be rational about the entire situation.

Blayne couldn't have very well gone to the office in a pair of jeans and a rumpled tee. The outfit looked even more inappropriate after spending the night piled on Ben's living room floor.

Regardless, Ben had not been thrilled to wake up alone with half the covers peeled back from his bed.

He could still feel Blayne's arms. He could still feel the shape of Blayne's shoulder where it had pressed against the side of his face as he'd slept. The other side of the bed was still warm.

It wasn't as if Blayne had deserted him in the middle of the night. Ben could hear the splash of water in the bathroom sink. He could see a sliver of golden light cutting across the floor in the early-morning darkness. Blayne was still there.

But as Ben lay in the half-empty bed half asleep, he felt abandoned.

"Honey," he called from the pillow.

Ben heard the familiar squeak of the faucet turning off. The bathroom door opened to spill light into the bedroom, and Ben came fully awake.

"What?" Blayne asked.

It was hard to tell whether he was responding to Ben's call or questioning his choice of words. Hopefully he hadn't heard that word at all.

Ben felt stupid and confused. He knew damned well that you don't call someone 'honey' on a first date. Hell, there had never even been a first date unless he counted coffee or pizza in his living room. And you sure as hell don't call a closeted, married coworker 'honey,' no matter how many 'dates' there may have been.

So Ben had just rolled back into the pillow and buried his face. He almost hoped that Blayne would go back to the sink. He almost hoped Blayne would go back to washing him off his skin and sneaking out into the early morning.

So Ben feigned sleep. There was nothing to stop Blayne from walking out into the purple dawn and locking the door behind him. Ben tried to remind himself what was really going on here. Blayne was married. Blayne was the boss' son. Blayne was 'straight.'

The only thing worse than sleeping with Blayne was calling him 'honey.' Ben would be damned if he let himself develop some childhood crush on an unattainable man. And he would be double-damned if he let it slip out and let that man know about it.

Then he had felt the solid weight of Blayne's hand on his back. Ben felt the softness of just-washed skin against him. Then he felt the gentlest touch of lips on the back of his neck. Blayne hadn't shaved. Ben could feel the slight tickle of whiskers around his kiss. And Ben could feel the slow, sleepy way Blayne let his lips linger there on the nape of his neck.

The feeling was almost too comfortable and wonderful for Ben to stand. He certainly couldn't resist it. Ben rolled over to face him.

Blayne had retrieved his boxers from the other room, but that was the only effort he had made to cover himself. Ben looked up at him sitting there in the bruised light of daybreak and the golden glow from the bathroom. The conflicting colors seemed to dance across his tan skin. The light wrapped around his wide shoulders and the creases of his broad, smooth chest. It traced every muscle along his arm and the tiny lines along the corners of his smile. It highlighted his uncharacteristically tousled hair. The strands of tan and gold were streaked with sunrise. His eyes were amber.

"I've got to go," Blayne said, "unless you have a tie that matches blue jeans."

But even as he said it, he crawled under the sheets with Ben. He held his naked body against him and kissed the backs of his shoulders.

Ben felt his body start to respond to the affection, but he knew by Blayne's breathing that this wasn't foreplay. This was good-bye. He really did have to go. So Ben just let Blayne hold him for one long moment as the sun peaked over the windowsill and the room was filled with gold.

After long kisses, he had left. And Ben had dreamed about him. All he had to do was dream that Blayne was still there in the bed as if he belonged there, and Ben felt safe and warm. Then he woke, and he felt stupid yet again. So he showered quickly and went to work early, earlier than Blayne Brandon.

Ben heard the speaker of the paging system click on again. Through the window of his office, he saw Garret Brandon stride impatiently toward the reception desk. The poor woman sitting there looked absolutely terrified with her finger on the button of the intercom. Before she could repeat the page or Garret could bark new orders at her, Blayne walked into the lobby with defiance on his face.

Ben almost laughed at the similarity in their walks. Father and son, pissed off and taking names. Neither of them looked particularly happy or prepared to see the other here, but neither was going to be caught off guard.

"Did you want to speak to me about something?" Blayne started the conversation. It didn't sound much like a question, and it didn't sound much like he wanted to hear the answer.

"The reports on product profitability," Garret said flatly. "Not on my desk."

"Because they were sent last week," Blayne said, "after you approved them. Twice."

Ben watched as the receptionist hunkered down behind her desk. She tried to busy herself when pens and papers, but he could tell she just wanted to disappear. Fortunately, the rest of the office hadn't gotten off to its usual bustling start. It was still early on a Monday, and the rest of the lobby was empty. It was turning out to be one hell of a Monday for this poor woman.

"Jeanette's products?" Garret asked, ignoring the insult. "You need to meet. I called. All weekend. Your wife called. Where were you?"

Blayne didn't even look the slightest bit guilty. He wasn't going to be attacked or surprised by Garret's tactics. He looked cool and collected. In fact, he looked absolutely dashing with his fresh shave, combed hair and crisp suit. The contrast to his early-morning casualness was charming. Ben was almost pleased he had left to clean himself up. Of course, there was nothing Ben wanted more than to unknot that tie and muss that hair, to peel off that suit and return Blayne to his disheveled nakedness.

"What is going on here?" Blayne questioned. "Profitability reports aren't due for a month. We're ahead of the game. And what do I have to do with England's products? If they need reports, send Jeanette back to deal with them."

"She's your wife." Garret pointed out.

That fact seemed to affect Ben more strongly than Blayne. When he thought about it, Ben realized it always had. Ben wasn't even part of this argument, but he felt a pang of regret when he heard Garret mention her name. Even if she was a complete bitch.

Blayne didn't even flinch.

"You're telling me to focus on this project," Blayne countered, "this project that is rapidly approaching a production deadline. But you seem to be doing everything you can to sabotage it. This isn't about me, and it isn't about Jeanette."

"About all of us. This company. This family."

"In case you've forgotten, those are two separate things," Blayne said. "This is about what's in there, dad."

He pointed straight at Ben through the window. Ben almost overlooked the fact that Blayne had called Garret Brandon 'dad' for the first time he could remember. He looked down quickly at whatever papers were sitting on the table in front of him. He had no idea what they said. He was just avoiding Blayne's insistent index finger and Garret's accusing stare that followed it.

"That's what really matters," Blayne continued. "That's what we have to figure out and make work. It's about this project. It's about Ben. And I for one plan on doing whatever I can to put it all together."

"No. Nothing to do with you," Garret insisted. "Just design. Need you in London. You and Jeannette. Plane leaves at noon."

Ben sneaked a peak out of the corner of his eye. At least Blayne had lowered his finger. Now his hands were on his hips. Blayne and Garret stood there in an absolute face off. They were two men in dark suits. They were adversaries. They were father and son.

In fact, they looked nothing alike. Blayne's warm good looks contrasted the severity of Garret's sharp edges. However, the determination in their eyes and the aggressive resistance in their stances were practically reflections as they stood there nose to nose.

"Jeanette and I aren't going anywhere," Blayne said definitively. "We're getting a divorce."

"Of course not," Garret barked.

"This is one business decision you are not going to make, dad," Blayne said. "It's over."

Blayne walked away. Sometimes the winner just leaves. He doesn't have to finish the fight or complete the kill. He just does what he has to do and recognizes when he's reached that point. Winning isn't always about defeating someone else. It's about triumphing for yourself.

Ben heard his door open without a knock. He looked up in surprise as Blayne walked boldly into his office, as if Ben were expecting him, as if they were familiar.

Out of the corner of his eye, Ben could see Garret Brandon standing alone in the lobby. Ben didn't even have to see him. He could feel those eyes cutting through the glass. He could feel that gaze piercing him.

"Good morning," Blayne said loud enough to be heard in the lobby.

Somehow that made it better. Ben no longer felt Garret's glare. He knew it was still there, watching, disapproving. Somehow Blayne's words and his smile made all of that irrelevant. Garret may still have been looking, but it didn't matter what he saw. They didn't care.

"Good morning," Ben responded. He smiled right back at him.

Their smiles had that knowing smirk in the corners, that secretive signal of shared insight. They were like schoolboys who knew who put the goat in the principal's office and then showed up to class as if nothing was amiss.

The conspiratorial smiles reflected in the sparkle of their eyes. But they had to be careful not to give away their secret. They shouldn't gaze at one another too long. The principal was still standing right outside the window, and he didn't look very happy. It was almost as if he knew, or he almost knew. He was just waiting for them to give it all away.

That brief moment was bliss, as if they were immune to Garret and his power and the rest of the world that wanted them to fail. But within seconds Ben could feel Garret's icy scowl on his back again.

He could almost hear the gears grinding away in that man's head. No, he could almost feel them. Garret's merciless business mind was churning away, and this time Ben was the target.

It was a paranoid thought. God only knew what his therapist would think about it. But it sent a shiver up Ben's spine regardless.

He had to look away from Blayne. In fact, he had to look back at Garret. It was not a challenge. He wasn't trying to start a fight. He was just trying to reassure himself that the stare he felt on his back was really there. Actually, he hoped he'd just been imagining the whole thing.

Unfortunately, his instincts had been dead on. Ben locked eyes with Garret Brandon through the glass. The man didn't even consider looking away. He peered into Ben in a way that felt like a violation. It seemed he looked straight into him and saw things he could use against him. It seemed Garret knew things, knew everything. It almost seemed he saw things there that Ben himself didn't even know.

At that moment, the moment before Ben had to look away to protect himself, the elevator doors opened onto the lobby. Todd and Emily spilled out of the shiny doors with laughter and coffee cups.

They stopped laughing as soon as they saw Garret standing solid and alone there, but it was enough of a disturbance to make the boss look away from Ben. He nodded at them and walked away. He left the two wide-eyed and silent.

They entered Ben's office with a hundred questions on their faces. They looked to Ben for answers, but he was too flustered to sum up the situation. So Blayne did it for him.

"Looks like you guys are stuck with me," he said.

Everyone but Ben laughed. This office was just the right size for four. But their laughter was a little high and tight. They knew that there would be something else hanging over them in this spacious room. And the shadow of Garret Brandon was much too large and foreboding to fit in here with them.

"Well, there's plenty of work for all of us," Todd said as he paced around the room, back and forth in front of the wide view of the awakening city. "Let's get started."

Ben couldn't tell if all that excess energy was nervousness or ambition. The sunlight from the window made Todd look like a little ball of energy. His orange tufts of hair glowed.

Ben noticed that Todd had taken an extra minute or two with his grooming this morning. He hadn't tamed all the wild streaks of hair, but most of it was plastered down and combed neatly to the side. His pants even looked ironed. Ben could tell by the fresh crease down the leg that was slightly off center.

Todd slapped his hands together and rubbed them briskly. Ben almost expected a pep talk.

"Well, Hot Toddy," Emily called out to him, "you're rearing to go as usual."

She chuckled under her breath at him. She didn't seem to realize that Ben and Blayne were starring at her with cocked eyebrows.

"Hot Toddy?" Ben asked. There was nothing that would distract him from this conversation. "Did I miss something?"

"Oh, Em just thinks it..." Todd began.

"Em?" Ben interrupted. Todd blushed. "When the hell did you two get so damned cute."

Ben looked back and forth between the two and finally let his accusation rest on Emily. For the first time he noticed that her hair was not in her signature ponytail. Hell, it even looked like she'd brushed it. Her dark brown hair fell around her shoulders softly. It framed her pale, fresh face and made her eyelashes stand out. She looked beautiful, but Ben was not about to let her get away with it for a second.

"Ben," she said with warning in her voice, "you're the one who said you wanted to make this project a success."

"Things were left a little unfinished last week," Todd tried to explain. He had stopped pacing, but he hadn't stopped blushing. "Mandatory doesn't like unfinished business."

Ben's question was still unanswered, and he just kept staring at the two of them, waiting. Even Blayne seemed interested in this story. He was still standing by the door, but now he leaned back against the frame and crossed his arms across his broad chest, watching the show.

"So we decided to figure it out," Emily said. "So we got together yesterday to talk about it."

"And give each other pet names?" Ben smirked, "And makeovers?"

"To look at some design ideas for the razor," she said through her teeth.

Right on cue, Todd hustled toward the table and spread rows of papers out for display. Ben stood to examine them, and Blayne joined him at the table. He was having a blast tormenting Emily for a change, but his curiosity about the razor was almost as intense.

"Really, Em?" Ben said with as many insinuating syllable as possible. "How interesting."

"Really," Emily said definitively.

She said it in a way, and with a warning look, that said, 'I didn't get laid, so shut the hell up.'

"What did you two do yesterday?" She added with feigned innocence in her voice.

Emily looked at how close Ben and Blayne stood. There was nothing overtly inappropriate about it, but two straight men certainly wouldn't be in each other's personal space like that. Moreover, a straight man tended to double his distance from all out gay men. It left more room for his masculinity and testosterone and his big giant cock. Or something like that. It also left plenty of room for homophobia and the kind of squeamish fear usually reserved for very small girls. Regardless, there was no such space between Ben and Blayne. They were close enough to feel heat and electricity and attraction.

Damn it, Ben thought. Emily could always tell. He made a mental note to stop disclosing sensitive information to his fag hag. He also considered the color of the pot and the kettle.

He may have been just as guilty as they were, if not more so, but he couldn't help teasing them. It was his nature. "Well, I guess Blayne and I will just have to come up with cute little nicknames, too."

"I don't know about the rest of you," Blayne came to the rescue, "but I think Blayne is a bad enough name all by itself. Sounds kind of effeminate, don't you think?"

"That's one way to put it," Ben joked. But there was really nothing mean about it. He kind of smiled and leaned toward Blayne. Their shoulders brushed against one another lightly. A straight guy probably would have punched him on the shoulder and guffawed with his mouth wide open. Ben opted for a softer touch and harsher words. He leaned back into Blayne one more time for good measure.

And honestly, Blayne didn't seem to mind. He smirked and shook his head, as if Ben was the naughtiest little smart-ass he'd ever encountered. Actually, it was quite possible that he was. Ben just wondered what his punishment was going to be.

He shook the thought from his head and looked back to Todd. The little man was off the hook thanks to Blayne.

"Just don't screw it up, Hot Toddy," Ben said to the frightened man's face. He could tell Todd had no idea whether he was talking about the project or Emily. And that confusion was exactly what Ben had intended.

But Todd didn't need Ben's permission to hit on his hag. Hell, Ben probably would have slipped him a wad of cash and a handful of condoms if he thought it would help any. He just didn't think any man had a chance with Emily. Todd wasn't even in her weight-class. But he was wiry. Maybe he could pull a few moves she wasn't expecting.

With that thought, Ben turned his attention to the pages on the table.

"Wow," he said. He was almost ashamed of his childish games that had distracted them from the project when he saw the amount of work in front of him.

Ben figured Emily really hadn't gotten laid. There simply wouldn't have been time for it. He didn't know where she had found the time to do this much work over the weekend.

There must have been a dozen different designs there, all meticulously arranged in rows by Todd. It even seemed that he had grouped them into categories. Each row seemed to have its own style.

There was a modern series across the top with shiny curves and geometric designs. However, there was nothing cliché or typical about them. These were not the slightly tweaked knock-offs Garret had shown Ben. Emily's were almost like sculpture.

The row under that was almost retro, but there was something fresh about the combinations, too. They were square or oblong, decorated with chrome-like accents and exaggerated details like cars from the fifties. They borrowed their color schemes from hippies and disco dancers—avocado and burnt orange and baby blue.

The bottom row traveled back further in time. These designs could only be called antique. Maybe Victorian. Possibly Egyptian. They were formal and ornate, scalloped and beaded, heavy and solid. They were beautiful.

Blayne gravitated immediately toward the bottom row. He reached for one of the designs on the right. It was a burnished silver rod with deep grooves carved into its length. Along each end, there was a protruding circle of darker metal, like two rings. Along the edges of the bands there were rows of finely beaded silver. it could have been the model for a grand column or a scepter. The blade seemed to grow out of it naturally, like a buttress or a jewel. The unique silvery patina was perfectly tarnished and antiqued, rich and luxurious.

"What is this made of?" Blayne asked.

"It's paper," Emily joked. She laughed nervously at her bad joke. She always seemed embarrassed when people looked at her work or complimented her talent. "Just kidding. It's pewter."

"It's amazing," he said.

He took the sheet of paper in both hands to examine it. He seemed so eager and mesmerized that he nearly dropped it. He fumbled. He sliced his thumb wide open on the edge of the paper.

"Shit!"

But with his thumb in his mouth, he actually could have said 'ship' or sheet' or 'shift.' Given the circumstances, Ben figured the vulgar form was the proper translation. Blayne nursed his wound, sucked his blood.

"If you're going to talk with your mouth full..." Ben quipped.

"I know," Blayne interrupted, "I should have something more interesting in there to talk about."

"What?" Ben asked, completely baffled.

How in the world had Blayne known what he was going to say? He was sure that that saying was a Ben-original. It wasn't even one of his good ones.

"It must be a Terrington thing," Blayne answered. His cut seemed to have stopped bleeding. At least he'd taken it out of his mouth. He was easier to understand without the speech impediment, but Ben still didn't quite grasp what he was saying.

"What?"

"Terrington College," he said. "I saw it on your resume. The Terrington Terrors? The good ol' alma mater?"

"Yeah, I know all that," Ben said, "but how the hell do you?"

He looked over at Blayne with the strangest expression. Half of him wanted to gaze at this handsome face endlessly. The other half didn't know what to think. Strangely, he felt so close to Blayne. Yet every time he though he knew what was going on in that beautiful, sandy head, Blayne came out with something as crazy and unexpected as the name of Ben's college.

"I went to Terrington, too." Blayne said. "So you don't remember me?"

He didn't expect a real answer. He was certain they had never met. He was almost certain. And he was almost teasing Ben with his question. He was just checking.

"No," but Ben didn't sound that sure of his answer. "But it is a pretty small school."

"The best of the best," Blayne piped in a common Terrington adage, "or so they say."

"Nothing but for a Brandon," Ben amended. He looked a little glassy-eyed at Blayne. He furrowed his brow and wrinkled his scar. "Do they say that, too?"

"Well, no," Blayne said, just as perplexed, "but we do."

And by 'we' he meant the Brandons. He didn't mean him and

Ben. Why would he and Ben share these sayings? It was a family tradition, a family joke. It was inside snobbery from his father who prided himself on having his name on a building at his old school.

The questioning look just wouldn't leave Ben's face. His dark, straight eyebrows practically met in the middle, he was so confused. Blayne took a moment to admire him. He ignored the presence of Emily and Todd. He just gazed at Ben's beautiful bewilderment. He loved the way the sharp, pale angles of his face could twist into such an adorable grimace. The line across his forehead and the worried expression of his brow only emphasized the white scar. It was tough and cute and rugged, but at the same time it troubled Blayne.

"It is weird we never met," Ben mused. "Maybe I saw you before, from across the quad, on the way to class. I mean, you seem..."

But he couldn't conjure up the right word. Familiar? Reminiscent? Intimate? Common? Forgettable? It was on the tip of his tongue, and it wouldn't come off. He was stuck.

"Maybe," Blayne said. "We must have traveled in different circles."

"I'm sure," Ben said. At least his old sarcasm managed to creep back into his comment. The backhanded insult managed to bring him into reality for a moment. He just wasn't sure. He didn't know. There was so much he couldn't remember.

What Ben did remember from college was probably not Blayne's cup of tea. Ben had his share of fun at Terrington; he just couldn't remember all their names. That had very little to do with amnesia.

Ben doubted any of his 'friends' would have become closeted, married businessmen. He figured there was no chance that Blayne had been part of his circle, or circle jerk for that matter.

Blayne was still uptight for a thirty-three-year-old. Ben couldn't imagine what kind of nervous nerd he had been at twenty. Maybe he hadn't stood out of the crowd then. Maybe he wasn't as handsome and altogether hot back then. It was possible. But it was still strange.

"Maybe," Blayne conceded. "It was a long time ago."

"It's all a little foggy really," Ben added. "You know—college. Half the time studying until you're cross-eyed. The other half, drinking till you're blind."

"Anything could have happened."

"Yeah," Ben agreed, "anything."

They paused. There really wasn't anything left to say. They just stared at each other as if the answer was going to materialize there between them.

"All right, boys," Emily interrupted, "thanks for the trip down memory lane, but it's going nowhere real fast."

"Yeah, guys," Todd jumped back into the conversation, "how about a detour onto Reality Street? This razor ain't designing itself."

Ben and Blayne looked over at their audience. It was as if they had forgotten that they weren't alone. They stared dumbly at the other two and then gazed down at the computer-generated drawing of an antique razor. There was a spot of blood in the margin.

"It's perfect," Ben said.

"Well, I don't know about that," Emily insisted. She tucked her hair behind her ear shyly. It was as close to a thank you as she got. "I've got a lot of fine tuning to do before it's presentable."

"Look, I don't know the first thing about design," Blayne said, "but this hits the target audience smack dab in the face. Look."

And with that, he rushed to the other end of the room and retrieved a stack of folders. Ben had looked at them days ago, but as far as he was concerned the reports weren't even in English. However, they seemed to be written in Blayne's native tongue.

"Look at these demographics," he insisted. "Are you sure you didn't read this marketing research?"

No one in the room answered. They didn't know what the hell he was talking about. Even if they had read it, they wouldn't have understood him any better.

"Look at these men," Blayne said as he opened the first thick report.

Everyone else in the room saw charts and graphs. They certainly didn't see men.

But as Blayne opened the booklets to lopsided charts, bar graphs and rows of numbers, he began to paint a picture of the men he saw in them.

"Look how their incomes skew," he pointed out. "They're way above average,"

It was true. The men who purchased Mandatory made twice as much as the guys who bought your run-of-the-mill grooming products. Their jobs were inevitably listed as business/professional. They spent inordinate amounts of money on fashion and travel and sports cars every year.

"Mandatory users aren't your everyday guy with stubble," Blayne said. "They want quality and luxury. But the guys who are going to buy this razor are even more exclusive than our average customer."

He flipped pages as the other three looked on. They weren't really grasping the data printed there. They were waiting for Blayne to translate.

Ben just watched his hands flip through research. He looked at the strong fingers, the smooth tan skin stretched across wide knuckles. He remembered what it felt like to be touched by those hands, to wake up with those arms around him.

"They are the cream of the crop," Blayne continued. "They are the snootiest of our market, and the richest. They have to be. Do you have any idea how much thing is going to cost?"

No one knew. They all looked dumbly at him, waiting for the revelation. Ben tried to focus on his job instead of the job he'd prefer to be performing on Blayne.

"At least five times the average razor," he answered himself. "We had to jack up the price to justify the start-up costs of production. We have manufacturing plants just sitting there empty, waiting for a design. And it can't just be good. It has to be expensive as hell."

"So we're selling an expensive razor to rich guys," Emily summed it up. "I don't get how that makes this design any better."

"These men could buy an electric razor for less," Blayne pointed out. "They don't want some flashy, modern toy. We're not trying to sell this to a fifteen-year-old with peach fuzz and hope he stays with our razor out of habit."

"Right," Ben said. He was beginning to see where Blayne was headed with this. "We've got to make this a real luxury product, almost a status symbol. Like a Rolls Royce or a Rolex. It's got to be a classic."

"Exactly," Blayne said. "This customer doesn't just want a fancy gadget and a good shave. He doesn't just want to look better. He wants a valuable collector's piece that actually makes him better for owning it. This customer is middle-aged, high-income and completely full of himself."

"Damn," Emily piped in, "who the hell is this guy?"

"It's my father."

Blayne was staring out into the lobby. They all turned to follow his gaze, and there was Garret Brandon glaring right back at them.

It was almost as if all four of them shivered at once. It was that same look Ben had seen earlier that morning. It was so accusing, so malignant.

Blayne walked over to the window and closed the blinds.

CHAPTER 11

Tuesday, they discovered the pewter problem. It was too soft, too heavy and too expensive. Unfortunately, it was exactly the look they wanted. And even more unfortunate was the fact that it wasn't the only problem they were having.

Blayne and Ben were having serious trouble focusing on the problem at hand. Every time they reached for some reference book on metals or leaned in to look at a computer screen, their hands would touch, their shoulders would rub.

It had been over twenty-four hours since they had kissed. It was driving them crazy.

Mandatory had managed to keep them apart the night before. At the end of the day Monday, Todd and Blayne had been pulled into other areas of the company to handle meetings and documents and responsibilities that existed outside this war room with its secretively closed blinds.

Emily and Ben had been left to walk home together. It wasn't quite the pairing either of them had imagined. So they just shared a beer and talked about their new jobs. They both avoided teasing or accusing or admitting a thing. They didn't have enough energy left to open that can of worms and mention the two absentee members of their group.

They didn't have much energy for anything. They left their beers unfinished on the bar and were both in their respective beds before ten. Alone.

Ben was glad he was tired. Otherwise, thoughts of Blayne would have kept him tossing and turning and jerking off all night long. As it was, he fell asleep thinking about Blayne's embrace. On the edge of sleep, he could almost convince himself that his pillow was as comfortable as the crook of Blayne's arm between bicep and chest.

Very similar thoughts made Blayne's additional work take twice as long as it should have. His lawyer had to repeat the details of divorce several times before Blayne understood the steps to take and finally hung up the receiver. He left the office about the same time Ben was falling asleep.

But Tuesday morning, there was no escaping those thoughts. The big room seemed too close for comfort. Ben and Blayne couldn't put enough space between them to weaken their attraction. The presence of Todd and Emily was the only thing keeping them from peeling off their clothes and devouring one another.

The other couple was tucked into a corner of the room, huddled at a computer making the smallest tweaks to the design. Todd and Emily were completely absorbed and just as oblivious to Ben and Blayne's struggle.

Emily was a perfectionist. She would fiddle with every millimeter and shadow of the thing until five minutes before a presentation. And Todd seemed absolutely enthralled by the process, or perhaps by the woman doing it. He stood right over her shoulder the whole time. Normally, she would rip someone's head off just for glancing at an unfinished project, let alone watching and commenting and hanging there like her conscience.

She didn't even let Ben do that. But he wasn't jealous. The entire process drove Ben crazy. But not nearly as crazy as the scent of Blayne and the tan shadow of stubble along his jaw.

Ben closed his eyes and inhaled. Blayne smelled clean and warm, like the beach or summer in the woods. There was something so comforting about the simple smell of man, this man.

It was redolent of flowering trees. Like a memory from years past of one specific tree that only grows in a certain climate he'd visited once long ago. Like something he thought he'd forgotten, but suddenly the combination of cologne and soap and the breeze hit him just right. Woody and floral and fresh like dew, like honey. Suddenly, he was back there.

Ben knew that scent was still clinging to his sheets. That must be what made it so familiar and exciting. But it also stuck to his thoughts like a reminder. Never forget this, it said. Don't lose this memory, too.

When Ben opened his eyes, Blayne was looking right at him. It figured. But Blayne wasn't accusing him of daydreaming or sleeping. He wasn't angry that Ben had looked away from the incredibly boring subject of metallurgy on the computer screen in front of them.

Despite that work, despite the pesky problem of pewter, they couldn't avoid the intensity of each other's presence. No matter what they read or where they turned, Ben and Blayne were right there side by side, inches apart and just out of reach.

"Well, silver tarnishes," Blayne said, "and it's more expensive anyway."

Blayne certainly wasn't thinking about silver or any other metal for that matter. Ben just nodded his head. Blayne was thinking about the shape of Ben's face, the high cheekbones and pale skin. He was thinking about the sharp angles of jaw and chin, the way they felt cradled in his hand as he brushed back those dark bangs and kissed those lips.

He was thinking about Ben's body above him, moving back and forth on him. He was thinking about the trickle of sweat down Ben's tight torso and the sound of breath in a still room. He couldn't get the sensation out of his head. He couldn't shake the memory of being inside Ben.

And there was a part of Blayne, somewhere behind these thoughts, deep inside himself, that couldn't help wondering what it would be like to have Ben deep inside him. The speculation was crazy, but it was almost a sensation all its own. Blayne could almost feel it. It was almost as if Blayne already knew what it would feel like to have a man inside him.

And of course, Blayne did know. A deep, stabbing guilt coursed through him. He did know subconsciously, even though he couldn't remember. His body knew what it was like to be penetrated and violated. Blayne didn't want to remember.

Blayne scolded himself. He screamed at himself from inside. Stop it! These were the tortured thoughts that crept into his head every time he saw a beautiful man jog by or caught a masculine smile thrown in his direction. These were the thoughts he couldn't remember. He didn't want to. They were thoughts he had been told about, warned about. He would do anything, ignore any desire, to keep them from coming back. Until now. Until Ben.

Blayne refused to let the two thoughts have anything to do with one another. Rape is not sex, he reminded himself. And it had nothing to do with the feeling Blayne was having now. It had nothing to do with Ben.

This sensation, this curiosity, was unique to Ben. He was the one making Blayne feel this way, putting these thoughts into his head. And if, after all, Blayne was going to have memories of men and sex and all those things he had feared for so long, he wanted them to be with Ben.

"Silver won't work," Ben announced to the room. He was just repeating the fact Blayne had discovered, but it was all he could do to focus on the task at hand in that small way. "Are you sure this thing can't be made out of plastic?"

That got Emily's attention. She swiveled her chair from the computer and shot him her bitchiest look. It was exactly what Ben would have expected from her while she was in the middle of a project. She couldn't resist his taunting, even with an adorable little redheaded admirer hanging on her every word and hanging directly above her.

"Don't mess with me, missy," she said. "Just find a solution."

"Aren't you supposed to be the designer?" he challenged.

"Exactly. I'm a designer. Which basically means I draw pictures," she quirked her eyebrow at him. He was in trouble now. "I make it pretty, but I don't know how the hell to make it. I could draw you a car, honey, but it doesn't make me a mechanic. And, by the way, aren't you supposed to be the almighty Creative Head?"

She didn't want an answer, and she didn't wait for one. She turned back to her computer and her design. She just turned her back on him. Todd followed suit and immediately pointed to something he thought was infinitely interesting on the screen.

But she was right. She had already done her part. And Todd had supplied all this research and reference materials on metal and the company and razors and every other little detail he could find to organize for them. Even Blayne, despite his own distractions, had been invaluable in helping them understand the consumer and select a design. He was also the one who insisted they couldn't leave the pewter problem up to the factory or the company or Garret Brandon. His father would use any excuse possible to reject them and their design. Their failure was the test of his success.

Everyone had played their part. Everyone had given their all. Ben hadn't done anything but cause a lot of trouble. He had disrupted Mandatory, Garret, Jeanette, the entire project. He had disrupted Emily's career, Blayne's sexuality and a marriage. He'd managed all this in a single week at the company. The only thing he hadn't done was his job.

Although Ben still wasn't exactly sure what that job was. But he figured it wasn't staring into space and daydreaming about the boss' son.

Ben looked over at Todd and Emily. They may have been flirting. Honestly, it was hard to tell. But they were definitely working, which more than could be said for Ben and Blayne. Somehow the magnetic pull they felt and the tension it took to resist falling into each other's arms was taking all their energy. Ben didn't know how Todd and Emily could multitask so efficiently.

Emily and Todd seemed so sweet, like puppy love, like young love. They didn't actually seem like children. It was their relationship that was youthful. Honestly, it wasn't even a relationship at this point. They were still flirting with the idea. They were still flirting with each other.

But it wasn't like that with Ben and Blayne. The air between them seemed charged at every moment. It wasn't just sex or attraction. This thing between them seemed tangible. It seemed like a well-established relationship.

It was a funny thought, especially considering the fact that Ben had never managed to date anyone longer than a few months. Even though Blayne had a ten-year marriage under his belt, it was anything but traditional or functional, and now it was over.

Neither of them knew what a real relationship felt like. But if they had to guess, both of them would have said it felt just like this. However, neither of them was willing to say that out loud or even whisper it to himself. It seemed so stupid, so impossible. But that's not how it felt.

Ben should have known better. He should have known not to let his desire cloud his better judgment. Blayne was married. Blayne was closeted. Blayne was the boss' son and everything Ben should be avoiding as a semi-stable gay man in his thirties. He knew all this. He kept repeating it to himself like a prayer, waiting for it to come true.

He knew that people don't fall in love over coffee. They don't fall in love in a week. Maybe if it was months or years of coffee and companionship. Maybe. But not on a weekday afternoon in a coffee shop.

He believed all these things. These were the lessons he had learned, the facts he lived by. He knew they were true. They just didn't feel that way.

When he looked at the way Blayne's shoulders tested the strength of his suit or the distracted way those big brown eyes kept glancing back at Ben, there was no amount of repeating these facts that would make Ben feel it. Instead, his head filled with memories of sex and kisses and laughter. His mind was flooded with images and emotions that he was sure there hadn't been time to create over the past week.

It was as if he had forgotten all the rules and lessons he had learned in the gay world. Pretty faces were a dime a dozen. And anyone could buy one from a plastic surgeon for a little bit more.

There were a lot of things Ben had forgotten in his life. But no matter how he tried to remind himself, he couldn't seem to remember to follow his own life lessons. There was something stronger than that sitting right here in front of him.

It felt stronger than desire. It felt like instinct, like knowledge. No matter how he tried to shake himself and bring his thoughts back to the present, his mind kept tugging him in another direction. I know where I'm going, it said, follow me.

It kept teasing him with sweaty thoughts and endless possibilities: Blayne with a tan; weekends in bed; a slow walk down a familiar path, hand in hand.

"I need index cards," Blayne blurted suddenly, "and a break."

He stood and stretched and headed for the door. Ben couldn't be sure if it had been Blayne's silly statement or his stretching body, but something gave Ben an immediate erection. He realized that it was the simple opportunity of the moment.

Ben counted to a hundred and excused himself to use the restroom.

Blayne walked down the hall toward the supply closet, but he wasn't thinking about index cards. He was trying to clear his head. He couldn't focus. Even thoughts of the supply closet brought back memories of Ben.

Almost kissing. Kissing. Ben on top of him. Ben in the morning. The aftertaste of Ben on his lips.

Blayne stared at rows of index cards and couldn't seem to choose a color. White would have been the obvious and normal choice, but he was fixated on pale blue. Half the shade of Ben's eyes, Blayne thought.

He was being ridiculous and he knew it. What was this obsession, this fling? Blayne didn't even know how to articulate the relationship in his own mind. Ben had picked him up in a coffee shop, for crying out loud.

And Blayne didn't know what that meant. He didn't know the rules of the gay world and gay relationships. Hell, quite honestly, he didn't even know if he was gay. Yes, another ridiculous thought, but it was the first and most obvious question that would come to anyone's mind if Blayne started gushing all these obsessive feelings for Ben to them.

Maybe it was just Ben. Maybe the intoxicating thrill of

touching male flesh for the first time had caused Blayne to exaggerating the events of the past week. Maybe it was Blayne's own twisted, half-blank mind playing Freudian games of revenge and self-torture. What did Dr. Carver call it, the rape mentality? The victim mentality? Bullshit?

There was nothing frightening or self-deprecating about these thoughts of Ben. They confused Blayne, but they didn't make him feel bad anymore. Instead, they caused a flutter of excitement and anticipation beneath his breastbone.

Ben sipping coffee. Ben eating pizza. Greasy lips and fingers. Caressing.

Ben's face as he cracked a joke or challenged authority. The quirk of a scarred eyebrow. The dark stripe of fur down Ben's flat stomach.

Ben in white briefs. Ben in the office. Ben in nothing but a Santa Claus hat and reindeer boxers...

It was the middle of summer. But in Blayne's mind, this is the odd thought that finally stuck—or came lose.

Dancing back and forth in front of a tiny Christmas tree, Ben smiled. He sang a carol that Blayne couldn't quite hear. He laughed as the floppy red hat slipped down over his eyes. He stopped dancing and shoved his costume back in place.

Then Blayne saw those blue, blue eyes in his mind. He saw Ben's dark eyebrows framing those eyes. He didn't see a scar.

***

Halfway down the hall, Ben realized he actually did need to use the restroom, especially if he had any hopes of successfully accosting Blayne in the supply room.

He hurried into the bright, empty room and trotted up to a urinal. He fumbled with his fly. Coaxing urine out of a half-hard penis takes some time, time he didn't have if he was going to catch Blayne.

As he was finishing, he was sure he'd missed his opportunity.

Then Blayne walked into the men's room holding a packet of

blue index cards . He looked dazed. He looked as if he didn't even see Ben standing there with his dick in his hand.

Blayne set the index cards down by the sink and turned on the tap. He leaned over and splashed water onto his face, blew long bubbling sighs into his cupped hands.

By the time he looked up, streams of water were pouring past his lips; bangs were plastered to his forehead.

He looked like a boy caught in the rain. He looked innocent and beautiful. For the briefest moment, Ben forgot the glaring white light of the bathroom. For just a second, he saw Blayne like this, soaked wet in the rain, framed in the golden spotlight of a street lamp, staring up at a window.

A moment later, Ben's attention returned to the bathroom. Blayne seemed to have snapped back to reality as well. The one thing that was certain, was Ben's erection was back in full force, hard in the palm of his hand.

They stared at one another, lost momentarily in the silence of the room. Ben squeezed the erection in his hand, felt the resistant flesh and surge of blood. He ran his thumb lightly along its length and felt the tickling tripping of each nerve as he gazed across the room into Blayne's eyes.

Blayne's focus broke as his eyes darted downward. He watched Ben stroke his long, straight hard-on. He followed the path Ben's fingers took from the engorged head to its base where it jutted from the fly of his pants.

Blayne closed the distance between them without further hesitation. A few hurried steps brought him right up against Ben's body. He pinned him against the wall between the urinals and kissed him hard.

Blayne was not usually this aggressive. There was nothing usual about this desire, however. The anticipation he had suffered through all morning long released itself into the rough, hungry kiss.

He held Ben's head from behind, to protect it from the hard tile wall and to pull him closer and harder into Blayne's wide-open mouth.

Stubble scratched at tender lips. Tongues probed and clashed frantically.

Blayne reveled in the desperate ruggedness of their action. He would never dare kiss a woman this hard. He wouldn't want to. But he could let the full force of his passion attack Ben's gaping mouth. He could kiss this man as hard as he wanted, as hard as he could. He could literally rub his face in it. And Ben could kiss him back just as hard.

Blayne could feel that erection pressed between them, Ben's hand still clenched around it, pumping faster. Blayne's own erection poked at his restricting fly and jabbed against Ben's stomach.

There was something else that turned Blayne on. There was something dirty and forbidden about fooling around in the restroom. The fear of getting caught and the novelty of the location.

There was nothing filthy about Mandatory's restrooms. In fact, they may have been the most meticulous in the city. They weren't just convenient facilities. At Mandatory, the men's room was a sparkling company showplace. The vanity was decorated like a cosmetics counter with a variety of soaps and lotions. The place even smelled pretty, like sandalwood and sage.

Regardless, the very fact of making out in the boy's room added an element of fantasy in Blayne's mind. It was naughty and dirty, and it made him lap even more hungrily at Ben's cavernous mouth.

Without letting the hot wetness of their kiss part, without releasing his grip on his own cock, Ben pushed and shuffled them across the bathroom and into the first stall. Blayne locked the door shut behind them.

Ben collapsed onto the toilet , gasping for air and fumbling to release Blayne's bulge that jutted in front of his face. Blayne was too dazed to help him. He ran the back of his hand across his mouth and wiped the sloppy remnants of their kiss from his chin.

When Blayne looked down, Ben had managed to free his erection, too. Ben was still running his hand up and down his own cock and had undone Blayne's pants one-handed. Blayne was impressed at his dexterity. Whereas Ben's penis stuck straight up through his open fly, Blayne's now bobbed freely because his pants were around his ankles.

Ben grabbed the thick base of Blayne's cock in his fist. He squeezed until the bulbous head throbbed purple, then released. Blayne moaned.

Ben's fingers moved up and down, just barely encircling Blayne's girth. He mirrored the motion of his other hand own his own yearning erection. Ben worked their cocks simultaneously, jerking his hand in his lap and pulling at Blayne roughly directly in front of his face.

Suddenly Ben leaned forward and dove in. He gripped the plump head of Blayne's penis with his lips. He teased the wide slit with his tongue. He twisted his head and his mouth in eager circles around the big, round knob. Then he pushed it to the back of his throat.

Blayne sighed in pleasure and release. It came out as a deep groan. Ben slid his head from one end of Blayne's shaft to the other in long, anxious mouthfuls. He pounded his fist along his own shaft in rhythm.

Blayne put his hand on the back of Ben's head once again. He followed its motion, guided its path as if Ben needed coaching or coaxing. As he did, Blayne's fingers dug into hair, rubbed at the nape of Ben's neck. He gripped harder.

Before he even knew what he was doing, he was pulling Ben's head insistently. He was grinding his hips into the man's face and feeding him his cock.

Ben slurped in compliance. He let his hand work faster on his own rod. He let Blayne fuck his face.

When Ben finally pushed back and pushed Blayne away, Blayne assumed he had gone too far. And perhaps Ben's mouth had taken as much pounding as it could. Ben gasped for breath and the opportunity to swallow. But at the same time, he was simply changing tactics.

He grabbed Blayne's hips and turned him around. He shoved

Blayne against the stall door, forcing him to reach forward and brace himself. Ben had pushed him into a wide-legged stance as if he was preparing to frisk him. Spread 'em.

Then Ben buried his face in Blayne's ass. Although Ben certainly couldn't see it from this position, Blayne's eyes widened in shock and electric sensation.

Ben's tongue prodded the tight hole. His hands spread Blayne's cheeks so he could delve deeper. He lapped and drooled in the warm musk of Blayne's ass. He wetted the entire length of the crevice, rubbed his face in the short, moist hairs.

Blayne leaned forward and pushed his ass toward this new, thrilling touch Ben was introducing him to. He was just about to let out another groan of appreciation when he heard the groan of the restroom door.

They both heard it. Ben lifted his head from his task of giving pleasure and quickly lifted his feet out of sight and onto the toilet seat.

Without thinking, Blayne followed suit and hopped onto the back of the toilet with Ben.

That was not how the game was supposed to be played. Now, instead of there appearing to be one person using the stall, there appeared to be no one inside a locked door. Despite the fact that this put Blayne's furry leg muscles within inches of Ben's face, it wasn't such a brilliant move.

Someone stepped into the room. Someone walked by slowly.

Don't choose this one, Ben thought. The footsteps returned to the front of the bright room, as if they had just been surveying the bathroom's occupants. They shuffled in front of a urinal for a while.

Blayne's precarious perch on the porcelain edge was becoming shaky. Ben looked up at him as he reached out and braced himself carefully against the walls of the stall.

Why won't this guy leave? Isn't he done pissing yet?

Blayne looked hilarious fluttering up there in his jacket and tie, especially since his pants and boxers were still around his ankles. Ben wondered if this is what semi-formal meant.

The urinal flushed. But when it stopped its splashing and hissing, the footsteps didn't leave. They shuffled, hesitated. Ben and Blayne held their breath.

The footsteps paced, turned toward them, turned back, approached the sink. This was torture. Ben's folded legs were starting to tingle. Blayne's bulging calf was quaking with pain or nerves or both.

Water poured into the sink. It stopped. It started. Stopped again. The intruder had resorted to water torture.

Did this guy know they were in here? Was he trying to flush them out? No better place for flushing than a bathroom, Ben thought. But the joke wasn't enough to cheer him. In fact, he was starting to get pretty worried. Gay men don't even spend this much time in the bathroom, not alone anyway.

The feet outside started tapping, waiting, contemplating. Ben hoped this guy was just combing his hair or picking his nose in the mirror. He hoped that anxious tapping wasn't meant for them.

"Emily, Emily, Emily," the tapping feet muttered into the mirror.

It was Todd. Ben stifled a laugh against Blayne's knee and nearly knocked him from the ledge of the toilet. Blayne teetered and looked down with wide-eyed accusation.

It wouldn't have been the worst situation in the world if Todd had discovered them here, Ben supposed. However, pantless and perverted probably wasn't the best way for Blayne to come out to his coworker.

Anyway, it sounded as if the poor kid had enough on his mind. Emily was more than enough to disturb a straight man. He didn't need gay drama on top of it all. He didn't need to witness Ben's 'creative head'… or his creative bottom.

Finally, the door squeaked shut behind Todd's footsteps. Blayne fell clumsily onto his feet and slammed against the locked stall door. He stood there shackled by his pants and glaring incriminatingly at Ben.

But it didn't take long for that look to go away, or for his erection to return, as Ben took him in his mouth again. Ben buried his face and felt Blayne grow and harden in the warmth of his mouth.

He was eager to resume his task. And Blayne was just as eager to release all that pent up anxiety. At least this was one job they were going to finish today.

When they walked back into the office together, Emily and Todd didn't even turn to notice. Todd just raised his arm toward them without meeting their eyes.

"Here, Blayne," he said. "You must have left these index cards in the men's room."

CHAPTER 12

Blayne was in the office bright and early on Wednesday morning. There was nothing new about that fact, but today the reason for it was completely different.

For the second time this week, he had spent the night in Ben's arms. That comforting embrace seemed to be the only cure for the thoughts and desires that had plagued his mind all day long.

But in the confusion of his ecstasy, not one of Blayne's thoughts had considered packing a bag for the overnight trip. So, yet again, he was forced to kiss Ben gently at dawn and sneak out into the purple light.

Fortunately, the gym occupied the same office tower as Mandatory. Blayne certainly wasn't up for a workout this morning. Ben had taken care of that excess energy. But Blayne managed to slip into the locker room for a shower amid all the early-morning exercise nuts. No one seemed to notice that his face wasn't covered in workout sweat. It was wearing a satisfied smile in its place.

Then Blayne walked silently to his office with wet hair and took the extra suit from its hook behind his office door. It was what any careful business man would do. You never knew when you'd spill coffee on your tie before a big meeting or have to jet off to a conference at a moment's notice.

He knotted his tie without a mirror in the dark office. It seemed like ages since he'd really worked here. This used to be where the majority of his time, his life, was spent. Now his days passed very differently at the other end of the company behind closed blinds.

Blayne walked out of his office without turning the lights on. Most of this entire floor was still in darkness. The summer sun was rising hot and orange beyond the glass walls, but most of the interior fluorescent bulbs were silent and dark.

There were a few lights down the hallway, safety lighting in public areas, behind the reception desk in the lobby, and spilling from the open blinds of Ben's office in slanted stripes onto the floor.

Blayne stopped at the far end of the lobby where he was still concealed in shadows. He knew that no one who worked in that office would have opened those blinds. They had been shut tight against Garret's prying eyes Monday.

It could have been the cleaning service or the maintenance staff. Maybe some one had dusted the blinds. Blayne just watched that rectangular window of light and waited.

He saw movement in the far corner. Someone bent at the computer screen and rushed toward the window. Blayne saw eyes peeking out from between the blinds, peering into the lobby. He saw blond hair and suspicious squinting. It was Jeanette's weasely little lover. He poked his head back into the room and hurried to the other side.

Blayne moved to confront him, to beat the shit out of the little snoop. But suddenly a light at the top of the elevator bank flickered on. The brass doors whooshed open. Blayne stepped back into darkness, waited.

It was Emily. She didn't seem to notice the blinds or the unusual light cutting across the floor. She walked with her typical determination, her ponytail bobbing behind her. Blayne could tell she'd been thinking about the design all night. She couldn't wait to get in here and make some miniscule change that had gnawed at her until she woke early and came in to fix it.

"What the fuck?" Emily stepped into the office.

Blayne smiled. He couldn't have said it better himself.

Blayne could see Emily's silhouette in the doorway with her hands on her hips. He could see nervous flickers of movement through the blinds as Jeanette's flunky stammered and stalled.

"Excuse me," his British accent stuttered, "I don't believe we've met. I work with Jeanette Brandon."

"Yeah, I know exactly who you are," Emily sneered as she strode in to confront him, "and what you are."

The truth was Emily had never met the man. She didn't have any idea what this creep's name was. But it was apparent to Blayne that she and Ben had traded enough gossip for her to recognize a sleaze ball with a British accent when she came across him.

"You're going to have to be a lot smarter than you look to find what you're searching for in there," she said as she approached the computer and switched it off. "See, I'm naturally distrustful. I'm used to getting screwed over. I'm a woman."

"And a very beautiful and talented one at that," the weasel oozed. He had regained some composure as he patted his thin, blonde hair and smoothed his tie. "I was just so curious to see your creation. I'm sure it is as breathtaking as its creator."

"I wouldn't hold my breath," Emily interrupted, "unless it's going to shut you up."

"We're all working for the same company, on the same project after all," he just kept going. "Maybe you could give me a sneak preview. A private showing."

This guy was absolute slime, Blayne thought. He had all he could do to keep himself from joining the confrontation . Somehow this was better. Letting Emily humiliate the idiot was perfect justice.

"The only thing you're going to get a private showing of is my fist," she offered. "It's breathtaking, really. Knocks the wind right out of you."

Blayne chuckled silently to himself.

The elevator doors opened again, and this time Todd stumbled into the half-darkness. Blayne had all he could do to contain his laughter as Todd shuffled by oblivious.

"I don't think a beautiful woman like you would really do that," the weasel cooed as Todd walked in unsuspecting.

"Well, I'm sure as hell not going to have a showing of privates or whatever," Emily said, "and I don't think my fiancé appreciates you talking to me that way."

The weasel turned around and faced Todd. They blushed at each other.

"Are you serious?" the British accent made it unclear whether he was questioning Emily's hostility or her relationship with Todd.

"I seriously have no interest in you," she insisted. "Besides, I don't have enough seniority here to help your career. You've slept your way as high as you can go."

Blayne couldn't see everything that was going on in there, despite the open blinds. However, he did notice the sudden silence as the truth of Emily's comment hit home and knocked the pasty little freak on his ass.

The pause in the entertainment gave other sounds the chance to drift through hallways towards Blayne's hiding place. Voices were creeping through offices. Computers were chiming awake. Nearly all the lights had come on by now.

Blayne's hiding place was no longer that hidden. It was just another corner of the lobby next to an increasingly busy elevator bank.

He took a seat near the reception desk and flipped absently through some men's exercise magazine. The receptionist pretended not to notice as she settled into her post in front of the phone. She had learned her lesson about ignoring the Brandons' peculiarities. She didn't so much as smile at him hidden there behind the magazine.

Ben was right. These ads and articles were little more than pornography. Shirtless men flexed and sweated on every page, whether they were selling after shave or demonstrating the latest chest exercise.

Why are these men topless in the gym?

Blayne could almost hear Ben's voice teasing him. Then Blayne did actually hear that voice, but there was nothing comical about it.

"Perhaps you've forgotten which department you work in," Ben boomed angrily, "or which country."

The pipsqueak murmured something about being curious and

wanting to help, but Blayne couldn't quite hear him from this side of the reception area. It didn't really matter. His English charm wasn't going to work on Ben either. He didn't have the brains or the balls to stand up to a real man. Besides, Blayne thought smugly, he isn't really Ben's type.

Blayne leaned forward on his knees, expecting to catch a glimpse of Ben's cute ass and defiant pose framed in the doorway. Instead, he saw the menacing silhouette of his wife obscuring his view.

"Mr. Abrahms," Jeanette's icy voice cut through the mumbling, "show me the designs. Otherwise you're doing nothing here but wasting everyone's time."

"Mrs. Brandon," Ben hissed back sarcastically, "It's my time, and I'm going to take it. It's also my job, and I plan on doing it without your help or interference."

"You can't come in here and pretend to understand this company and our customers," Jeanette said. "I may not be in the 'creative' department, but I have been in this company for twelve years, which makes me an authority and your superior."

"I'm sure it makes you a lot of things," Ben agreed, "but I tend to question authority and unsolicited opinions."

"Expert advice is hardly an opinion," Jeanette growled. "I can tell you immediately whether your designs complement our audience. You need to learn to take what is given to you from someone above you."

"That's what Blayne is for."

In Blayne's mind, he could see the evil grin spread across Ben's face. He almost wished Jeanette understood the double meaning in Ben's statement. At the very least, he hoped the thought crossed her mind.

Regardless of what was going on in her head, Blayne knew exactly what stoic stare of intimidation Jeanette was giving Ben right this moment. He was sure Ben would just smile back disobediently. This was one stalemate that could go on forever.

You sure know how to pick them, Blayne thought to himself.

And no matter which one he chose in the end, no matter which side he took, he was the only one who was going to be able to break up their staring contest.

Blayne threw down his mag full of sweaty men and headed toward the conference room.

"Is there a problem here?" he asked as he stepped into the center of the room.

Blayne had pushed beyond Jeanette and Ben to take center stage and the center of attention. He wasn't about to hang in the hall and peer over their shoulders. This conversation had already gone on too long and spilled too far into the rest of the company.

Both Jeanette and Ben started talking at once. They were like tattling children, and Blayne raise his hand for silence just like an impatient father.

"Everyone just get back to your own job," Blayne ordered. "This isn't about seniority or secrecy. Everyone has a job to do. So do it."

"Providing marketing recommendations is my job," Jeanette insisted. "That's what I'm trying to do."

She was persistent, but it was obvious that Blayne's outspoken dominance had caught her off guard. She wasn't used to him being so strong-willed. She certainly wasn't used to taking orders from her own husband.

"I can handle it," Blayne said. "It's my job, too. And this is my market. You're not in England anymore, Jeanette. Although perhaps you should be."

The look on her tight-lipped face was barely restrained. Tension rolled across her brow. Anger seethed in her eyes. From somewhere behind, her lover gasped audibly.

Blayne's impression of the domineering father was convincing, and it appeared as if it was actually going to work. But suddenly his performance was upstaged by someone with a lot more experience playing that role.

"Problems?" Garret Brandon asked accusingly.

This time, no one answered. The office was packed but silent. It wasn't possible to cram any more people or attitude into the room.

Emily and Todd and the weasel had faded into the background as louder and older enemies had taken over the battle. Now they were a captive audience. There was nowhere for them to run or hide, no way to escape.

The only exit was blocked by the triangle of Ben, Blayne and Jeanette. They all held their positions. No one budged. And no one moved to answer Garret where he stood surveying the scene, threatening to choose sides.

"Jeanette?" he insisted an explanation.

"We've delayed an entire week," She said turning toward him. "I think it's time we saw some progress. Our guidance is critical to the success of the design."

"Didn't your guidance result in that last round of designs?" Ben snapped. Jeanette's icy glare snapped back toward him.

"And what has your brilliance resulted in over the past week?" she counterattacked.

"How long did the previous designs take?" Blayne challenged. He didn't want an answer. He knew. "We've had a designer on staff for only two days."

"We?" Jeanette sneered. She looked back and forth between Blayne and Ben. "Since when have 'you' become 'we'?"

"Enough!" Garret erupted. Silence returned to the room, and a uniquely unprofessional shade of red crept into Garret's face as he addressed Ben. "I ask for solutions. You create problems. I ask for designs. You make excuses."

"And they break into our office and make demands," Ben shot back.

"This isn't a battle," the blonde British weasel piped in from the peanut gallery. "We're all on the same side."

No one turned to acknowledge his two cents. It was a completely logical and completely obvious statement. It was also completely idiotic. No one in the room believed it.

"Can't win without enemies," Garret said. "Can't test your strength without a fight."

"Well you can't go to battle without a plan, without a leader,"

Jeanette tried to follow his metaphor. She tried to play to his ego. She tried to get the boss on her side.

"Leader? Who?" Garret asked suspiciously. Perhaps he smelled treason. "Me? You? Blayne?"

"Blayne," Ben said quickly. It was the obvious choice, but he had no argument to back it up. Blayne was on his side. Blayne would protect him. Blayne would be there with his arms around him when Ben woke up in the morning.

"Why, Blayne?" Garret asked his son, ignoring Ben.

Blayne stared back confused. It wasn't clear what Garret was asking, but he seemed very interested in Blayne's answer.

"They need marketing advice," he said weakly. It didn't seem like a good answer; it didn't seem like the correct one; it didn't seem like the truth.

"That's exactly what I'm trying to provide," Jeanette butted in.

"Impartial advice," Blayne amended his statement bitterly.

"Impartial?" Jeanette scoffed. "I've never seen you choose sides like this before. It's not like you. It's not professional. It is, in no way, impartial. You are choosing this group of inexperienced hacks over your father and your wife!"

Jeanette had worked herself into business hysterics. Professional outrage was as close to emotional as she could get. Bringing familial relations into her argument was the most desperate maneuver Blayne had ever witnessed.

"You really are the Ice Queen," he marveled. "You'll say anything in the name of business. Go back to London, Jeanette. We do much better with the Atlantic separating us. And we'll do even better when we have a real separation."

It was the first time most of the people in the room had heard a word relating to the divorce. Even those who had heard looked surprised. Jeanette herself seemed to have been caught off guard by the mention of it. Garret fumed. Ben's heart jumped.

Blayne had said it out loud, in front of witnesses. He was making his threat a reality. No one had expected that kind of defiance and determination.

"But why?" Garret practically roared. "Why this battle? Why this project? Why this man?"

This is what it came down to. Why had Blayne chosen Ben?

As far as Garret was concerned, Ben's gut business instincts and creative expertise were not enough to warrant Blayne's support. They weren't enough to make him switch sides.

It wasn't about a design or a deadline. Maybe it wasn't even about the divorce. Garret needed complete control. He needed to know exactly what had led his son astray. Not why they were standing here arguing about a hypothetical razor. But why Blayne was standing here beside Ben at all.

He needed to know why his son had joined forces with the enemy. He needed to understand the enemy mind so he could destroy them. He needed to know why he was going to have to destroy his own son.

Garret waited. He let the angry color drain from his face, but he never unclenched his teeth. He again looked professional and threatening in his perfect suit, not a hair out of place.

And Ben waited, too. He was sure he didn't quite cut the impressive figure that Garret Brandon did. He was sure he was rumpled and flustered. But he watched Blayne just as intently.

All eyes were on Blayne. Jeanette's icy glare. Her lover's gaping bewilderment. Emily and Todd' nervous expectation. They looked as if they may already know the answer, as if they suspected, as if they feared Garret did as well.

This was the moment of truth.

This was the dramatic coming-out scene that Ben had never experienced. Ben had written it in a letter like a coward. He had written and rewritten until the words and penmanship were perfect. His parents never acknowledged it. They never mentioned it one way or the other. So he figured it must have been some of the best writing he'd ever done.

But it wasn't this good. Blayne had a live audience. Blayne had no escape except the truth. The possibility of that truth thrilled Ben. He almost felt guilty delighting in the drama of it all. But he was swept up by the moment and the anticipation of Blayne's words and did not give a thought to the consequences. Blayne had already chosen Ben. Now he just had to say it.

His father was standing there with the closet door flung open, and the only way past him was out.

Still, Blayne never lost his composure. That wasn't like him. He was a result of his father's blood and lifelong business training. He didn't sweat it under the bare bulb of the third degree. He only sweated in close proximity to Ben. In bed. In bathroom stalls. In supply closets. Even in a coffee shop on a midweek afternoon.

Ben only stood a step away from him now. He could have reached out to touch him. But this was business Blayne. Suit and tie and a fresh shave. He looked calm and collected and handsome. He looked thoughtful, as if this long, silent consideration was normal and necessary.

"Can't remember?" Garret prodded his son. "Can't remember why you're choosing this stranger over your wife?"

Ben couldn't help it. Now he did reach out to Blayne. He didn't actually touch him. He reached halfway across the distance between them. He held out his hand to show support. Blayne didn't have to do this alone. He could take Ben's hand and they could step out of the closet together.

Of course, Ben didn't actually expect Blayne to hold his hand, although it would have been nice. It was just a gesture. It was a symbol of camaraderie. It didn't even appear affectionate. It looked completely appropriate. Ben's movement made a simple point.

And so did Blayne's. He turned abruptly from Ben as if his hand would burn.

"I didn't," Blayne said. "I did not choose anyone. I chose Mandatory."

Ben's hand dropped. His hopes fell to the floor. Garret's eyes lit up.

No one in the room was stupid enough to believe Blayne's claim, except perhaps Jeanette's moronic lover. However, half of them appeared completely satisfied by it. Even Jeanette seemed to relax a little.

"I'm sorry if this seems like rebellion," Blayne continued, "but I have to do what I believe is right for the company. A lot depends on this project."

"More than most of you even know," Garret declared. He was practically agreeing with his son now. He was almost welcoming him as an enemy.

"This is an internal test before it goes into production. Before it hits the market. My decision to see this experiment through is a safeguard to our company," Blayne was really on a roll now. "This is my dedication to Mandatory. This is not a betrayal."

Blayne looked determined, invigorated, excited. He stood there with his tie and his back absolutely straight. He looked like an enthusiastic salesman trying a little too hard to sell his position and his product, but the audience already seemed sold.

It was exactly the answer everyone wanted to hear. Blayne was not trying to sabotage the company, or his father, or his wife. Blayne was not going to give up Emily's design before it was time. All for one, and one for all. Maybe everyone was on the same side after all.

Everyone but Ben. Ben charged out of the room, right past Garret's protective guard at the door. He deserted the battle. He went AWOL.

Normally, no one would have breached Garret's stance, but right now he seemed calmed by his son's sudden allegiance. His guard was down, and he let Ben pass.

No one would get fired today. That would be too easy. Complete destruction takes a little more time. The bloodiest wars take soldiers and bayonets and double agents. Bombs sweep everything too clean, too easily. Garret was in it for the sake of battle.

Ben was more than happy to retreat from the field this time. He couldn't accept the conditions of the treaty that would allow them all to get along for a while and temporarily put aside their weapons and bickering.

Lies and denial and hurt feelings. Those were not terms Ben could live with. Peace and quiet and employment were not worth those allowances.

Ben knew he shouldn't be so sensitive. He was just being a typical gay man. But that was the problem. Ben was gay. Blayne was not, at least not when there was anyone but Ben around. He should have known better than to expect anything more from this married man. This closet case.

He should have followed his instincts right from the beginning. Not the instincts that made him stalk Blayne from across the coffee shop and flirt shamelessly. He should have followed the instinct of disgust and repulsion that overcame him the moment he found out Blayne was 'married' and 'straight.'

He was halfway down the hall when he heard footsteps behind him. Ben picked up the pace even though he had no idea where he was headed. The footsteps could have been anyone. The office was almost full by now.

But something told him it was Blayne. The sound and the rhythm were familiar and persistent. The fact that Ben could identify Blayne by the echo of his footfalls was infuriating. Blayne wouldn't acknowledge their relationship in the slightest way, but Ben could recognize the sound of him in the dark.

"Ben," Blayne called down the hall, "hold on."

There was no way Ben was stopping to have this conversation in the hall. There was also no escape. He had passed the elevators, and he had no idea where the nearest stairwell was. He would have been screwed in case of a fire. This emergency suddenly seemed much more serious. He was trapped.

"Ben," Blayne called again, louder, "wait!"

Ben couldn't very well keep running aimlessly and let Blayne keep yelling through the halls. He had to face this. Someone did. If Blayne wasn't going to be honest about the situation, Ben was going to have to be. He staggered left and then right before finding a side hall ahead to duck into and await those familiar footsteps.

When Blayne appeared before him, Ben had just realized that this was the hall that led to the supply closet. He was standing right beside its doorway.

Blayne put out his hand to usher Ben inside the closet for some privacy. Ben shrugged his shoulder away roughly. If he was going into the closet again, he could do it all by himself.

This time, the meeting among the pens and pads was going to be very different from before. Ben would step into this closet one more time with Blayne. He would have this conversation in here to protect it from the ears of those outside. But after it was said and done, Ben was coming out and leaving Blayne in there without a second glance back.

"What? I'm waiting," Ben's eyes flashed angry and blue in the dim light.

"You don't understand," Blayne began. His eyes were soft and brown, doleful, pleading.

The pained expression only angered Ben more. Blayne could switch his emotions and his appearance at the drop of a hat. Mad, sad, gay, straight. When it came down to it, Blayne was a good businessman, but Ben wasn't buying the sales pitch.

"I think I understand perfectly," he said. "I think I've heard more than enough."

"You don't understand my father or his business," Blayne said slowly, trying to pace the situation, trying to calm Ben. "Your instincts are right, but my father won't believe that. And he would put an end to everything if he suspected there was anything else going on."

"Don't try to protect me," Ben hissed. "I don't need a knight in shining armor, thanks very much. I can stand up for myself."

"It wouldn't work, Ben. He wouldn't listen to you. This is the only way we have a chance."

"We?" Ben sneered.

"Our project. Emily's design. Your career."

Ben just glowered at him. He hated him. He hated him for standing there beautiful and calm. He hated him for being gullible and simplistic. He hated him for boiling the word 'we' down to so little, for diluting it with so many things that were not them.

"If you think I give a shit about this razor, you're as stupid as those people in there who think that's why you're doing this," Ben paused and breathed. He tried to keep every emotion but contempt out of his voice. "The sad thing is, you've convinced yourself that you are one of those people."

Ben tried to push past him without touching, but Blayne stood strong. He stood firmer than his father, and he wouldn't let Ben escape. Those damn Brandons wouldn't budge until they'd heard what they wanted to hear.

"That's not true," Blayne sounded genuinely hurt. He was brilliant at his act. "This isn't about them. It's about us."

Ben was tired of words like 'we' and 'us.' He didn't want to be lumped together with Blayne into a single pronoun. It was too intimate. It was too close for comfort. It was too familiar.

"This isn't about anyone but you, Blayne," Ben said, and his looked pierced deep into Blayne. "If this was about 'us,' you could have just said it. And if this was about the 'company,' you could have just kept hiding behind your father and your wife forever. Razor or no razor, Mandatory makes a nice, safe closet. And as far as I'm concerned, you can stay there."

Ben shoved Blayne out of the way. If Blayne found words to respond, Ben was too far down the hall to hear them. He was in the elevator before he could gather his thoughts, and he was in a cab before he realized the only place left to go today was therapy. And that wasn't for hours.

As he wandered the city, he wondered absently if Melissa would have him committed.

CHAPTER 13

Ben caught Melissa off guard when he barged into her office. She jumped a little and smiled nervously up from her desk. He was early, but Melissa wasn't usually so high-strung. He didn't mean to surprise her. He just didn't have anywhere else to go after blowing off work and avoiding the entire Brandon family tree all day.

He'd stomped around town angrily. He'd scowled at strangers, even the cute ones. He'd stuffed a burger and beer into his gut to reward himself for being so forceful, but they weren't settling in his stomach no matter how slowly he'd chewed to kill time.

He tried to tell himself this feeling had nothing to do with regret. It was just a bunch of greasy suds floating around. It wasn't pleasant, but it was better than the thoughts that stewed in his mind.

"You seem different this week," Melissa said as he settled into the couch.

"Well, I'm sober."

"I mean generally, Ben. You seem troubled," she paused, "in a different way."

"Are you a shrink or a psychic?" Ben asked accusingly.

"Ben, it's my job to notice the slightest changes in you," She put on her professional voice, as if reading out of an instruction manual. "It could be nothing. But it could also be the first sign of some psychological or physical manifestation."

He really wasn't in the mood to be 'read' or 'psychoanalyzed' or anything else for that matter. Maybe there was something different. But he didn't really know what that was.

Okay, it was Blayne Brandon, the bastard. But it was also

something more. Ben didn't know how to pinpoint the change that had occurred over the past week, but he really didn't feel like exploring it with Melissa. He looked up at her frizzy red curls. The usual pencil hair accessory wasn't doing much to restrain them today.

"I could just be having a bad day."

"Sure," she said, "and I hope that's all it is. And I hope it gets better. That's why I'm trying to rule out the obvious."

"Oh, now I'm obvious?"

Ben would have found a way to turn anything she said into an attack.

"You certainly seem like someone in emotional distress," she said, "like someone who is having relationship problems. Have you met someone at work?"

Now it was Ben's turn to be caught off guard. He looked up at her expectant gaze and wondered where the hell that question had come from.

Well, even if she was a psychic, there was no way Ben was in the mood to rehash his pseudo-relationship with Blayne. Whatever it had been, it was over now. Anyway, he was here to provide some twisted insight into his wounded mind, not his wounded heart. This was not couples therapy.

Ben settled back into the leather couch and put on his best bitch face. She could pry all she wanted; he was not going to budge. Bedsides, there was something eerie about her snooping questions and her searching eyes. She didn't need to know any more than she already suspected.

"You're nosier than a fag hag," Ben said, "and I have enough trouble keeping the one I've got in line."

"Are you having problems with your friend then?" She asked. "Or is it a man?"

What was this? Ben wasn't exactly a serial dater. He wasn't just bad at relationships; he just didn't do them. He couldn't remember if he and Melissa had ever talked about a man at all. However, she certainly seemed fixated on the subject all of a sudden.

"Yes, fine, I admit it," Ben threw his hands up in surrender. "I've met Mr. Right."

Melissa looked intent, concerned. No matter how pretty her copper curls made her, there was still something disquieting about red eyebrows to Ben. The way she knitted them together in close examination looked almost freakish. It reminded Ben of Todd's silly thatch of a red rooster's tail.

"Tell me about him," Melissa seemed to be taking this very seriously.

"Oh, he's great, does whatever I say," Ben indulged her. "He'd make a nice little wife, but I think Emily is going to screw him first."

"Who?" she asked.

He'd completely lost her with that one.

"Todd."

"Todd?" She looked even more perplexed.

"Todd. At work. And Emily. My fag hag," Ben explained. "I think they've got a case of puppy love. In my opinion, he's the perfect man, funny, obedient, sincere. But he's not really my type. He's a redhead. No offense."

"None taken"

"Well, at least he's a man."

"I'm not looking for a date, Ben," she resumed her professional voice. "There isn't anyone else?"

Was this woman's sole purpose to torture him? Hell, yes, there was someone. There was Blayne Brandon with his soft brown eyes and hot muscled bod. There was Blayne Brandon with his wife and father and closeted, twisted mentality. There was Blayne Brandon, the man Ben had sworn off completely.

"No one worth mentioning. No."

"So, is this about your father?" she changed tactics.

Once again, she caught Ben way off guard. In his horrid mood, he hadn't even thought about Pete. That felt miles and years away. He had come to terms with it and laid him to rest.

But having his therapist throw his father's death in his face, gave him a tinge of guilt, as if he should be feeling something more. Ben felt guilty for having made peace with his dad and moving on.

"How do you know about that?" Ben asked. He was sure he hadn't mentioned it. He was sure, as guilty as she was now making him feel, that the memory of his father had not crossed his mind at all today.

"I must have read it in the paper," she answered.

"Oh," he responded. The truth was, Ben hadn't seen the obituary himself. He hadn't even known it had been in the paper at all.

"Were there any unexpected emotions or discoveries you want to discuss?" she probed.

"No. This isn't about him. That's over. It wasn't a surprise."

Ben didn't feel like going into it. This was one healing process he had managed all by himself. He didn't need to rehash it now. He didn't need to give Melissa the credit for his recovery.

For all he knew, reliving the whole experience would just stir things up and unsettle his mind. Sure, he had been surprised to have the smallest moment of resolution with his father. He was also surprised to discover an inheritance. But the last thing he wanted was to dredge all that up today. It would only aggravate his mood.

"I'm fine with that," he insisted.

"Good," she said. "I'm glad to hear it. And I'm sorry to hear about your father."

"Thanks."

Ben was starting to loosen up again. He leaned back into the sofa, although he resisted the urge to lie down as he had last Wednesday in his drunken stupor.

The room always seemed dim. Ben guessed it was supposed to be relaxing or secretive like a confessional. Today the ambience wasn't really helping his mood. Therapy just wasn't helping the situation, just as it had never helped him reclaim a single memory from his past.

Melissa wasn't solving any problem for him, but Ben felt better talking to someone who wasn't wrapped up in Mandatory. Anything was a welcome distraction at this point. Maybe that was enough. Maybe therapy was working just a little.

"Have you been having more flashbacks?" Melissa changed the subject.

Ben sat right back up, as stiff as a board. Melissa never brought up his flashbacks. She never encouraged discussions about them. But what had really thrown him for a loop was the fact that she had never ever ever referred to them as 'flashbacks.'

For once, he decided not to challenge her or make a smart-ass remark. He decided to overlook his foul mood and his tendency toward sarcasm. He decided to see this as an opportunity.

"Yes," he answered, "a lot more."

"The accident still?"

"No."

His answer even surprised him. Melissa looked terrified.

He hadn't realized the change until now, but all the dreams and moments of déjà vu he'd been experiencing didn't involve the crash. They seemed similar, related perhaps, but it wasn't the crash. He hadn't had that old, familiar dream since the day he met Blayne in the coffee shop.

That fact struck him suddenly. But he had already decided to avoid that subject. He switched his focus back to the flashbacks themselves.

"Actually, they've been different," he said. "It's more like a feeling of familiarity."

"How?" she asked. She leaned forward and took the pencil from her hair. Curls bounced down around her face, and she tucked them behind her ears. She jotted down something on her pad. Ben couldn't remember her ever taking notes before.

"And pain," he added.

"You've been having pain?" she interrupted. "Perhaps we should run some tests."

"No, not real pain," he tried to explain. "More like the memory of pain."

Ben tried to focus on that morning in the office. The screeching sound. The searing pain that seemed to pulse through his head. The entire experience had been disorienting. Recalling the details wasn't easy.

"Light maybe," he said, "or electricity. Something bright, and a shooting pain right through my head. But it wasn't like the accident. It was somewhere else. Somewhere with high-pitched equipment. Could it have been an operating room?"

Melissa didn't answer right away. She kept scribbling on her pad quickly. Ben tried to search her downturned face, but her hair had fallen again into a shield of privacy, like a veil.

"I doubt it, Ben," she said, looking back at him. "Yes, you had quite a lot of surgery, of course. You were sedated for days, heavily. Look, Ben I don't believe you truly remember anything from that time. Not the accident or the months immediately preceding it. But there is no way you remember surgery during which time you not only had amnesia, but anesthesia as well."

"I don't know," he admitted. "It's not like I remember scalpels or anything. Just a bright burning, like a shock."

"Ben, it's impossible," she cut him off. "If you're having real pain, now, then you should go to the hospital tonight for examination. I can make a call. They'll admit you immediately."

"No no no," he insisted. "It was days ago. It was just a memory, like remembering a painful experience. It wasn't real."

Ben rubbed his head and let his thumb pass over his scar. He held up his hand to Melissa in a weak indication that everything was fine now. She didn't need to do anything about it.

"You're right," she agreed. "It probably wasn't real. Neither real pain nor a real memory."

"Maybe," he acknowledged. "I really don't know."

This was one point he could concede. He didn't know what the hell it was, and he certainly didn't want to explore it. He didn't need more migraines, real or imagined. Even if it was a genuine memory, Ben was willing to let it sink back into the dark depths of his mind. He didn't need to remember it.

"What else?" she asked immediately. "You said there had been a lot more recently. What else has been familiar?"

Melissa was still leaning forward with her elbows on her knees and her notepad in her lap. She was poised for information. She was almost crouching, getting ready to pounce. She looked nervous and anxious to get to the bottom of the issue.

For the first time, Ben noticed one side of her blouse was untucked. Her eyes looked a little hollowed, concerned almost. It was as if she had been worrying for days, not just about this one moment, this one session.

Ben wondered what was going on in Melissa's life. He was sure he was the least of her worries at the moment. Something personal must have been bothering her.

Suddenly Ben felt bad. He had come in here with his bad attitude and made her evening even more difficult. He leaned back and relaxed a little. She wasn't attacking or interrogating him. She just wanted to go home and have a telephone fight with her own boyfriend.

No wonder she had been so suspicious. Ben decided to be as honest as possible. He decided to make this as easy for her as he could.

"It's hard to explain," he started. "None of it is as concrete as the old dream was. It's just a feeling. When I wake up or turn a corner or gaze off into space. It's like there's going to be something there. Someone. That's what it's like. I keep expecting someone to be there. It feels like they should be."

"Who, Ben?" she pressed, "Who is supposed to be there? Who is there?"

"I don't know," Ben exhaled loudly in frustration. He tried to focus. He didn't want Melissa to think he was pissed off at her. He didn't want to make things worse. He tried to think, to give her something concrete.

"It's like I've had something on the tip of my tongue for ten years," he said. "A name maybe. A face? It's this feeling, and now I feel like I'm about to spit it out."

"No, Ben," she sounded like she was forbidding him from remembering. "I don't think it's that close to the surface.

Unfortunately, I don't think it's buried any deeper either. If you haven't remembered after all this time, it's highly unlikely you'll recover any of your memories now. It's not just going to come to mind or roll off your tongue. You just want it to."

She looked absolutely frazzled. Ben wished she'd stop taking notes and pin back her unruly hair. It looked a lot frizzier than normal. Her entire persona seemed to be buzzing with static and tension.

"Well, that's not how it feels," he said. "It's not just fading into the past. In fact, it feels stronger."

He didn't want to be difficult. He wanted to be as honest as possible.

"You know what it feels like?" he asked. "It feels exactly like when you meet someone and you know you've met them before. You know their name. You know where you first met them. But you can't remember. It's just a feeling of knowing, but it's so strong. And if you just keep talking to them long enough, it will come to you. You'll just throw their name into the conversation naturally, eventually. You know it's going to happen. You just don't know how long you have to keep talking, how long you have to keep making a fool of yourself before it all makes sense."

"Who are you talking about?"

"What?"

"Who's name are you trying to remember?"

"Sorry, Doc. I don't remember," he said ironically. "It's just an example, an analogy, you know? Aren't you supposed to be the one interpreting all these symbols for me?"

"I have, Ben," she said. She actually raised her voice. She sounded hopeless. "I have told you over and over again that these are not memories. They are not real. You are grasping at nothing. You are creating these feelings like you'd make up a story. You've already forgotten it all, Ben. The safest thing you could do now is forget about forgetting it. Drop it and move on."

"Sorry," Ben said.

He normally wouldn't have given up so easily. He didn't like being scolded, and it wasn't like Melissa at all.

He really wasn't sorry about his feelings or his dreams or his memories, real or not. He was just sorry she was having such a shitty day.

He looked up at the clock on the wall. They'd gone way over time. He knew Melissa was tired of this. In fact, this was the most tired he had ever seen her. He didn't have any desire to keep the conversation going.

Everyone has bad days. Ben and Melissa just happened to be having them on the same day. And all this time, he thought he'd had it rough. From the looks of things, Melissa had gotten the shit end of the stick today. He figured they should both just head home to bed.

"It's probably just the new job," he suggested. "We've got deadlines and office politics, and I'm just not used to it yet. Unemployment doesn't look so bad anymore. I guess I'm just under a lot of stress."

"You're probably right," she said. She seemed to calm a bit at his cooperation. "Just don't jump to any conclusions. Don't sacrifice the future for some irrational hope of regaining the past, Ben. I've said it before. You have nothing to gain from the past. But it would so easy to throw everything away looking backwards."

Ben wasn't exactly sure what she meant. She had said similar things before, all her 'focus on the future' nonsense, but this sounded like some apocalyptic pronouncement. He wasn't about to argue.

"I know," he said, "and I won't. I'm just glad to talk about something other than work, I guess. Thank God you have nothing to do with Mandatory."

He tried to laugh and lighten the mood, but it was beyond hope now. The sun was setting, and Melissa's little office of leather furniture seemed darker and colder than it should have. It had lost its warmth.

"It's getting late," she said.

"Yeah," Ben agreed as he stood to leave. "I'll see you next week."

On his way out, Ben looked back. He was trying to see what

Melissa was doing, give her a reassuring smile or a wave good-bye. But it was too dim in the office. From the outside, the entire room looked black.

All Ben could see was the sign next to the door, its gold letters lit up by the setting sun. Dr. Melissa Carver.

CHAPTER 14

As soon as he awoke alone in his own bed, Blayne knew that the brightness of Thursday morning wasn't going to bring any clarity to his mind. He was still groggy with confusion and the piles of work he had used to distract himself late into the night.

Of course, work was not the problem. It was his excuse. It always had been, and he wasn't about to give up his safe haven now.

Blayne didn't care if work was a diversion. It still mattered to him. At least it was something rational to focus on amid the blurry mess of his personal life. He wasn't about to let this project fail just because everyone seemed to be fighting against him.

Everyone included Ben Abrahms. Blayne just didn't understand. He couldn't fit Ben into some neat category. Was he an enemy? A friend? An ally in the Mandatory battle? A lover?

He was tired of trying to wrap his mind around the situation. He was tired of the constant struggle with Ben and himself. They always seemed to be halfway between fighting and fucking.

Blayne wasn't comfortable with either of those extremes. He certainly couldn't focus while being pulled in opposite directions. He simply couldn't focus with Ben close to him.

Blayne didn't get to the office as early as he would have liked. The halls were bustling with people, and Mandatory churned along efficiently as if there were no internal malfunction threatening to break it down.

Blayne had intended to avoid Ben completely. He didn't know if Ben was in yet, but just to be safe he headed toward his own office this morning. He didn't know how he was going to resolve the situation with Ben, or if he was even going to try. He just knew he couldn't make any decisions with Ben right there.

The decision he finally made was to get out of the office, to get away from Ben, and make some real progress on this project. Blayne may not have been able to make up his mind or solve his life, but he sure as hell was going to solve the pewter problem.

"Stephen," Blayne said into his phone, "could you come by my office? I have some design questions for you."

He put the receiver back in its cradle decisively. It was simple acts like this that reassured Blayne he wasn't losing his mind. He was still curt and professional. He could still get the job done.

Unfortunately, Stephen was the last person Blayne wanted to see. Well, the second to last person actually. Stephen was the flitty little designer who had come up with all that crap Garret and Jeanette wanted to manufacture. He was the slinky little wisp of a thing who had so blatantly flirted with Ben.

Blayne met him at the door. There was no reason to make this intimate or let it take any longer than absolutely necessary. Stephen knew better than to flirt with the boss' son, but Blayne didn't see any reason to invite him to sit down and get comfortable.

"I've got some questions about metal," Blayne began.

He grabbed his briefcase and headed down the hall. There was no reason this conversation couldn't happen on his way out the door.

Stephen didn't seem hurried or bothered at all. He prattled on eagerly about jewelry and lampshades and any other whimsical piece of metallic clutter he had ever designed. He gestured extravagantly and flapped his silk shirt.

Blayne just ignored the display and jotted down names of jewelers and welders and metal shops. By the time they'd reached the elevator, he had quite a list.

"Thank you, Stephen. You've been quite helpful."

Blayne hit the down button and left the little designer fluttering in the lobby.

***

162

Sleep had dulled Ben's anger. Maybe it was time or perspective that cooled his temper a bit. It could also have been the sweet dreams that filled his night and contradicted his mood.

There hadn't been much to it really. Again, there were no specifics. The dream was more like a concept of happiness. Summertime. A sandy beach. The sounds of laughter and waves in the distance. The tastes of strawberries and white wine. The warmth of sunshine and holding hands with his eyes closed.

That was it. Ben had practically awoken smiling. No matter how he tried, he couldn't recapture the roiling rage from yesterday.

As he entered the office, he found himself making excuses for Blayne. He found himself almost understanding.

Coming out at twenty hadn't been easy. And Ben certainly hadn't been put on the spot with his wife, his father, his lover and his career on the line and in the same room.

It was too easy to forget just how hard it could be. It wasn't even about the drama and the pressure. Coming out had a lot more to do with coming to terms with yourself.

Ben certainly wasn't making that very easy for Blayne. Instead of being the experienced, compassionate gay man who understood what he was going through, Ben had acted like a spoiled brat and a drama queen. He had tried to make Blayne's coming-out experience all about himself.

The last thing Blayne needed was more pressure, Ben realized. And even though it stabbed him in the gut when he considered it, Ben realized Blayne probably didn't need a boyfriend either.

Ben wasn't about to tell Blayne this, and he didn't even intend to apologize. His epiphany and dream-induced benevolence were not strong enough to overcome his pride completely.

He'd just try to be polite and professional. If Blayne wanted to talk about homosexuality or coming out or the price of tea in China, Ben would try to give him honest, objective advice. They might not create a romantic relationship out of all this mess, but they could at least create a working relationship and an overpriced razor.

Todd and Emily were huddled even closer together over the

monitor when Ben entered. If they noticed his entrance, they didn't bother to pull away from one another when they heard him come in. Todd's hand was practically touching Emily's shoulder where is rested on the back of her chair.

Good for them. Straight people can be so cute sometimes, Ben thought.

"Morning, folks," he called out.

"Good morning," they answered in unison.

The cheeriness in Ben's voice surprised them all, including him. No one was about to acknowledge it and question the good luck. No one mentioned yesterday or the way Ben had stormed out and disappeared.

"Where's Blayne?" Ben asked nonchalantly

There was a definite pause in the room. Neither Todd nor Emily turned to face Ben. Neither said a word for several nervous seconds.

Ben pretended he didn't notice. He absently shuffled papers and rearranged piles of reference books. He turned on another computer. It bonged and hummed to life. That electronic response seemed to be the only one he was going to get.

"He isn't in yet?" Ben prodded.

"I think he's been working in his own office," Todd threw over his shoulder.

He acted as if the comment was a grenade. Todd actually ducked and leaned closer to Emily for protection. He was waiting for the explosion.

"Oh," Ben said.

No surprise crept into his voice. Nothing exploded. It was so matter-of-fact that Ben felt immensely proud of himself. It was almost as if he hadn't thrown a tantrum and stomped out of here yesterday.

"I think I'll swing by and see how things are going," Ben said. "How are things on your end?"

'Just hunky-dory," Emily answered sarcastically. "How are your things?"

"Fine."

Ben stepped into the hall. He was being very adult and professional about this whole thing. He could easily go talk to Blayne about pewter or deadlines. Switching from their usual topic of conversation would just make it clear that it was all water under the bridge.

Ben didn't need to apologize. He just needed to move on. He could get over it. This too shall pass.

Ben stopped dead in his tracks.

He saw them, but they obviously didn't notice him. Ben was just steps from Blayne's empty office, but he could clearly see Blayne's back retreating down the hall. And it was even easier to see the brightly patterned shirt of that slutty designer walking next to him.

Ben watched as they walked and chatted. He couldn't hear their conversation, but he could see the way the designer kept reaching up and touching Blayne's elbow, punctuating each sentence with physical contact.

Ben noticed that Blayne wasn't shying away from the attention. He also noticed that he had his briefcase with him. Blayne wasn't planning on returning any time soon. Ben wasn't exactly sure what he was planning, but several possibilities immediately came to mind.

Ben already knew how Blayne's midweek, out-of-office trips could go. He wondered if Blayne was taking this guy out for 'coffee.'

No matter how Ben tried to rationalize it, no matter how he tried to tell himself he was getting over this silly infatuation, he couldn't ignore the stabbing pain in his chest. The ache went straight through him.

He should have known better. He shouldn't have allowed some closeted, married jerk to make him feel this way. He shouldn't be suffering over this man as if this were a real relationship, or even a remote possibility.

It was becoming increasingly obvious that a relationship was the last thing Blayne Brandon had on his mind.

SCOTT&SCOTT

Ben took one last look at the pair parading down the hall, and then he stepped into Blayne's office and out of sight. He doubted Blayne had the good sense to watch his back, but Ben didn't want to get caught if they turned around. He didn't want Blayne to know he had caught them.

The lights were off in Blayne's office. The dim outlines of books and folders and picture frames surrounded Ben. Every sight infuriated him. He didn't have to turn on the lights to know that those were pictures of Blayne's wife. Those were piles of work that had nothing to do with their razor.

Ben was standing in the middle of Blayne's lies. These were the things he used to distract himself from the truth. This dark office was Blayne's closet.

And if Blayne wanted to stay in that closet, that was fine with Ben. Ben didn't need a boyfriend. He didn't need to be the gay, white knight.

He had resolved to make up and play nice, not to push so hard and fast. Ben didn't want to shove Blayne out of the closest at such a critical velocity that he'd fall flat on his face.

But if Ben couldn't lure Blayne out, he didn't want to watch him sleep his way out of the closet with every flamboyant designer in the company. This was too much. Blayne was going straight, well 'directly,' from the closet to the meat market.

Ben knocked a pile of papers off Blayne's desk on his way out. He left them there scattered across the floor. It was almost an accident.

Ben stormed back across the lobby toward his own office. If Blayne just wanted to get off where it was easy, there was nothing Ben could do about it. If he wanted to go from married man to gay slut in one fell swoop, Ben couldn't stand in his way. And he didn't want to.

If Blayne ever found his way out of the closet, he still had years of practice ahead of him before he became eligible for serious dating. But Blayne sure wasn't wasting any time. He seemed to be getting a pretty good start on his 'practice.'

Ben sat down hard at his desk, but he didn't say a word. Emily and Todd didn't budge. They didn't even look up. They remained just as silent as they had been before.

They ignored Ben's heavy footsteps. They ignored his angry sighs. They had been ignoring quite a lot over the past week, and they weren't about to speak up now. They were just doing their job.

Ben had a job to do, too. It was a job he'd been ignoring all a week, one that had nothing to do with Blayne or designers. Ben was the ad guy. Let Emily and Todd fiddle with the angles and colors of this razor until the cows come home; Ben was the one who was supposed to convince men they actually needed this silly thing. He had to make them want it.

He grabbed a notebook and a handful of pens. He doodled in the margins. He drew heavy, distracted lines that had nothing to do with razors or advertising. He scribbled angrily.

Ben needed to come up with an idea, a campaign. What he didn't need was to be Blayne's ongoing experiment. Ben was an adult, a gay adult. He was a seasoned homosexual. He didn't need Blayne's newfound confusion complicating his life. He didn't need to be anyone's mentor or gay guide. Ben had earned his scars, and he deserved more.

He rubbed the scar in his brow and tried to focus his cluttered mind on the page in front of him. He needed to create an image for this razor or it would never sell, he reminded himself again. But right this second the only thing Ben could think to do with a razor was to cut Blayne's throat.

***

Somewhere between his second jeweler and a metal shop, Blayne's cell phone rang.

This pewter problem was turning out to be the least of his worries. All he'd had to do was ask the right people. It turned out there were countless coatings and oxidizing chemicals that could give any shade of a faux finish to almost any metal. Hell, they could probably make this razor out of tin foil and have it appear perfectly pewter.

His phone rang again. Blayne reached over to the passenger's side and grabbed his briefcase. He fished the buzzing phone out from among several samples of differently colored metallic squares.

"Blayne Brandon," he answered professionally.

It took him a moment to recognize the voice on the other end. It wasn't the hollow static of his phone's reception as much as the strange edge in his therapist's voice that made it difficult.

"Oh, Dr. Carver, I'm sorry. I completely forgot about our session today."

"I'm worried about you, Blayne," the voice hissed. "You seem so distracted."

"There's just a lot going on right now."

"That's what concerns me. Your marriage, your job, your homophobia. It all seems to be spiraling at once. And it seems to be wrapped up in avoidance and denial relating to your past trauma. I don't want you avoiding therapy as well, not when you need it most."

She paused. Blayne came to a red light and tapped his foot against the brake several times, harder than he needed to.

Dr. Carver's speech seemed so prepared. It seemed rushed and nervous. On top of everything else, it seemed completely wrong. Blayne felt more in control. He was finally dealing with the present, solving problems, moving ahead. Calling all of that into question and digging up ancient history absolutely infuriated Blayne.

How in the world could she attribute every aspect of his life to some incident he couldn't even remember? Why did she insist on dwelling on the past? She seemed more affected by the event than Blayne himself. She seemed to want him to be more affected by it.

Blayne just didn't understand how reliving old pain was going to make anything happening now less painful.

"Dr. Carver," he began slowly; he tried to sound rational. "What could rape possibly have to do with my divorce and my job?"

"I'm your therapist, Blayne. I need to explore your past and how it affects these decisions you're making now."

Blayne stared up at the red light. Maybe he just didn't buy into psychotherapy after all these years. Maybe Dr. Carver was just a bad therapist. Maybe he should tell her that this homophobic rape victim had just started an affair with a man. Now that was progress.

"It's the past," he said instead. "Forget it. I did. Why don't you ever bring up my father, my childhood, why my mother deserted us thirty years ago? At least I remember all that pain."

"Blayne, professionally, I believe your repression and fear surrounding the rape are key factors in understanding your current and possibly harmful behavior."

God, how long had she rehearsed that comeback? It hadn't made it sound any more genuine. It just sounded desperate.

The light turned green, and Blayne stomped onto the gas pedal roughly.

"I've heard your professional opinion, Dr. Carver, for ten years," he said firmly. "Now I think it's time for a second opinion—Mine. And in my opinion, Dr. Carver, that's horseshit. I won't be coming in today. I won't be coming in again."

Blayne tossed the phone back into his open briefcase. He pushed the gas a little harder. He edged the speedometer up a few notches. The streets were practically empty on a Thursday morning, and there were open miles ahead of him.

Blayne turned off the AC, rolled down the window, and breathed a deep breath of summer air.

He felt relieved. He felt as if a weight had been lifted from him. He had made a decision, and it felt good. He knew he was going to have to make a lot more.

Blayne just didn't know what those decisions were. Divorce? Rebellion? Homosexuality?

It was the first time he had even let him think that thought in his own head. Until now, he'd never even allowed himself that possibility. Until Ben, he'd never let himself think it. Gay. What if?

Even if he was sure. Even if he wanted to come out of the closet and start dating men, he wasn't sure he wanted to do that with Ben. It was a silly thought. But there was almost something too close about their entire relationship. Too serious.

Blayne didn't want to admit it, but he didn't want Ben to become his gay experiment. He didn't want this to be the trial-and-error relationship where he figured out the mysteries of this whole 'gay thing' and then proceeded to fuck it all up.

What if this all really was an illusion? What if he really was just torturing himself over the rape and the loss of memory? What if he didn't understand what was really going on in his own head? Crazy people don't actually think they're crazy, do they?

Maybe he wasn't gay. Maybe his attraction to men really was some twisted form of posttraumatic-stress syndrome. Dr. Carver had some convoluted explanation for everything. What if she was right?

But there was no explanation for Ben. Blayne stared at the open road ahead of him and saw Ben's smart-ass smile hanging there. Of all the doubts and possibilities, that memory was the only one that felt real.

"Fuck it," Blayne said aloud to the wind and the road and every obstacle in his life.

None of Blayne's losses and traumas could explain what he felt now. It wasn't just attraction to men; it was a distinct attraction to this man. Ben.

And with that thought, Blayne made another decision. He decided on Ben.

CHAPTER 15

Nothing pissed Ben off like an empty notebook and a mind full of distracting ideas that had nothing to do with the job at hand. And by Friday morning, Ben had something even worse. He had a notebook full of scribbles and a head full of anger.

The doodles along the margins didn't even resemble a razor. They may as well have been hearts and smiley faces and B.A. + B.B. 4ever.

But the deep scratches of ink that filled the pages had no such adolescent charm and innocence. They matched his dark thoughts completely.

He didn't mind a one-night stand. He didn't mind being an experiment. What infuriated him was having to stand by and watch that experiment go completely awry. He hated having everything blow up in his face. He couldn't tolerate just standing there with soot on is face and watching Blayne tramp around with every convenient experimental subject that came by.

It was more than his pride could stand. It was more than insulting. Somehow it felt like betrayal. That's what made Ben feel stupid.

Anger was fine. That was justified and empowering. But betrayal made Ben the victim. It made him feel violated and weak.

The thought of Blayne with a stranger—kissing lips that didn't matter—stabbed Ben deep inside his gut. And the guilt for feeling what he knew he shouldn't hurt him almost as much.

These combined pains had driven Ben into an absolute fury over the past twenty-four hours. His empty notebook stared back at him blankly as if it were taunting him with his own stupidity.

Ben felt like a fool, and he knew he was going to make an even bigger fool of himself as soon as he caught sight of Blayne Brandon stepping out of the elevator.

He glimpsed the crisp creases of Blayne's pants out of the corner of his eye. Ben hadn't even known he'd been watching, staring expectantly through the window into the lobby. But Todd and Emily didn't issue a single sound of surprise as Ben whipped his head toward the sight of Blayne's approaching steps.

"We need to talk alone," Ben said hoarsely.

Neither Todd nor Emily questioned why or who 'we' was exactly. They exited silently from the room before Blayne was halfway across the lobby. They didn't even glance up as they passed him.

Blayne looked over his shoulder at them quizzically. He knitted his brows together and shrugged at what he assumed had to be some strange act of puppy love. He had no idea what they were up to, and he had no idea what he was about to walk into.

He actually stepped into the office with a smile on his face. But that didn't last long.

"So, fucking the designer shows your commitment to the company?"

Ben got up and slammed the door shut. He walked right past Blayne without touching him, without even looking at him.

He slammed the door so hard that it actually bounced back from its frame and stood ajar, but Ben didn't notice. By the time the door had stopped swinging, Ben had already stomped to the other side of the room. He turned and fixed his gaze on Blayne.

Blayne stood there blankly with his briefcase in his hand. He was so confused that an expression didn't even register on his face. His mouth was half open as if he wanted to say something but didn't know where to begin.

"I don't give a fuck what you do," Ben's voice was guttural with anger. "And I don't care who you fuck. But don't you dare expect me to sit here and watch it while you pretend you're working on my project."

Ben's eyes were on fire, blue like propane flames.

"I refuse to be your cover," he continued. "I don't need this job. And I certainly don't need your shit. I'm quitting."

Ben turned and sat at the long table in the middle on the room. His back was facing Blayne. He'd said everything he needed to. There was no reason for him to torture himself with the sight of the man at the other end of the room.

He stared out at the city through the tall glass wall. He watched the silent buildings full of people awaiting the weekend. Nothing seemed to move. It was like a landscape, a picture. It was as if the entire city was holding its breath in anticipation, not of the weekend but of some other impending moment.

Ben wondered how long time could hold its breath. He wondered how long things could wait. He figured some people spend their whole lives waiting for something that never happens. He wondered if they ever even knew what it was they were waiting for in the first place.

It's kind of like amnesia, he thought. Because that's how Ben felt all the time. Waiting. Expecting. But never really believing that the mystery would ever reveal itself.

Déjà vu. Past lives. Flashbacks. It was all just a bunch of hopes and dreams that never happened in the past and would never come true in the future. Maybe waiting endlessly was better than facing reality

So Ben kept his back turned to his reality and just watched the window.

Suddenly a shimmering shower fell in front of Ben's eyes. Dozens of metal chips flickered and tinkled in the air before they clanged onto the table.

Blayne let the metal samples pour from his hands. He'd scooped them from his briefcase like water from a silver stream, and now he stood over Ben and splashed the proof of yesterday's work right in front of his face.

Ben watched as every shade of metal reflected sunlight like a disco ball. Bronze and chrome. Antiqued brass and brushed steel.

The static world he'd been watching was suddenly alive with light and color. Everything was liquid and fluid, but the edges were sharp.

"In case you give a fuck," Blayne said from behind him, "this is what I was doing yesterday. I solved the pewter problem."

Ben didn't say a word. He didn't turn to face Blayne. He didn't have to. Blayne could see the surprise blush across Ben's ears and the back of his neck. The deep pink embarrassment contrasted with his dark hairline.

Blayne decided to take the unique shade of skin as an apology. He decided to take Ben's outburst as a sign that he was still interested.

"By the way, I solved another problem," Blayne said. "I figured out that I'm falling in love with you."

This time, Ben turned. He swiveled around in his chair so fast that he had to reach out and grab the corner of the table to stop himself.

Blayne pulled up a chair of his own and sat facing Ben's surprised look. He stared straight into those wide eyes as if he'd figured everything out over the past twenty-four hours.

"You were right," he told Ben. "This isn't about the project or the company. It is about me. But what I had to understand was that it had a lot to do with you, too."

"But what about everything else?" Ben couldn't find the words. "Your father and Jeanette and... everything?"

When it came right down to it, Ben was tripping over the same obstacles and excuses Blayne had been using all along. They were real problems, but they weren't as real as the truth that stared them in the face right now.

Ben blinked and wrinkled his forehead in confusion. Blayne didn't bat an eye. His gaze was solid.

"I don't care if they fire us both. I don't care if Mandatory never makes a razor and ends up bankrupt."

Ben was dumbstruck. He'd already opened his big mouth a few too many times today. He didn't want to say the wrong thing again.

He just gazed across the short distance between them. He marveled at the steadfast look that was chiseled into Blayne's square jaw. He saw compassion in those soft, brown eyes. There was truth there, he could tell. But he still didn't know what to say.

"But it wasn't just about them," Blayne continued, "There's something else you should know."

"What is it?" Ben's voice returned when he noticed the serious look of worry on Blayne's beautiful face. It was still filled with determination and honestly, but now there seemed to be pain tingeing the corners of his mouth where before there had been a smile.

The pause seemed longer after Blayne actually spoke.

"I was raped."

"What?" Ben barely whispered his shock. He forgot to close his mouth after the word left his lips.

"I was attacked when I was in college."

Ben just sat there in horror. But he couldn't look away from Blayne's face. He wanted to absorb the pain he saw there. He wanted to take away as much of it as he could, but he knew it wasn't possible. Blayne's scar went deeper than Ben's ever could.

Underneath his shock and sympathy, Ben felt guilt rise inside him. He couldn't believe he had been so selfish. Of course there was no way for him to have known. But his jealousy and impatience seemed so petty and small now.

He felt guilty for trying to shove Blayne out of the closet, when he had no idea what skeletons were in there with him, holding him back.

Ben may have been gay and out for years, he may have dealt with stereotypes and misconceptions and bad dates, but he'd never had to deal with such a violation. Ben couldn't imagine having his sexuality entangled with such a painful memory.

Ben no longer blamed Blayne for installing a big, giant deadbolt on his closet and staying in there as long as possible. There was just one thing Ben didn't understand. Ben had no idea how he had managed to pick that lock and enter Blayne's life.

Ben felt closer to Blayne than ever. Sharing this pain only deepened the strangely familiar feeling of intimacy that Ben felt every time he looked at Blayne.

And Ben looked at him now, those soft eyes and that warm skin. From his sandy head to the stubble on his chin, Blayne's every feature looked as if it had been kissed by the sun.

There had been something unmistakable from the very beginning. It wasn't love at first sight or anything that cliché. It was something more. Somehow, it was recognition. And this revelation only emphasized that. Something that belonged to Ben had been hurt, damaged, wronged.

Blayne leaned forward. Their faces were less than a foot apart where they sat staring into each other's eyes. This wasn't the moment before a kiss. It was more than romance. It was much more intimate. It was more vulnerable and beautiful than being naked.

It felt good to tell someone, Blayne thought. It was like a sigh, like a deep breath after all these years. The look on Ben's face was exactly what Blayne needed to see. It wasn't understanding. It couldn't be. But it was sincere and warm. It was reciprocal pain, that stabbing look of hurt that is reflected in a person's face when someone he cares about is suffering.

Ben's forehead was wrinkled in concern. Those dark eyebrows were drawn tight together like two lines of worry broken by the white stripe of his scar. The fire had gone out of his bright blue eyes. They seemed to deepen and darken like the ocean when clouds roll in.

Blayne wanted to hold that face in his hands. He wanted to caress the sad lines away. He wanted to put kisses on eyelids and melt Ben's troubled expression. He had wanted to share the truth, not the pain.

He didn't want to dwell in the past any longer. He didn't need to rehash and relive details he couldn't even recall. That's why he had stopped therapy. It was time to move on. It was time to embrace the future. And the future was Ben.

"But I don't remember any of it," Blayne reassured.

"You don't?"

The silence was broken. The motionless moment passed. Ben reached over and put his hand on Blayne's knees. He squeezed and rubbed.

He was worried that Blayne might jump or shy away. Ben himself was fairly shaken by the conversation. But Blayne didn't budge. He was solid. He reached down and placed his own hand on top of Ben's. He ran his palm over those long, thin fingers and laced their grips together. He locked them tight, like a handshake, like a deal, like a secret.

It was a secret they shared but couldn't remember.

"I have amnesia," Blayne explained, "partial amnesia anyway. I can't remember that night or anything else for about six months before I woke up in the hospital."

"You're kidding," Ben said, amazed.

"Not about this," he said. "Maybe I'm blocking it out. Maybe it was the head injuries. No one knows. I certainly don't remember. And I don't want to."

"How in the world is this possible?" Ben asked, looking deep into Blayne's eyes, searching for an explanation.

"Supposedly, it's not as rare as you'd think."

"I guess not," Ben said. He took his free hand, the one that wasn't holding on to Blayne for dear life, and pointed to the scar through his eyebrow. "Senior year. Car crash."

"That's where that's from," Blayne said. It sounded like a revelation, as if he had been trying to figure out that scar's origin for ages.

"That's where my amnesia came from."

"Your amnesia?"

The unbelievable coincidence hung in the air. It filled the short distance between them. But before either of them could grasp its meaning, before they could try to fill in the blanks, their solitude was shattered.

Neither of them had noticed that the door was standing open. And they had no idea that Garret Brandon was standing there.

"What's going on here?" he demanded loudly.

Ben and Blayne both jumped. But they didn't take their hands away from one another. They didn't break their bond. As Garret boomed into the room and shut the door behind him, each felt the other flinch through entwined fingers.

Garret stood over them, arms crossed, legs spread wide. He was like a bully in a designer suit. Its charcoal material matched his hair. The flaming red of his silk tie matched his temper.

Ben took in these details instead of focusing on the moment. These colors and moods seemed more real than the surreal situation. Amnesia and passion. Fathers and sons. The confusion of it all swirled together.

They both looked up at Garret's demanding stance. Ben saw more than anger there, spread thick across that meticulously scrubbed countenance. He saw something much closer to hate.

And in that same moment, he felt Blayne's hold on his hand tighten. He felt the hesitation, the determined intake of breath that would be used to say something much too important. Ben looked over and saw the resolve on Blayne's face.

He was about to come out with the truth. Come out to his father.

"My father died last week," Ben said. "I'm sorry. I've just been having a hard time."

Ben didn't know why he had said it. He didn't know what had made him join the lying. His father had died, but he couldn't pretend that it had anything to do with the current conversation or his hand on Blayne's knee.

For some reason, he'd had to speak before Blayne admitted anything, and he couldn't understand why. Then he looked back up at Garret, and it made complete sense.

The contempt and hollow pity on his face was nothing short of evil. This was not the kind of man who needed to know your secrets. This was not the kind of father you came out to. Ben could tell from his icy expression that this was the kind of man who would manipulate any truth you told him. He would find a way to use it against you.

"I see," was as much sympathy as Garret mustered. "Well, enough consoling, Blayne. More than enough."

Garret uncrossed his arms and turned to leave. But the anger and spite never left his steely eyes. When he reached the door, he paused. He turned back and saw that his intimidating presence hadn't broken the hold Ben and Blayne had on each other. He glared down at their joined hands and spoke without looking them in the eye.

"No time for mourning now. Better be ready to meet with the board on Monday."

Blayne hadn't said a word to his father. He sat there speechless with the truth on the tip of his tongue. Ben had interrupted his revelation. And although Blayne didn't know why, he had decided to remain silent until he figured it out.

But this was too much. Now Garret had pushed things too far.

"There isn't a board meeting Monday," Blayne said.

"There is now," Garret stepped halfway out the door. "If your campaign is not ready," he shrugged. "Our original concepts are."

He stormed out into the lobby. He had made a scene and shaken the company in typical Brandon fashion. But no matter how loudly he had shouted, no matter how he had stomped and scowled, Ben and Blayne were still holding hands when he left.

So that was it, Ben thought. This was the final bell. His job was completed by Monday or his job was gone. Ben was actually surprised his career at Mandatory had lasted over a week. And suddenly he didn't care.

"Well," he said, "we have a long weekend ahead of us. There's no reason to start right away. I need a break already."

Ben stood and tugged Blayne by the hand. Blayne just smiled in silent confusion as Ben led him toward the elevator.

Emily and Todd were sitting near each other on the couch in the reception area. They shared a magazine and a look of complete bewilderment as the pair of men walked by them.

"How do you two feel about overtime?" Ben asked as he hit the elevator's down button.

"What?" Emily squawked.

"See you tomorrow morning, eight a.m. sharp." He smiled. "Take the rest of the afternoon off. We are."

Ben gave Blayne a quick, playful kiss near his ear just as the elevator doors were sliding shut in front of them.

"By the way," he whispered, "I'm falling in love with you, too."

The ten-minute cab ride to Ben's apartment was an excruciating eternity.

***

There was something exciting about the afternoon light as it crept across the floor of Ben's bedroom. It emphasized the fact that they were playing hooky. Ben and Blayne were breaking the rules. They weren't supposed to be wrapped in sheets and each other's arms as broad daylight poured in unashamed.

They had work and responsibilities and a deadline that was breathing down their necks. But none of that mattered when they felt the hot reality of actual breath on their necks. Metaphors were lost. The entire world could wait until tomorrow.

"Why did you lie like that to my father?" Blayne asked.

They were somewhere between kisses. Blayne sat with his broad shoulders against the headboard. Ben nestled his hand between the hard muscles of Blayne's chest. He stroked the smooth skin there with fingertips. He kissed the corner of his mouth.

"I wanted you all to myself," he answered. "There doesn't need to be anyone else to complicate that. Just us and the truth."

Blayne kissed him back. He took his head in his hand and kissed him slow and long, savoring. He licked at the stubble of Ben's upper lip and kissed the tip on his slender chin.

Ben blinked his dark lashes and revealed his blue, blue eyes. He just couldn't keep them closed. He wanted to keep reminding himself that this was true. This moment was happening. And Blayne was looking right back at him with his liquid brown eyes.

They both forgot why it was that people closed their eyes while kissing.

Blayne just looked at him. He didn't release his gentle hold on Ben's face. Blayne's gaze always felt like a smile, soft and warm. He let it pass over Ben's lips and neck, just looking. And then it settled on the thin, white stripe cut through Ben's dark eyebrow.

Blayne followed his gaze with a touch just as soft. He grazed the tip of his thumb over that scar. Back and forth.

"Amnesia, huh?" he almost laughed, because it was almost funny. "I guess we have more in common than we thought."

"I guess so," Ben said. He straddled Blayne's lap where he sat against the bed. He pressed against his body. He prepared to kiss again, maybe more. Then he stopped, halfway to those lips. "You know, I always worried that I had forgotten something really important. I'm glad I'm right here now. I'm glad I'm not missing this."

And the kiss that followed was made with their entire bodies. Ben pressed against Blayne's warmth as their mouths met. Their hold on one another was desperate and determined. There would be no more conversation, and they both knew it.

Ben squeezed his spread legs around Blayne's thick thighs. He felt the breadth of shoulders envelope him. He felt the surge of their kiss and the moment overtake him.

Ben felt the solid excitement of Blayne pressing against his stomach. That hot shaft pressed inline with the dark stripe of hair along Ben's stomach, as if it were following a map, a path, a course it knew it had to take.

Ben grabbed those tan, wide shoulders and pulled Blayne down onto the bed. He relieved him from his seated position and laid him on that broad back. Ben stayed on top. He straddled him. He felt Blayne's erection under him, and he rocked slowly along its length.

Ben braced himself. He placed both hands against the hard shelf of Blayne's chest with locked elbows. He strategically placed his thumbs over those perfect, tawny nipples and pressed ever so slightly into the firm flesh.

Ben pressed against Blayne. He rocked against his chest and

his cock. He waited until the moment was right. He knew what was coming. He felt it under him. He felt it pressing along the crack of his ass.

And then all his expectations were turned upside-down.

Blayne pulled Ben to him. He held him close. And he kissed him. Then Blayne rolled over. He rolled underneath Ben so that Ben was not just on top, he was the top.

The hemisphere of Blayne's firm, round ass rose above the white sheets and the midday sun. And Ben's hard-on hovered above that smooth globe expectantly.

He was in complete disbelief, but he wasn't about to question his good luck. He glanced up at the muscles of Blayne's shoulders and the place where his hands disappeared under the pillow. Ben saw the taper of his waist and the tilt of his hips that pushed that perfect ass upwards.

Fine. Ben wasn't about to say no. He wasn't about to turn down this opportunity. And he wasn't overlooking the importance of the moment.

Ben knew what this meant, or at least he thought he did. Blayne was making himself completely vulnerable to him. Blayne had already confessed the secrets of his past. Now he was giving up all his fears and reluctance to Ben. And Ben wasn't going to make him regret it.

He grabbed the bottle of lube as subtly as he could. Blayne rolled his handsome face against the pillow, but he kept his eyes closed. Ben dribbled the cool lubricant into the crevice of Blayne's ass, and he felt the shiver of surprise pour through the body under him.

Ben took a breath; he let the moment pass. He rubbed his thumb between the greasy cheeks and let the tip of his finger penetrate Blayne ever so slightly. Just a little. The tip. Slowly.

Ben felt the ring of muscle relax around his finger as he pushed his second knuckle softly inside. Blayne even pivoted his hips upward to welcome the sensation.

Ben withdrew just as slowly and reached for a condom. His

hand was shaking as he tore open the package. The lube on his fingers didn't help. He wondered to himself if he could be even more nervous than Blayne.

Blayne lay there silently, apparently relaxed and expectant. His beautiful body was stretched across Ben's bed, mounds of muscle and tan skin rose and fell slowly with his breath.

Ben felt his own heart beat a million miles an hour. It wasn't as if he had never done this. It wasn't as if this were *his* first time.

He couldn't tell if it was nerves or anticipation that made this moment seem so important. Maybe it was simply that this moment was important, to him, to Blayne, to them.

But as he rolled the condom over his rock-hard erection, desire made his blood pump even faster.

He laid himself across Blayne's back. He nestled his cock between Blayne's slippery ass cheeks. He kissed the back of his neck. He kissed the corner of his stubbled jaw. He breathed a sigh of reassurance near his ear.

Blayne stretched warmly under him and reached a hand back to grasp Ben's thigh. He stroked the dark hair there and pulled him even closer. But Ben was already pressed on top of him. There was only one way for them to come closer together.

Ben rocked his hips and felt the hot friction of his cock and Blayne's ass. He felt the inviting squeeze of Blayne's muscled cheeks. And then he felt the pause, the moment when the head of his cock bumped against the tight divot of Blayne's hole. It had found its target, and it waited there for the inevitable.

Ben pressed gently, and he felt Blayne exhale under him. Ever so slowly, he eased the tip into the narrow warmth. He held it there as he held Blayne under him. He pressed further. He withdrew slightly. He moved the round head in and out of Blayne and waited for the delicious pressure surrounding his cock to subside a bit.

Ben let Blayne adjust to the sensation. He continued in slow motion, despite the wild tickle of passion that enveloped him. The tightness of Blayne's hole and the firm cushion of his muscled ass were driving Ben crazy. But Ben wouldn't allow his desire to go too fast. He wouldn't plow into that delicate ass the way every fiber of his instincts begged him to.

Instead, he kissed the space between shoulder blades and stroked the roundness of those big shoulders. The gentle attention relaxed Blayne, and Ben felt him open suddenly.

He felt the relaxation pass through the huge body under him. Every muscle seemed to soften and sigh. And Ben settled into him in the same gentle way. He just stopped resisting the pull of gravity and passion. He let the weight of his body push him deeper. He let the length of his hard shaft disappear entirely into Blayne.

Blayne inhaled silently. He held his breath in surprise. The feeling of a man inside him was so new. No amount of wondering or fantasizing could have prepared him for this reality.

Ben's weight pressed him into the warm, summer sheets, and Blayne fixated on the unique sensation inside him. This wasn't what he expected. This tender warmth and fullness was not what he had anticipated.

The initial tinge of pain vanished as he relaxed and accepted Ben inside him. Every inch of Ben touched a new nerve and created a new kind of pleasure that Blayne never imagined he could experience.

Blayne realized he was still holding his breath. He exhaled, and the shivering breath that escaped him turned to motion. It flattened him against the bed and lowered their joined bodies. It brought Ben down on top of him again, closer, deeper. And it set their hips in motion, rocking in unison, thrusting together.

Ben's long, slow fucking came faster with the chorus of their breath. The building sensation and sound of passion pushed them on.

Blayne raised his hips, spread his ass and gave Ben complete access to him. Ben lifted himself up and held that ass as he thrust into it again and again.

He reached around and grasped the thick base of Blayne's cock. He felt the reassuring hardness that told him Blayne's jagged panting wasn't lying. He pumped harder as his pumped Blayne's solid erection in his fist.

The scent of sweat and man filled their sunny afternoon. Ben's dark bangs plastered against his forehead and concealed his scar. Droplets of sweat fell onto Blayne's slick back. They pooled in the furrow of his spine and trickled toward his tailbone, toward the spot where Ben pressed himself eagerly.

And as he poured his desire into the tip of the condom, he collapsed onto that sweaty back. He felt Blayne's hole pulse in response to his throbbing orgasm. And he felt Blayne's own surge of desire spill hot and wet into the palm of his hand.

"By the way," Ben said as they drifted somewhere near sleep, "I think I'm done falling."

"What?"

"I've hit bottom. I don't think I'm falling in love anymore," he said. "I think I'm right in the middle of it."

CHAPTER 16

Saturday morning was actually quite bright in the empty office tower. Sun spilled in from each of its glass sides. However, the main lights had not been switched on. So hallways and conference rooms and the lobby itself were little pockets of shadow hiding inside the sunny day.

It was like being at school on the weekend. There were no classes. There was no crowded recess. And there were no teachers to tell you what to do.

For the second day in a row, Ben and Blayne felt as if they were kids breaking the rules. This childish joy seemed to mirror the youthful excitement of their relationship.

It was the skipping of heartbeats and the rush of passion every time they touched. They actually held hands as they stepped into Mandatory's vacant halls.

It was more than puppy love though. Ben and Blayne actually were breaking the rules—Garret's rules and social norms.

They were both breaking their own rules as well—Homosexuality, married men, coworkers. But all those logical restrictions seemed silly now. There were things that transcended rules. There were always exceptions.

And there was definitely something exceptional about all this. There was something beyond infatuation and experimentation. It was as if they were discovering the truth. Every time they looked at one another, they felt a thrill deep inside their bodies and minds that they just couldn't put a finger on.

The two had barely been able to drag themselves out of bed. They hadn't been tired. They'd been asleep on and off since early evening. But there were restless distractions other than slumber that kept pulling them back into the sheets and long, slow kisses.

Once they had actually gotten into the shower, they were convinced that they would never leave.

The sight of warm water washing over bodies was torture enough. Rivulets poured down through the crevices of Blayne's thick, muscled body, flattening the patch of tawny pubic hair and gathering at the base of his thick shaft. They were both half-hard, and the sensations and sights rapidly put the situation on the rise.

Ben grabbed the soap and lathered Blayne's chest with both hands. He kissed wet lips softly. The water only emphasized the porcelain leanness of Ben's body. It dripped from his angular jaw. It coursed down his tight stomach, following his trail of fur. It slicked the peppering of dark hairs against the white skin of his runner's thighs.

Blayne pulled Ben to him. The soap and water between them let their bodies slide against each other in a brand-new way.

Ben's soapy hand clenched Blayne's hard cock, slipping up and around its broad head in breathless tickles of bubbles and fingers. He pressed his own long erection against the soapy shelf of Blayne's abs. Blayne held him there, running a sudsy hand along his ass, sliding a finger into the wet warmth of his hairy crack.

The room was full of steam and sighs. Neither of them wanted to catch his breath.

Fortunately for their careers and unfortunately for them, the hot water had run out suddenly and sent them gasping for air and scampering out to rub their goose bumps away with towels. In the chill of the moment, the shivers weren't the only thing to shrink away. But at least they got to work on time.

In fact, they seemed to have beaten Todd and Emily. Ben wondered if they were locked in a bathroom somewhere waiting for their water to go cold. It was an amusing thought, but not an image he wanted to entertain for long.

He was glad when the elevator bell announced their arrival and wiped his imagination clean of heterosexual shenanigans.

"Good morning, men," Emily echoed into the empty office.

The two of them spilled into the lobby all smiles and giggles. Emily had even set her hair free from its usual ponytail. And Todd had abandoned his crooked-tie look for a more weekend-casual tee-shirt.

No one mentioned that Blayne was wearing the same pants and shirt from yesterday. His jacket and tie were crumpled somewhere on Ben's floor. The omission of those articles and the detail of their location seemed to be enough of a disguise.

"Coffee?" Todd asked, holding out a third cup to Ben.

"Thanks."

He gulped greedily. With all the distractions of the morning, he had completely forgotten. The natural high he and Blayne shared had gotten him from the bed to the shower and all the way to work. But now it was time to get cracking, and Ben welcomed the scalding caffeine.

Blayne looked around the shady lobby at Ben and Emily and Todd as they sipped at their cups and blew at fragrant steam. Sunlight spilled softly across the floor to light their sleepy Saturday expressions. But there was also a glow of excitement and conspiracy radiating from everyone.

He had to smile to himself. Only Ben could have brought this dysfunctional group together: the office oddball; the wild woman; the boss' son and the handsome smart-ass.

They were quite a team. But it was the only kind of ragtag group of rebels that could ever hope to challenge Garret Brandon. Business competitors and government regulators didn't stand a chance. Only a bunch this crazy could come up with a way to beat him. They were the only ones crazy enough to try.

Ben looked up from his cup suddenly and realized that Blayne was the only one not sharing in this moment of caffeine-addiction.

"You guys didn't get the memo?" Ben asked sarcastically. "We're not mad at Blayne anymore. You could have brought him some coffee, too."

"Honey, we were never mad at Blayne. You were," Emily pointed out. "Maybe you didn't get that memo."

The two friends smirked at each other over their cups of coffee for a moment of silence.

"Oh, Blayne doesn't drink coffee," Todd came to the rescue.

"Really?" Ben asked. But he was looking at Blayne smugly, almost accusingly.

In Ben's mind, he was remembering what this handsome, rumpled man looked like less than two weeks ago. He remembered how Blayne sat stiffly in his perfectly starched shirt holding a full cup of coffee that midweek afternoon. Funny place to find a non-coffee-drinker.

"That was decaf," Blayne answered. He knew exactly what was going through Ben's mischievous mind. But no one else had a clue.

"What the hell are you talking about?" Emily said.

"Nothing," Blayne answered. "I don't drink coffee. Period. It makes me hyper. And then I make stupid mistakes."

He shot a sassy look at Ben.

"Well then," Ben said, "get the man a double espresso."

They all laughed even though Todd and Emily weren't exactly sure what was so funny. The one thing they were certain of, was that they had better not leave these two alone for a moment if they hoped to get any work done at all today. They may not have completely gotten the inside jokes, but there was no mistaking the playful looks these two were giving one another.

"Enough fun and game, boys," Emily said in her best schoolmarm/dominatrix voice.

She ushered them all into their shared office. She actually slapped Todd on the ass to hurry him along.

All bets were off. Everything was out in the open now. Ben leaned over and gave Blayne a peck on the cheek before they stepped into the sunny room. He smelled like Ben's shaving cream. And even though it was a Mandatory product, it made Ben smile.

The bright conference room had become their headquarters. Over the past week, they had made it their own with files and computers and notebooks and clutter. But today it really felt like their own little world.

The hollow silence of the rest of the building emphasized the sunlit warmth of their little space and their little group. Outside the window the city was sleeping in late on a Saturday. Families were getting ready to drive to the beach. College kids were sleeping off hangovers.

And here they were above it all, working. But somehow it was the perfect place. None of them seemed to want to be anywhere else. This was the last hoorah. It was like a farewell party that no one wanted to admit meant goodbye. Whether they succeeded or failed in Monday's meeting, there was very little chance that it would ever be like this again—working together, discovering friends, falling in love.

The four of them went about spreading out designs and charts and notebooks. Emily pushed a few buttons and woke the computers with electronic beeps and bongs.

"Time to get down to business, men," she said.

Little did Emily know that 'business' was going to be so much fun.

By noon the walls were covered in sheets of paper, and the four of them were in another fit of laughter.

Prints of the design from every conceivable angle were taped to the walls. And huge sheets of blank paper hung here and there between them.

They took turns scrawling ideas in marker across the white background of paper. Then they took turns laughing at each other's horrible concepts.

Emily's design looked perfect. There was no angle that wasn't flattering.

The burnished pewter was flawlessly shadowed and sculpted along its grooved length. The protruding bands at each end were rimmed in glistening, silvery beadwork. It was classic, timeless. It looked as sharp as the shiny blade it held.

However, the forecast for their brainstorm wasn't looking so good.

None of their ideas could compare to the design. The razor

looked amazing, but they weren't going to be able to sell it without an advertising platform. They weren't even going to be able to sell the idea to Mandatory's own board.

Creating a campaign, an image for this project, was the number-one thing Ben was hired to do. That was what he was supposed to have done for one of Garret's original designs. Emily's new razor was better than anything Garret had imagined, but it didn't have anything to do with Ben's job description.

Ben crossed out a list of words he'd been making on the giant paper. High-class. Classy. Classic. High-classy. High-Classic.

Now the words had two things in common: they all had lines drawn though them, and they all sucked.

The others in the room chuckled. That poor attempt didn't even warrant a full laugh. Then Blayne grabbed a marker, and they all burst into wild hysterics.

"You did not just write that," Emily insisted through her guffaws.

They all looked up at the paper through teary eyes. In blue marker, Blayne had written 'Stubble-licious.'

Todd was doubled over, bracing himself on his knees.

"Don't quit your day job," he said.

"Yeah," Ben chimed in, "Someone has to support us when we all get fired."

"You can always go back to waiting tables, Mr. Hotshot Ad Guy," Blayne said.

He raised his eyebrows and pursed his lips.

The laughter subsided just a bit. It could have been the mention of unemployment. It could have been that they were simply running out of breath. But there was also something out of place about Blayne's comment.

"When was the last time you waited tables, Ben?" Emily asked.

She'd known him for years, and she couldn't remember him ever mentioning it. Waiting tables wasn't the most uncommon job, but she just found it odd that Blayne knew something about Ben's history that she didn't.

"I haven't waited tables since college," he said. "And I have no plans to be a servant any time soon."

"You two went to college together, right?" Todd asked. He quirked his orange eyebrows together in confusion. They had mentioned the coincidence before, but since then it seemed to have fallen through the cracks.

"Well, we went to the same college," Ben said, "but I wouldn't exactly say 'together.'"

"Yeah, I have a feeling I'd remember Ben," Blayne added.

Emily chuckled. She shared Todd's confusion. It just seemed so uncanny. She watched the two of them together, and they were so comfortable and familiar with each other. All four of them were around the big center table now, but Ben and Blayne were practically in their own world. It was hard to believe that they had only known each other for a matter of weeks.

"Well, actually that's not all we have in common," Blayne continued. "Turns out we both have 'partial amnesia.'"

Ben was surprised to hear him say it. It wasn't a secret, but Ben wasn't going to mention the common detail. His amnesia was a usual and tired subject of conversation, but he didn't know whether Blayne wanted to share his painful memory, or lack of memory actually.

"You're shitting me," Emily insisted, always the lady. This was just too much.

"What are you two talking about?" Todd asked. He hadn't even heard about Ben's memory loss. Blayne certainly hadn't made his own public company information in the years Todd had been at Mandatory.

"Don't you think that's a pretty odd twist of fate?" Emily asked. "I mean it's not like discovering you both had the same English professor."

"It's not that unusual," Blayne explained, "and trust me, that's where the similarity ends. We couldn't have gotten our amnesia in more different ways. Ben was in a car accident. I was attacked."

The seriousness of his comments seemed to erase the doubt

that had been spread across Todd and Emily's faces. They couldn't dispute the facts, and Ben and Blayne simply couldn't remember them.

"Neither of you remember a thing?" Todd asked.

"Not for a couple months, no," Blayne explained.

"Every once in a while I think I do," Ben said thoughtfully. "But it's more of a feeling or a dream than a memory. At least that's what my therapist keeps insisting. A hell of a lot of good ten years of psycho babble has done."

"You, too?" Blayne asked incredulously.

"Of course," he answered, "but honestly, I think she's getting tired of the subject. She never wants to talk about."

"Really? It's all mine ever talks about. I was the one getting tired of it, and her. I actually just stopped going. Crazy redhead. No offense, Todd."

Todd smiled and brushed off the joke. He was used to it, and Blayne's fondness for redheads was not a big concern. Some people in the room didn't seem to have any problems with it.

"Wait, your therapist is a redhead?" Ben blurted out. "What's her name?"

"Dr. Carver."

"Dr. Melissa Carver?"

"Yes."

"Wow," Ben said, "I must admit, the coincidences are getting a little thick in here."

"Well, it must be her specialty or something," Blayne speculated. "I mean, how many amnesia shrinks can there be in one city?"

"For that matter," Emily added, "how many guys with amnesia can there be?"

"I guess we'll have to ask Melissa," Ben said. "Damn. Imagine the things she must know about us."

He looked at Blayne and nearly blushed. No wonder she had been so suspicious about Ben's love life. She must have known all along but couldn't bring it up and betray confidentiality.

"Well, I don't tell her everything," Blayne reassured.

"That's good to know."

They all laughed. They laughed it off. There wasn't really anything else they could do. There were no answers. Coincidences happen. People win the lottery and get struck by lightning. Sometimes it even happens more than once.

So Ben grabbed the blue marker from Blayne's hand and went back to the drawing board.

The rest of the afternoon wasn't much more productive. By the time they had finished listing every cheesy wordplay they could imagine, it was time for dinner.

When Todd returned with the bags of Chinese food, the walls were covered with phrases like 'cutting edge,' 'look sharp' and 'shaving face.'

When every oversized sheet of paper was filled with doodles and scribbles and crossed-out words, they called it quits. They were exhausted from laughter and frustration and unspoken anxiety.

"It's fine," Ben said as he dug into his Styrofoam container of fried rice. "It's good we got all the crap out of our systems today. Tomorrow we can really get to work."

"Might as well," Emily snorted. "If not, we'll have plenty of free time after Monday."

Todd laughed nervously and spilled duck sauce on his pants. No one was quite sure how entangled his career had become in this little group of dissidents. It was uncertain how their success or failure would impact his future.

But from the look of things, he was fairly entangled with one of the rebels at least. He sat about half an inch from Emily, and she reached over to dab at his stained thigh with her napkin.

"Don't worry. We'll come up with something," Blayne said. "Right, Ben?"

He patted Ben's leg encouragingly. It was reassuring the way Blayne mirrored Emily's gesture. They were both patting their men on the leg, showing support and affection.

They couldn't really fail. At the very least, it appeared two relationships would come out of this project. The razor's future wasn't necessarily so rosy. Ben needed to pair it up with a compatible concept before there could be any real sparks.

"Sure," Ben answered. "Tomorrow."

So they finished their spicy chicken and tangerine beef. They shut off the lights, set the alarm behind them and left the entire office reeking of Chinese take-out.

No one even questioned the division of the troops as Emily and Todd headed in one direction together and Ben and Blayne in another.

Sunday morning, when they arrived in the same configuration, all they said was 'Hello.'

Saturday was bright. Sunday it rained. Other than that, the two days flowed into one another. It must have clouded over sometime during the night, but as soon as the four of them got into their office the outlook appeared much brighter.

The ideas were coming faster, and a few of them even made sense.

Emily wanted to do an antique theme. She wanted Victorian boudoirs and golden lighting.

"I'm not so sure men are going to want to buy a razor from a guy in a wig and face powder," Ben said. "Call me a homophobe, but it's just my gut reaction."

Emily tossed her dark hair defiantly and pouted about how pretty it would be.

Todd was voting for a luxury barbershop scenario where the men are treated to a shave and pampered with the new razor.

"So is it a spa?" Blayne asked. "Or is there a barbershop poll and quartet out front."

"I guess it is a little confusing," Todd confessed.

He sat down next to Emily and waited for the next idea to hit.

Blayne was still a fan of the traditional Mandatory advertising. Nipples and muscles and steamy mirrors. He never said the word 'porn.' He said 'real-life scenario' and 'product demonstration.'

Ben wasn't so subtle.

"I like naked men as much the next guy," he said. "Well, okay, maybe a little more than the next guy. But I have a feeling that this market is more refined than your typical Mandatory man."

"But Mandatory has an image," Blayne insisted. "We can't stray from that completely. That makes no marketing sense at all."

Ben looked across the table at him. He was right. Ben knew that, and that just made him more attractive. A smart, strong man. His square jaw and wide shoulders were set and thoughtful. He was more relaxed here with them, sitting with his shirt untucked and his collar unbuttoned. Ben could see the soft, tan hollow of his throat, and even that vulnerable spot looked powerful. Ben felt safe and proud.

Maybe all the good ones weren't married. Maybe at least one of them was getting divorced. Maybe he'd even turn out to be gay.

"Okay, Mr. Smarty Pants," Ben smirked and quirked his scarred eyebrow, "then tell me who's going to buy this razor. Who is this guy? What is Mandatory?"

Emily and Todd smiled at the two of them. It could have been the cute way Ben and Blayne even managed to turn business talk into flirtation. Then again, it could have been Emily's hand resting on Todd's knee under the conference table.

"It's the same answer," Blayne said. "This customer and this company are both the same person. Mandatory is Garret Brandon."

Ben didn't argue. He didn't challenge him. He simply grabbed a red marker from the center of the table and approached a giant, blank sheet on paper hanging on the wall next to a poster-sized print of the razor.

He wrote, 'Garret Brandon is Mandatory.'

"That's for sure," Todd called out. "There's no avoiding Garret. He's a requirement all right."

The room exploded in laughter. It was the obvious joke that no one had dared to make. Saying it out loud was exactly the release they needed.

Todd was practically snorting for breath. He bobbed his red

head back and forth, tears spilling from the corners of his eyes. He never thought he'd say anything against Garret, let alone in front of the boss' son.

But Blayne was laughing just as hard. He knew the truth of the statement better than anyone else here. He was the one who knew it was so true that it shouldn't be so funny.

But it was Ben who stopped laughing first. He sat staring at what he had written in red and waited for the others to subside. He waited until Blayne took a deep breath and kicked his feet up on the table. He waited until Todd wiped his eyes, and Emily fell silently exhausted against his shoulder.

"And who is he?" Ben asked. "Really? Why did he hire me? What's Garret Brandon thinking?"

"'You can't win without an enemy,'" Blayne mocked one of Garret's favorite sayings.

"But he doesn't have to win," Be insisted. "He's the boss."

"He thinks he has to," Todd added. "And from what I've seen, he usually does."

"Men," Emily scoffed. "Don't you ever get tired of butting heads and bossing each other around?"

"Maybe it's what keeps him at the top," Todd said. "Maybe everyone's so afraid of his bark that no one dares to chance his bite."

"Or maybe his bite really is that bad," Ben suggested.

"He's testing himself and the company," Blayne said. "He'd do anything to protect Mandatory. He always has. Do you know what the name of this company was before he took it over?"

No one in the room went back that far. No one knew Garret like Blayne. No one knew his hunger and drive. No one knew that he had sacrificed his family to build an empire on after shave.

"Choices, Incorporated," Blayne told them. "'Don't give people choices,' Garret would say. 'Tell them what to do. Tell them what to buy. Be in control. Make it mandatory.'"

Something rattled inside Ben's head. He couldn't tell if it was a flashback or just the uncanny impression Blayne did of his father. It was as if he had forgotten something important or missed something obvious. He put his hand to his scarred brow.

Then something clicked. Something Blayne had said suddenly made perfect sense.

"It's about control," Ben said, almost to himself.

He stood and went to the sheet of paper with 'Garret Brandon is Mandatory' scrawled across it. Ben uncapped the marker, and above the boss' name he wrote 'Control.'

Then he crossed out Garret's name.

The other three looked up at him for a moment. They wrinkled their brows, and then they dropped their jaws.

"Control is Mandatory," he read. "Ladies and gentlemen, introducing the first razor from Mandatory, 'Control.'"

The applause was so loud that it was hard to believe there were only three people clapping.

CHAPTER 17

I t had seemed like a miracle when the idea struck them so early in the morning. But by the time the sun set on Sunday, the four of them realized that they'd bought just enough time for themselves.

The afternoon had been packed with revisions and preparations. 'Control' had to be integrated into every poster, ever printout, every sheet of paper that would be handed out at Monday's meeting.

Emily had practically gone blind incorporating all the changes on the computer. When the light started to fade from the sky, she rubbed her fatigued eyes and flipped off the glowing monitor. She popped the disk out of the machine as it hummed asleep.

"There you go, boys," she said. "I'll drop this off at the printer and pick up the posters in the morning."

Todd stood behind her and rubbed her tight shoulders. He had spent the day pulling every bit of research he could scrounge up on business men and megalomaniacs. Emily groaned at his massage. They were both exhausted.

"Go home, you two," Ben said. "Good work."

"Are you sure, Ben?" Todd asked. "Is there anything else I can do?"

"No," Blayne insisted. "Ben and I just have to integrate all this marketing information into the presentation folder. Your work is done. From here on, Ben is the show pony. I just have to groom him with some facts to back up his fireworks."

They said their goodbyes and peeled the sheets of paper from the walls. Emily took the old posters to show the printers what they wanted and to hide any evidence from prying Mandatory eyes that may want a sneak preview before the meeting.

It was amazing how much they'd accomplished in one day, especially considering the snail's pace Ben had been working at over the last week. Aside from incorporating the new name and message into the posters and presentation booklets, they had even designed ads to follow Mandatory's current campaign.

Ben was determined that this would not be the fluffy gay porn that had been churned out over the years for after shave and shaving cream and deodorant. But Blayne was right; the image still had to fit the company.

Emily had taken the classic steamy mirror image and manipulated it. The razor and 'Control is Mandatory' filled the foggy bottom of the ad. However, in the clear swath that had been wiped away with a hand, there was not a shirtless twenty-year-old model as usual. The reflection was an image of the perfect business man—crisp suit, perfectly knotted tie, his hand raised as if he had just wiped the mirror clean or dismissed an entire conference room of fired employees.

Only the bottom half of the man's face was visible. His expression was stern, and his shave was flawless. However, you couldn't see who he was or his gaze of power. Only the four of them knew exactly who was in that photo. They had dug it out of the company's archive of publicity shots. It was Garret Brandon.

Ben tucked smaller versions of the ad into the folder behind charts of demographic information and wondered if any of the board members would recognize the boss.

"I hope they still have energy for sex," Ben said as soon as the elevator doors slid shut behind Emily and Todd.

"I hope you have energy to think about something else for a change," Blayne said as he ran his hand along Ben's leg warmly.

"And how exactly am I supposed to do that with you right here?" Ben asked.

He leaned over and kissed Blayne. He felt the slight stubble of his upper lip and the soft touch of his warm mouth. It was just a small taste. They both knew there was work to do.

They were assembling presentation booklets: copies of ads;

marketing research; income charts; production estimate; shots of the razor from every angle.

Ben didn't know what half the stuff was, but Blayne insisted on it. He also insisted on having two copies.

"Always have a backup," he said. "You never know."

Ben stuffed the pages together obediently.

"Wow," Ben said, "I never really thought tomorrow was going to happen. Now I'm getting nervous."

Blayne looked up from his booklet with the softest brown eyes. He spent a moment just looking at Ben. He took his time just thinking about the short time they had spent together and the depths of emotion that had developed in mere weeks.

Ben did look scared now. He looked young and vulnerable. He didn't look a thing like that smart-ass who had been so brazen in the coffee shop. His blue eyes sparkled crystalline against pale white skin. His dark bangs fell across his forehead and made the contrast even sharper.

Blayne reached out his big hand and placed it gently on Ben's long, white fingers. He stopped the nervous motion of Ben's hand. He looked him straight in the eye.

"I can't be up there with you, you know," Blayne said. "Tomorrow is your job. I can support you some, but it can't look like I'm deserting the company to the board. It would all backfire. I can't look like a traitor."

Blayne looked so sad that it almost made Ben want to cry. It wasn't as if Blayne hadn't already given up enough. He'd rebelled against everything that had kept him safe over the years—his job, his company, his father, his wife, his life.

Ben didn't expect anything other than this simple moment. He didn't want more than Blayne's hand on his and those honest eyes staring at him. The only thing he could have asked for was a smile.

"You're right," he said. "You're better behind enemy lines. You can be my double agent."

Blayne smiled, and Ben kissed him. They finished assembling their identical booklets in silence as the sun finished setting beyond the transparent walls of the glass tower.

"Well, that's it," Ben said as he slid his completed packet into a manila envelope.

"That's it," Blayne did the same with his booklet. " You did a great job, no matter what happens tomorrow. Hopefully my father loves this company so much that he'll do what's right even if it means admitting he's wrong."

Ben appreciated the praise from a businessman as smart and experienced as Blayne, because he knew he was telling the truth. But honestly, Ben was thinking about something else. It was something he had forgotten about until now.

"What was it you said about the company before he took over?" Ben asked thoughtfully. "There was something about it. I just can't remember."

"Choices?" Blayne asked with surprise.

"There's something so familiar about it," Ben said.

"I doubt it. Choices, inc. was not a very successful company."

Suddenly Ben's mouth fell open. His eyes went wide with recognition.

"That's it," he said in amazement. "Choices, inc. That's the name on the checks I found in my father's apartment."

Hundreds of thousands of dollars had piled up in Pete Abrahms bank account over the years. All of those checks were issued by Choices, inc. None of those checks were written during the years that Choices was actually a functioning company. Mandatory had taken over years earlier.

"What are you talking about?" Blayne asked.

"Shhh!"

Ben's hand flew to Blayne chest to silence him. If the look in his blue eyes had been nervousness before, now it was sheer horror.

He looked over Blayne's shoulder toward the huge lobby window. They hadn't shut the blinds all weekend long. There hadn't been any need to. Besides, the interior of the building had remained in darkness as the daylight filled their room. They couldn't even see beyond the sunlight into the shadows there.

But now the sun had set. Now Ben saw shadows inside the shadows of the lobby.

Near the elevator banks, something moved. Someone.

"Don't turn around," he told Blayne, "but there's someone out there."

It could have been anyone coming in to work. People put in plenty of overtime here. This weekend had actually been quite quiet. But Ben had a bad feeling about it that crawled up the back of his neck. It seemed to crawl inside his head.

If someone was near the elevators, why hadn't they heard the dinging announcement of doors opening onto this floor? Who walks up forty-two flights of stairs? No one's that much of an exercise freak.

Shadows shifted out there, more than one.

"They're guarding the elevators."

Logically, Blayne should have questioned his paranoia.

But logically, they shouldn't be working all weekend to wage war against his own father. Logically, two people from the same college don't get amnesia, move to the same town, have the same therapist, work for the same company and then fall in love.

"Which side?" Blayne whispered.

"What?" Ben looked back to Blayne's wide eyes.

"Which side of the elevator banks are they on?"

"Left."

"Then we go right. Here," Blayne handed Ben an envelope containing their presentation. He took the other copy and tucked it into the back of his pants. "Just say 'me, too.'"

"Me too?"

"Not now." Blayne walked to the door and paused.

Ben saw shadows shuffling. He tucked his manila envelope into the back of his pants.

"I left the presentation there on the desk," Blayne called back into the room loudly, louder than he had to. "I've got to hit the john."

"Me, too," Ben boomed as he stood to follow.

The only thing left on the desk was a bag of leftover Chinese food.

They walked quickly down the hall. Not too quickly though. Ben had to concentrate to keep himself from running. He had to try even harder to keep from looking behind him. He could feel movement there. He could feel shadows. It was like something creeping in the dark, something he could feel but not see.

He hoped they liked fried rice.

Blayne walked past the bathroom. He opened the next windowless door, and Ben followed him into the stairwell. Now they ran.

Ben didn't know if he could run down 42 flights of stairs. But he didn't know what was behind them either. There didn't seem to be any alternative.

Luckily Blayne had another option. He stopped at the very next floor and quickly punched a code into the keypad next to the door. A green light flashed approval, and he pulled open the door.

"Where are we?" Ben whispered. His voice echoed in the hollow shaft of the stairwell.

Blayne led him into the dark forty-first floor, and pulled the door shut behind them. A red light flashed as it locked.

"The sales floor," He said as he navigated through rows of darkened desks. "Mandatory has four floors."

"Oh," Ben said as he stumbled after him. "Do they have the code?"

"That depends on who 'they' are."

Blayne's heart beat in his chest like a drum in a barrel. But he could swear he could heard footsteps rumbling down the stairs, even over the thumping sound of his fear.

He didn't know who they were or why he was so terrified. Something inside him just clicked. Something told him that being chased was the most horrifying thing that could happen. It was like a phobia he never knew he had.

He hit the down button on the elevator.

"They'll have someone waiting at the front door," Ben's eyes burned like propane in the darkness, enflamed with the same fear.

"We're not going out the front door."

Blayne kissed him quick as he jumped in the elevator and punched the door-close button several times before pressing 'P.'

The underground parking level seemed empty. Overly bright fluorescent lights buzzed and hummed loudly in the stillness. Each hurried step they took echoed their presence over and over again.

Blayne ran up to one the of the few cars in the lot on a Sunday night. It was a black and polished sedan with pretentiously tinted windows. The license plate read 'MAND2.'

Blayne fished the keys out of his pocket with jittery hands and prayed he had the right set for this company car. He selected one and the locks clicked open on the first try. He hoped he wasn't using up all their good luck.

He hit the locks again immediately once they were inside. Then he took a split second to take a breath. He heard Ben do the same beside him, and he put his hand over his for a moment before sliding the key into the ignition.

The engine roared through the cavernous garage. Now the clock was ticking. Pedestrians on the street would even be able to hear that echo.

He pulled up to the exit gate, just short of squealing the tires. He fumbled with the electric window. He fumbled with the keypad. He entered the code, and then they waited an eternity.

Ben tapped his long fingers nervously against the passenger's door. He looked behind them, beside them and back again. Finally, the gate lifted slowly.

They pulled onto the dark city streets.

"Where are we going?" Ben asked.

"I'm open to suggestions. But I don't think crossing the state line is going to help much in this case."

"How about another world?"

"Perfect," Blayne tried to laugh. "Just give me directions."

"Afterglow."

"What?"

"It's a gay bar."

"Fabulous."

Their conversation was cut short by the aggressive sound of an accelerating engine. Blayne looked in the rearview. Ben turned to the back window.

When Ben looked behind them, and it was like double déjà vu. The black car behind them was identical to the one they were riding in. He couldn't read the license plate, but he didn't have to. The recognition went beyond that similarity. He felt as if he'd been sitting here, looking at this same view before.

"It's another company car?" Ben asked. But he knew the answer.

"Why do I feel like we've had this conversation before?"

Pools of streetlights glistened in the rain-slicked pavement and flashed over the hood of the car as Blayne drove faster.

Panic gripped Ben. What the hell was happening? What did those people behind them want? And what would they do once they finally caught up with them?

"People from the company?" Ben marveled. "Can this all be about the design?"

"I doubt it," Blayne said flatly.

Despite the speed, he took a split second to look over at Ben. The honestly in those sad brown eyes was chilling.

Blayne knew better. Blayne knew Garret. He'd do anything to protect the company. And the company included the family and the family name.

What he didn't know was just how far Garret was willing to go. He didn't know what Garret was willing to do to keep him and Ben apart.

Garret seemed capable of anything. Blayne had never seen him reach a threshold. He'd never seen him give up or back off. There had to be a limit to his desire for complete control. There had to be, but Blayne didn't know where that line was. He didn't want to think about it. He just drove.

"Take a left."

Blayne cranked the wheel.

The car behind them matched them turn for turn.

The road opened up after they emerged from the maze of skyscrapers in the business district. The streetlights were farther apart. Regardless, Blayne switched off the headlights. He pushed the gas harder.

Ben could still see the headlights behind them. Whoever they were, they weren't trying to hide, and they were gaining.

He directed Blayne past projects, through winding turns and cavernous puddles. Every time he thought they'd lost their pursuers, they'd come to an open stretch of road and within moments the headlights reappeared behind them.

"Shortcut," Ben said. "Well, not really, but if we come from the back, they won't know where we're going even if they're regulars at Afterglow."

They took several turns between warehouses. It was getting harder and harder to see without headlights, and the streets here were little more than alleys dinged with potholes.

They passed vacant lots and even a few trees. This was not a section of town frequented by anyone but truck drivers and heroine addicts. At this time of night, no one was making deliveries, and even the addicts didn't want to brave the rain.

They took several more turns. Blayne saw the sharp corner and the guardrail too late. He never even saw the deep puddle that had gathered there.

He just felt the splash and the pull of the tires floating off the road. He felt the wheel go slack in his hands. He turned it uselessly to the right as the car scraped along the metal rail. The brakes seemed to make them skid even faster.

Ben gripped Blayne's thigh. He felt the tight muscle there driving the brake to the floor. He felt the car scrape harder.

They could hear metal buckling and grinding in those few second. Then the sound stopped. The guardrail ended, but their skid didn't.

The car flew over the edge of the banking. It hit the bottom of the deep gutter with an incredible thud.

Ben and Blayne were thrown forward. Seatbelts locked.

Airbags punched them in the face. Glass shattered. And the car finally came to a stop.

The crunch and tinkle of the smashed windshield seemed to go on forever. Everything went dark and silent except for that sound.

Ben didn't know how long he listened to the echo of the accident. It was a sound that seemed to reach back ten years. Maybe it had never stopped. Maybe it had always been there, quietly, in the back of his mind.

When the darkness of night replaced the darkness in his mind, Ben realized that his hand was still on Blayne's leg. He looked over and saw that Blayne's eyes were still closed; his hands had fallen from the wheel; a trickle of blood oozed from his nose and dripped from his upper lip.

"Blayne!"

When he got no response, Ben jumped from the car and ran around its destroyed front. He ripped open the driver's door.

"Blayne!"

He yanked at the seatbelt and pulled Blayne's limp, heavy body from behind the wheel.

Ben knelt in the wet earth. He held Blayne's head in his lap and wiped the blood from the divot of his lip.

"Blayne! Blayne!"

He rocked him back and forth. Tears fell like rain, and he bent to kiss Blayne's forehead. If only he really were Prince Charming.

Ben didn't know what else to do there in that deep gully. Rain gathered around his knees, and trash speckled the sopping grass. But the banking was high enough to hide them completely from the road.

Ben looked away from Blayne's beautiful face when he saw the headlights on the guardrail above. He heard the splash of water followed by the squeal of brakes. The car made the turn successfully. And it kept going.

"Blayne!"

The voice came from a million miles away. It came from years ago, from somewhere deep inside his mind and very close to his heart.

And before Blayne opened his eyes, he heard that voice again. He heard both their voices in a different place and time that seemed so close to this night.

'Those guys work for my father.'

'What?'

'The car behind us. It's a company car.'

'You're kidding. Why?'

'Daddy's little boy is breaking the rules.'

'So, we're being followed by hired thugs?'

'Or very loyal employees.'

'Your dad's a bit of a drama queen for a homophobe.'

'He's a little extreme, but he has the money and the ego to make it happen.'

'Like hell. Let's lose them.'

And then the night shattered. His mind shattered. That's the night when the sound of smashing glass started.

And now it finally went silent.

Blayne opened his eyes, and he saw Ben above him. He saw those teary blue eyes and the thrilling flash when their gazes locked. He didn't just see Ben. He recognized him.

He remembered.

Blayne kissed Ben despite his headache. He kept kissing him despite the fact that Ben's relief and concern erupted into shuddering sobs. They kissed among tears and rain.

"I was in the car accident," Blayne said.

"No shit," Ben laughed through his tears. He looked up at the crumpled hood of the car in front of them.

"No, not this accident," Blayne explained. "Your accident. At Terrington. I was with you. I remember, Ben."

"What are you talking about?"

"I wasn't raped, Ben. And you weren't drunk that night. We were being chased when we crashed, just like tonight. My father was trying to split us up. He found out we were together. We were together, Ben."

"We were?"

211

"Don't you see? It makes so much sense. The amnesia. Terrington. Everything about us. Can't you remember?"

"No."

And the truth of that word made Ben want to start crying again. It made perfect sense, despite its sheer insanity. And now Blayne was able to explain it. He could answer all the questions Ben had asked over and over again in the last decade. But he just sat there, confused and wet. He didn't understand. He didn't remember.

"You will," Blayne said as he held Ben tightly. "I remembered for both of us."

They clung to each other, wet and emotionally exhausted in the darkness. Blayne was overcome with memories: the first time they met at a party; dates at pizza parlors and concerts; trying to study next to each other in the library; the love they had made in the campus garden that night before they got into the car.

Ben was in shock. He couldn't speak, or he just couldn't think of what he should say. He had never been so thrilled and scared and surprised in his life. But he didn't know how to react. He was not sharing the flood of remembrance with Blayne. In fact, he was actually feeling jealous. Why had Blayne found the cure by repeating the cause? Why hadn't the antidote work for Ben?

He kept trying. He kept closing his eyes and trying to think back. He kept inserting the details. He tried to think of Blayne in the car. He tried to think of what their kisses had been like ten years ago. But there was nothing there. The inside of his mind was still blank. The only thing he found was the painful void of trying. It was like an electric buzz, a piercing scream that grated and whispered from a million miles away.

"It doesn't make sense," Ben stammered. "I mean it makes sense. But why? Why would he chase us? Why would he hire me and start this all over again?"

"Control."

And then headlights hit the guardrail again. This time they came from the opposite direction. This time they were going slower.

But somehow, they both knew it was the same car. Whoever was in that car must have realized they'd missed something. They were retracing their steps, and if Ben and Blayne didn't move it would only be a matter of time before they were found.

"Afterglow is just down the block," Ben said. "I think we can get there without going back to the road."

Sometimes it's good to be gay. Sure, thugs might chase you. Society may frown upon you. Fathers may disown you and cause you to have a decade of amnesia. But there's nothing quite like a good old gay bar.

Afterglow was quintessential. It had evolved with the times. It had a dance floor and a DJ who played the latest remixes. It shut down the bar and turned up the music at last call to transition to an after-hours stop for the tireless younger crowd.

But there was something timeless about it. It was tucked into a row of warehouses and supply companies. Half of it was underground. It didn't have a sign. It didn't encourage casual walk-ins. No one would even know it was there if he hadn't been told. It was the perfect hiding place.

From the outside, no one would have guessed that the dim bar was already packed. Men of all shapes and sizes pressed against the bar, ordered another drink, waited to press against each other.

Afterglow wasn't a place to discriminate. There was no type here. Business men and guys in boots stood next to pretty young things with pierced lips. Lesbians hung on the edges, dancing to slow songs before the beat took over and kids swarmed the floor.

The only people who wouldn't be welcome here were the types who chased two guys through the city streets with ill intent. Hired homophobes would be walking into enemy trenches if they descended those stairs. The added security should have comforted them more.

Ben and Blayne wove their way through blue lights and friendly gazes. They wiped back their rain-slicked bangs and shivered against one another. They pushed past bar chatter to the less-crowded dance floor and the slow pulse of early-night music.

Ben practically collapsed against Blayne. He held his head to the soaked shirt and tried to find comfort in the warmth beneath, the heartbeat under muscle. Blayne held him in an embrace of dance. They wrapped their arms around each other, placing protective hands in the smalls of backs and feeling the crinkle of manila envelopes where they had stowed their secret presentations in waistbands.

It was as if Blayne hadn't just been unconscious. It was as if he hadn't just had the biggest revelation of his life. He swayed strong and solid to the music as he held Ben's confused head to his breast.

He was overcome with everything: the memories; the moment; the feeling of reclaiming this love that he held against him now. He could almost forget the fear and the unknown.

He could take comfort in the fact that this wasn't the first time he'd been in a gay bar. This wasn't the first time he and Ben had danced. He could remember many nights.

The fact that Ben couldn't tore at Blayne's newly sensitized heart. He wanted to share all of these memories, these truths that had replaced all the lies and doubts and fears.

But those doubts were all Ben had. While Blayne felt love, Ben felt scared. He was left with a million questions.

Why had Garret done this? How had he done it? What exactly was it that he had done? And how had he and Blayne traveled ten years away from each other to end up in each other's arms rocking slowly to some haunting song about forever?

"Honey," Blayne whispered. He lifted Ben's head and kissed him softly. "It's going to be all right."

"I hope so."

His blue eyes looked so scared, searching for some answer in Blayne's reassuring gaze. Blayne ran his thumb along the dark stubble of Ben's jaw. He smiled.

"No matter what," he said, "we fell in love twice. That's all you need to remember."

Colored lights swirled across Blayne's warm face. They lit his sandy hair shades of gold and red. They sparkled in his eyes. And

Ben did love him. He was sure that he had loved him before. He couldn't imagine meeting this man and not falling head over heels.

But there was more. There were things more frightening than forgetting. There were things other than love that they weren't supposed to remember. Ben could feel it.

"We can't just live happily ever after, Blayne." He didn't mean to sound bitter. "They're chasing us. They chased us ten years ago. He's not going to stop. He paid my father off for a decade under the old company name. He put us in therapy. He told you that you were raped, Blayne. For Chrissake, what kind of father is he?"

"I honestly don't know."

And that was the most horrifying truth. Blayne knew Garret better than anyone. And he knew the things Ben was saying had to be true. He had no idea how far Garret would take it. He never dreamed he would go this far. He didn't know what, or who, his father would sacrifice for complete control.

"But I bet I know where we can find out."

The bouncer called them a cab and watched through the tiny window until it arrived. As far as he was concerned, he hadn't seen Ben and Blayne at all that night. But if anyone in a black sedan came around asking, he wasn't planning on being very friendly when he told them that.

"What's the address at Dr. Carver's office?" Blayne asked as they slid into the backseat of the cab.

"It's the middle of the night," Ben said. "She's not going to be there."

"Exactly."

CHAPTER 18

"It was a whirlwind," Blayne said.

The rain had stopped sometime while they were in the club. The streets were wet and shiny with puddles of golden streetlights. It was the cleanest this end of town ever got.

The backseat of the cab was dark. Irregular swatches of light passed over their faces as the driver headed from the warehouse district to the ritzy end of town. The trip wouldn't be long, but it would be enough.

They both looked straight ahead at the road. Maybe they were nervous of riding in cars. Maybe they were just trying to envision the past somewhere out there in the darkness. Blayne reached over and took Ben's hand without looking.

"It was almost as fast as this time," he squeezed Ben's fingers. "We met at this horrible party. Girls were puking in the bushes. Guys were doing keg stands. And you were your usual obnoxious and charming self. Somehow you managed to drag me away from all that fun. You kept me up all night over coffee talking about the meaning of life and religion and genetic metaphysics, or whatever crap angst-ridden college kids talk about. You waited until I was sober and exhausted and completely amazed with you. Then you took me to your room, and we fell asleep. That was it. Next to each other with all our clothes on. It was probably the most erotic night of my life.

"We did everything together that semester. Just a few months of passion and bliss. But it seemed so right. It seemed so right that I told my father. I sent him a letter and a picture of us tucked into my graduation announcement. It was a stupid decision made in ignorant happiness. But I don't think it would have mattered now. It wasn't my happiness he cared about.

"He called me from the office one night. He told me he had the perfect job and the perfect girl waiting for me after graduation. He never mentioned the letter or you. I hung up on him. That was the last time I talked to him before the accident. I think it was the only time I disobeyed him until you showed up again."

The cab came to a stop outside Melissa's office.

The quaint little street was deserted. All the shops were shut. The restaurants had closed. There were no bars within blocks. No one lived around here, because they couldn't afford it or because they could afford much, much better.

Blayne paid the driver and walked past the brass plate declaring Dr. Melissa Carver. The door looked more like the front door to a house in the country. It was wooden with windows and blinds. It was probably all part of the homey, psychotherapy décor. It was probably because there was nothing inside to protect. Just a room, a couch some books, maybe a few filing cabinets.

Blayne kicked the door hard near the handle. There was no deadbolt. There was no shrieking alarm. The flimsy lock ripped cleanly from the door jam on the first try. It barely even made a sound.

Ben wondered if there could be anything in there at all, as he watched Blayne step into the office. He followed him into the familiar space reluctantly. He just couldn't believe that answers were so easy to find.

Maybe Melissa didn't have anything to do with Garret. Maybe she really was an amnesia expert provided by Terrington College. But maybe Ben was just scared to find those answers.

There was something close to panic hovering in the back of his mind. It seemed much, much closer than any lost memory of happiness. He wanted more than anything to share those moments of youthful love with Blayne. But there was something inside him whispering that not all the secrets were passion and bliss. It echoed Melissa's warning to leave painful memories in the past.

Blayne switched on a brass desk lamp, and that small corner of the room filled with soft, gold light. The couch and the bookcases remained in shadows. The office where they had spent so many hours of fruitless therapy looked hollow and fake. So much wasted time. So many wasted years.

The filing cabinets were lined behind the desk. The rich, wooden drawers could have been part of the décor instead of receptacles for any clinical information.

Blayne looked back at Ben's scared face and smiled.

"It will be kind of like looking at your old yearbook."

Ben walked up beside him and faced the files. He slid an arm around Blayne's waist and rested his chin on his shoulder.

"Yeah. Most likely to have amnesia and a fucked up life. That should be easy to find."

Blayne opened the top drawer.

"There's no Abrahms," he flipped through folders. "There's no Brandon or Ben or Blayne."

"Young ends here."

"What?"

Ben was standing at the other end of the short row. He stood in front of the next-to-last filing cabinet.

"Catherine Young's files," Ben said. "I'm assuming last names starting with Z don't take up that entire last cabinet."

Ben shut Catherine's files, and Blayne came up beside him. They stood in front of that final filing cabinet for a moment, as if to catch their breath before taking the plunge.

Their faces were framed in light and fear, golden halos of anticipation. Ben's dark hair and Blayne's sandy bangs were fringed with energy and possibility. Their blue and brown eyes locked for a moment in resolute agreement.

Ben opened the top drawer.

Again, there was no Abrahms; there was no Brandon; there was no Ben, no Blayne.

However, there were dates. They opened lower drawers. Rows of years stretched back for over a decade. One folder's tab read 'Terrington.'

When they spread the contents out across the floor, they thought they might still have the wrong file. They stooped there in confusion, staring at the papers in the dim light, not knowing what they were looking at.

It wasn't what they expected. This didn't look like college memorabilia. They didn't even look like a therapist's notes. The forms were too official, with distinct sections and charts and numbers along the top and bottom. But they had Ben's name all over them.

"These are patient records," Blayne said. "They're medical charts."

There were weeks of them. Stacks of forms and long lists of medications that neither of them could decipher. The only words that stood out were 'broken rib,' 'minor bruising,' 'stable,' 'sedated.'

That word was repeated for days and days—'Sedated'—with no other indication of treatment or condition.

Then something changed in the progression of forms. Halfway through the pile, there was a single stack of papers clipped together. Blayne's name was on top.

'Severe head trauma.' 'Critical.' 'Major concussion.' 'Coma.'

From these forms, it certainly seemed that Blayne had been in much worse condition than Ben. However, for every day the word 'coma' was written on his chart, the word 'sedated' was scrawled on Ben's.

"Why would they have kept me sedated in stable condition?" Ben asked.

"I don't know."

Blayne scowled at the forms as if he could decipher all the medical jargon if he just concentrated.

Ben rubbed his temples. He let his thumb pass over his scar again and again. No wonder he didn't remember. He had been drugged out of his mind for days. Those drug cocktails were much more potent than anything that could have led to drunk driving.

But there was something else lying under his scar that ached with fear. There was something other than the accident and their relationship that Ben had forgotten.

He looked back to Blayne's fingers flipping through pages.

After several days Blayne had stabilized, but the coma appeared to drag on for a solid week. When that word finally stopped appearing on the charts, a new word took its place.

'Amnesia.'

Then it appeared he had been thrown straight into therapy. Actually, it seemed he had been thrown on a plane first and shipped back home. Those were the first groggy memories he had. As soon as Blayne's eyes had opened, someone made sure they never caught sight of Ben Abrahms again.

That's where Blayne's charts stopped. Despite the severity of his condition, his records were contained within a neat little packet in the middle of the folder.

But that was just the beginning of Ben's forms. It was just the beginning of long, complicated lists of medications and treatments. It was just the beginning of the horror.

"Oh my God," Blayne whispered. "What did they do to you?"

Ben saw the same thing, but he couldn't bring himself to speak. He couldn't find the words. He rubbed his scar and felt the throbbing pain of his dreams and flashbacks flood over him. The searing screech of high-pitched electricity boomed in his mind.

All these years he had thought he was catching glimpses of his lost life. He thought the pain and fear were tied to the accident. He thought the darkness was just the absence of memory.

All these years, he had thought he actually wanted to remember.

'Shock therapy.' 'Isolation chamber.' 'Surgery.'

Pain screamed through his memory. Panic seized his heart, took his breath.

Blayne flipped through pages faster and faster. It was all a blur, like falling rain or shattered glass. It was like sand pouring uncontrollably through an hourglass, time slipping through his hands.

A picture fell from the folder upside down onto the carpet.

Ben grabbed it quickly, holding on for dear life. He turned the photo over and let out a long, choking sob.

"Don't look, Ben."

Blayne imagined horror. He imagined surgery, a shaved head, a metal table with straps. Then he watched Ben lose control, pouring tears and clutching the picture protectively to his chest.

For all Blayne's childish, romantic memories he had discovered, Ben had nothing but pain. Now Blayne wanted more than anything to take that pain away. He wished they had never come here. He wished they had gone along blissfully with their new romance. He wished they hadn't reopened the scars of the past. He wished he hadn't even remembered.

"Were we ever that young?" Ben said hoarsely.

He put the photo on the floor. Ben and Blayne stared up at themselves from some beach years ago, tan and young and smiling. Their arms were around each other. Their entire world was happiness.

"I remember."

"You do?" Blayne's eyes lit in that dim room.

"Perhaps not as much as you. Not as clearly," he said. "But I remember this. I remember us, the way you felt and the newness of everything. Those months are coming into focus, like feelings and snapshots of moments."

"Ben, I'm so sorry," Blayne looked down at the piles of medical forms.

"No. None of that matters now," Ben put his hand on Blayne's thigh. "It's all worth it for this. For us."

They fell into each other's arms there sitting on the floor. Their embrace was so tight that there wasn't even space to kiss. They just clung to each other, cheeks pressed together, listening to breath against their ears.

They reveled in the reality of the moment. They clutched the solid fact of one another. They were together, complete, memories and all.

The phone clanged so loudly from the desk that it made them jump. The ring echoed throughout the shadowy office.

"We've got to get the hell out here."

They stood quickly, kicking pages of medical information and torture across the floor.

"Hello."

They froze when they heard Melissa answer the phone.

And it was a good thing they did, because as she stepped from the shadows she pointed a gun directly at them. Her aim didn't waver as she spoke into the receiver.

"Yes, I'm here."

Her red hair was in wild disarray. Her eyes were wide. She didn't even look directly at them, but they could tell she was watching. She must have been watching from the dark this entire time.

"Of course. I expect you to come. I can't do this all by myself," she snapped into the phone.

Ben and Blayne stood in silence. They held their breath and each other's hand. They stared into the barrel of her gun.

"You can see for yourself when you arrive," she said. "The files are still here."

She glanced at the littered floor nervously. Then she looked up and looked them straight in the eye.

"I panicked," she said. "I forgot my keys after you called. I had to break in. That's why the alarm was tripped."

Ben looked to the doorway, confused. He saw a small console blinking beside the door. The red light bounced off Melissa's red hair in the dark.

"Why would they come here?" she scoffed at the person on the line. "Even if they are together, there is no way they could have remembered. Trust me. I'm the only one who knows what they're thinking."

Melissa lowered the receiver and the gun.

"Don't go," she said softly. "I'm sorry about the gun. I didn't know what else to do. You had to stay. You have to listen."

They didn't know what to say. They didn't know if they should even believe her. How many lies could she tell? How many lies had she told them over the years? Were they just standing there waiting for whoever had been on the phone to show up?

"It was the worst mistake I ever made," she said. "Going along with them. Thinking I could clean up this mess. For almost ten years, you two have been my therapy. I thought if I could get you beyond it, make you truly forget it and move on, then maybe I could forget it all, too. But I can't. And I can't make up for it."

"Just tell us what we're up against," Blayne said.

"Just tell us the truth," Ben added.

Melissa looked across the desk at them. She looked absolutely terrified. But somewhere under her fear, there was a look of relief. She looked amazed and scared and delighted to be done with lying. Now she saw the truth, the two of them together again, holding hands after all these years.

"I don't really know," she answered. "All this time I thought there was something more important than the truth. And I was wrong. I bought into their lies and bribes and promises. I accepted veiled threats from people I admired. Doctors and professors. I never even met him until I was too far into it. I honestly don't know what would have happened if I'd said no. In a way, I really thought I was protecting you."

"How?" Ben couldn't hide his disbelief. Fear and curiosity were the only things holding his anger back. They needed answers and they needed to make it through tonight.

"They just would have found someone else," she said. "The damage had already been done. I didn't think therapy could undo all that. I didn't think I could undo it. And honestly, I didn't know what would have happened if I could."

She looked at her feet for a moment. She didn't have time to pause, to make things easy. She looked up at Ben quickly and swallowed hard.

"No one ever said it," she continued, "but they would have killed you. If Blayne had died, if he'd just remembered you when he woke. His amnesia saved your life. If they hadn't been able to recreate it in you. Those treatments alone, those experiments, they could have killed you. I don't know why they insisted on trying. I guess they thought it made them something better than murderers."

"No," Blayne said. "It's something much worse."

"Control," Ben finished the thought, the truth. "Control is Mandatory. Our minds. Our lives. Everything."

The three of them stood in silence. They could feel time tick by. They could sense the night passing and danger approaching.

"No one can control everything," Melissa said. "You two have proven that. Leave. Don't go home. Don't tell me where you're going. I don't know what he'll do. All I can tell you is just love each other. It's the one thing he's afraid of. It's the one thing he's never been able to do."

Before they ran through the busted door, they paused again in silence. As they held hands, Ben and Blayne both reached up to touch Melissa on opposite shoulders. They didn't have time to smile. They didn't have time to decide whether they should thank or forgive her. They just acknowledged the truth she had handed them and left her to clean up the files.

They poured into the night and the darkness. They prayed it was dark enough to hide them from hate.

CHAPTER 19

Y ou two have the most amazing bodies," the tailor said as
     he took measurements and stuck pins. "Strictly speaking
     as a designer, of course. Broad and muscular. Tall and lean.
You're like two completely different athletes. In the right suits,
you'd make a beautiful pair."

"Thank you, Maurice," Blayne tried not to blush.

He and Ben just stood there obediently with their arms
outstretched and their legs spread. It was kind of like being frisked,
except for the fact that Maurice was a diminutive tailor instead of
a burly cop.

The exclusive little shop had large, sunny windows that opened
onto a trendy city street. It wasn't the first place that came to mind
when they thought of hiding out. However, when they staggered by
his front door at dawn, the little man was already bustling around
inside. Blayne had been coming to Maurice for years, and he was
more than willing to open his shop early for his favorite customer
and a handsome friend.

After all, they couldn't show up to the big presentation wearing
their weekend casuals. Not only were they the furthest things from
power suits; their jeans and shirts were covered in grease and grass
stains and mud.

Ben and Blayne had alternately found themselves in parks
and alleys and all-night diners. They never spotted another black
company car that night. But every time some bum emerged from
the shadows or the summer wind blew across manicured gardens,
they had grabbed each other's hand and moved on.

It could have almost been romantic. There were roses in the
park, moonlight on the river; the breeze was warm and fragrant with

summer. For moments when they dozed under a tree or kissed softly in the embrace of darkness, it was tender and exciting. It was like that night at Terrington in the garden. That night they had made love before the accident. That night they both now remembered.

And that memory was what had kept them from losing themselves in the romance of the evening. That was the fear that had kept them jumping at shadows and running from one hiding place to the next.

So as the sunrise crept across the marble floor of Maurice's shop, Ben and Blayne felt completely wild-eyed and out of place in these designer suits. Their fear and determination were stronger stimulants than any caffeinated product.

"I only wish I had time to make custom suits for you two men," Maurice whimpered as he whisked at the sharp lines of fabric.

It was a ridiculous expectation at this hour and an even more ridiculous complaint. Every suit in this shop had been made by the little man, and they were all flawless. The fact that these two suits had been fitted precisely to their bodies instead of built directly onto them from scratch was irrelevant.

Despite their wired expressions and stubbled faces, they looked amazing.

Ben's suit was the deepest charcoal, all but black. Its four buttons fitted the jacket high and lean to his breastbone. It left just enough space for the electric blue of his tie to highlight his eyes.

Blayne looked more dapper than ever in his slate, double-breasted suit. It emphasized the V from his wide shoulders to his narrow waist. And his pale blue tie both echoed the gray of his jacket and complemented the color of Ben's.

They matched subtly and perfectly. No one would ever know they were together. But if they were standing side by side, there was no mistaking that they'd make the most handsome couple in the world.

"Thank you so much, Maurice," Ben said as they shook hands. "They're beautiful. I'll keep you in mind for the wedding."

They laughed as they rushed out the door into the morning

light. The meeting wasn't for a couple of hours, but they had gotten too used to running to slow down now.

However, neither of them ever thought of running away. They never considered skipping this meeting and evading Garret Brandon all together. They knew it just wasn't possible. Garret Brandon was Mandatory.

For all they knew, he could have an army waiting for them at the office. But if they didn't show up, he'd definitely have an army after them again soon. Garret just wouldn't give up.

But neither would Ben and Blayne. They weren't about to let him win without a fight. This wasn't just about a razor. It wasn't about business. This was about control.

Once and for all, Ben and Blayne were going to have to determine who was in control of their lives.

***

They paused in the shaving aisle of the drugstore. They stared at all the products and packages. Then they laughed nervously when they realized they didn't even have enough combined cash left to buy shaving cream produced by Mandatory.

Blayne reached out and grabbed a competitor's can that didn't look much different than the Mandatory version sitting next to it. He had enough money left over to pick up a couple discount razors to go with it.

"Garret hates this company," he said. "They make more money than he does."

***

In the mall restroom, the two of them were quite a sight—two men in expensive suits lathering their faces side by side in a public bathroom.

Before Blayne ripped open the plastic packaging of the razors, he flipped it over and examined the back. He took the manila envelopes they had been carrying all night and piled them on the bright countertop between sinks. Then he pulled a pen from his pocket.

"Just in case," he said.

He wrote the competitor's address across the front of the envelope, and he reached over and tucked it into the into the back of Ben's pants under the flare of his sleek jacket. He patted the curve of Ben's backside through the expensive material and smiled.

"Always have a back-up."

They looked in the mirror and winked at each other as they shaved. They tried not to be nervous as they scraped the stubble from their faces and thought about the day ahead of them.

Neither of them knew what to expect. It could be a trap. It could be business as usual. They didn't know what Garret knew. They didn't know how much he suspected.

But they did know the truth. And the one thing they knew for certain was they couldn't be afraid of him.

Everyone else played that role quite well. Everyone feared the big boss, and they had good reason to. Garret was a heartless business man, and that was only half the story.

However, Ben and Blayne had stopped cowering before the boss a week ago. Ben had stood up to him at their first meeting. And Blayne had finally stood up to his father after all these years.

Today, the trick was keeping up that cocky defiance. If they were suddenly afraid, he would know something had changed. He would know something was going on, if they showed the slightest sign of knowing the truth.

Because everyone else's fear was rooted somewhere in respect. But Ben and Blayne had more reason than any of them to be afraid, and that's why they couldn't be. They knew what he was capable of. They remembered.

They looked at each other, handsome and clean-faced in the mirror. They took a collective breath.

"We've been living a lie for a decade," Blayne said to Ben's reflection. "We can do it for one more day."

"This has got to be the best lie we ever tell."

***

"Good morning, ladies and gentlemen," Ben said to the audience.

There must have been thirty people in the conference room. These were the stuffed shirts and the stuffy blouses he had to impress. The board. The investors. These were the people who were waiting for him to fail so that they could feel justified supporting Garret's decision.

There were familiar faces sprinkled throughout the crowd, but they weren't really any comfort to Ben.

Garret sat front and center, scrutinizing, holding court. He looked so stony and resolute that he could have been the mastermind behind some evil empire or the boss of a successful company, or both.

Jeanette was right there beside him, looking cold and harsh. Ben had hoped she'd returned to England, but he wasn't surprised to see her. He knew she would have flown around the world to watch him fall. It was also no surprise that she sat completely across the room from her husband, soon-to-be-ex. She hadn't even glanced over when he entered the room.

Blayne had arrived twenty minutes before Ben. That was the plan. They weren't together. They didn't know anything. Everything was going according to plan. And as long as Garret thought it was his plan and not theirs, everything would be fine.

Emily and Todd huddled in the corner closest to the door. They smiled and winked and gave silent encouragement from across the room. Todd's tie was on straight, and Emily had even committed the ultimate self-betrayal of wearing a skirt.

They were completely oblivious to the drama of last night, and Ben was glad. They had been here early. They had hung posters and charts and covered them with blank sheets for the unveiling.

Ben was to have them spared last night's scare. But the fact that no one had intercepted Emily and Todd, the fact that the posters and printouts had been left undisturbed at the print shop all night long, only emphasized the frightening truth that all this had nothing to do with the razor. This project may have meant millions to every other person in this room, but Garret was willing to risk it all to destroy what Ben and Blayne had discovered.

Ben smiled.

"Sorry I'm late, folks," he said. "But I had quite an exciting night."

A few people in the audience managed to look vaguely interested. But they all had meetings and deadlines and better things to do than listen to this guy's bad jokes and awkward icebreakers.

"But I'll tell you something," he went on. "I already know you're going to love this product. Because whoever broke into the office yesterday and chased us all over town certainly seemed interested."

That perked the audience up a bit. A murmur rippled through the crowd. Emily and Todd looked completely horrified from their corner. If they only knew.

Ben could swear he even heard a couple people breathing out there now. The Ice Queen herself managed to look concerned. Jeanette wrung her hands. She looked as if she'd be glad to be back in London, divorced from this entire situation.

Garret didn't blink. He looked stoic, suspicious, free of guilt.

"Sorry about the car, Garret. But don't worry. I assure you no one outside this room has seen a single page of this."

With that, Ben pulled the report from its envelope. He held it up for a moment, just for effect. Then he laid it and the blank envelope down in front of Garret. Ben felt the crinkle of the back-up copy in his waistband every time he took a step.

He smoothed his jacket and checked his buttons. The precise lines of the dark fabric emphasized his slender frame and concealed the hidden package perfectly.

The idea that the competition would send burglars to steal their razor was pretty farfetched. But it was all Ben could come up with, and it wasn't nearly as unbelievable as the truth. If Ben had failed to mention their wild adventure, Garret might suspect that the seal of amnesia had sprung a leak.

Ben didn't give Garret another minute to contemplate that possibility. He turned and removed the sheet covering an oversized poster on the wall behind him. He revealed a four-foot image of the razor for the first time.

In all the excitement and horror and hard work, Ben had forgotten the effect Emily's design had. It was unexpected and sophisticated and beautiful. It was perfect.

Everyone on the board was there to do what Garret wanted. They were all waiting for his approval, his permission to like the design. However, that fact couldn't stop their immediate reaction.

The wave of sounds that flowed through the audience was overwhelmingly positive. 'Ooh.' 'Ah.' 'Hmm.' 'Oh.'

The heavy metal. The dark grooves. The solid lines. Ben let the masculine beauty of the razor speak for itself for a few moments. Then he went in for the second punch before they could catch their breath.

"Allow me to introduce Mandatory's first razor," he paused, "Control."

Immediately he unveiled a second poster. The buttoned-up torso of a business man was reflected out at the audience from a steamy mirror. The razor was positioned prominently in the ad, as was the tagline.

"Control is Mandatory," Ben read.

A few people nodded their heads silently. Todd and Emily smiled. Garret sat motionless.

Ben didn't wait for objections or acceptance. He dove right into his argument. He talked numbers and demographics and competitive marketing. He put up charts and graphs to support the flair with solid facts.

Ben wondered if the board members recognized Garret in the ad. Only a small portion of his jaw showed, and it was fairly obscured in the steamy mirror. It was more likely that they identified him from the description of Control's intended purchaser.

People even shot glances in Garret's direction as Ben explained the consumer profile.

"Rich, powerful, demanding, ruthless," he continued. "This man will do absolutely anything to be in control. The only way to sell him anything is to make him believe you're helping him do that, you're helping him stay in control because he's even controlling you.

"Control is not an option. And this razor is a requisite part of being in control. Control is Mandatory."

Ben paused. He looked out at the audience. If he and Emily and Todd had done their jobs correctly, there shouldn't be a problem. These were exactly the type of people Control had been designed for. Ben wouldn't be surprised if some of these tight-bunned women started shaving their legs and pits with this razor.

But like everything else in life, the truth of the matter didn't matter half as much as the perception. These people would do whatever Garret wanted, no matter what they truly believed.

The entire room waited for the boss to speak, to give his blessing or his curse. But there was one person in the audience who was tired of Garret's life-or-death power.

"It seems a little heavy-handed to me," Blayne said. He broke the silence. "Using the company name like that. It makes the entire image of Mandatory seem... well, bossy."

"That's who these people are," Ben shot back with perfect contempt. "They're bosses, businessmen, management. You don't lay down this kind of cash for a razor if you work in the mailroom."

He stared at Blayne. He noticed again how handsome he looked in his new suit, one foot propped casually and defiantly on the other knee. But he didn't let his admiration show on his face. He tried to glare. They weren't friends. They weren't lovers. They could play enemies as well any two businessmen.

You can't win without an enemy. If a battle was what Garret wanted, they would give him one. They would disagree with each other so he didn't have to. They would fight with each other to protect themselves from Garret and the truth.

"So you're bossing around the bosses?" Blayne asked sarcastically and wrinkled his brow in confused disagreement. "What's the logic behind that?"

"We're enabling them, empowering them," Ben explained to Blayne, to Garret, to the entire board. "We're telling them what they already know and giving them permission, giving them a tool, to be cocky jackasses. This razor is like a scepter. It's powerful and valuable simply because we say so. It's a symbol of control."

This time Garret almost seemed to nod. There was an nearly imperceptible movement as he listened to Ben argue with his son.

"That's just the thing." Blayne continued. "It has nothing to do with control. There is no special feature in this handle or this blade that improves shaving control. It's just a razor in a fancy package."

"And you're just a guy in an expensive suit with a close shave. But you get the job done," Ben answered. "What special feature gives you control?"

There was quiet, businesslike laughter from several areas of the audience. Then the room fell into complete silence as Garret lifted a finger slowly, as if he were knighting someone or condemning him to death.

"Enough, Blayne," he said. "Not a feature. A fact of life. No one buys your marketing numbers. Something deeper than that. Control."

With that pronouncement, the court had permission to erupt into applause. Somehow they were cheering for Garret, as if his clipped summation had sold them on the entire project.

Reluctantly, Blayne joined the clapping. As the audience broke into chattering groups of handshaking and back-patting, he shot Ben a quick, secret smile from across the room.

Garret never came to congratulate Ben directly. However, the excited buzz and encouragement from everyone in the room seemed to connect them all. People congratulated Garret. People congratulated Ben. They shook the same hands. It was almost the same thing. It was almost as if they were both playing for the same side. It was almost as if Garret weren't trying to destroy his life for the second time.

Emily and Todd worked their way through the crowd. Instinctively, they avoided Blayne as much as Garret and Jeanette or the plague. They left him to contend with all the big wigs and found Ben.

"Very impressive, Mr. Creative Head," Todd said as he shook his hand officially.

Ben nodded graciously and smiled.

"I do my best."

"OK, congratulations and all that good shit," Emily butted in, "But what the hell is the whole car chase thing about?"

"That's another story for another day," Ben said.

The smile didn't quite come across in his voice. Ben raised his scarred brow and gave her an exaggerated look that said more than enough. It said that there was too much to say and it was too dangerous to say a thing.

God, she'd never believe it all, Ben thought. He didn't even know if he could let himself believe that crazy past. But he had to if he believed he and Blayne had any chance of building a future together.

He closed his eyes and took a breath, just for a moment. But he took that moment to do something he hadn't been able to do for years. He closed his eyes and remembered.

He shut out the noisy business banter and called up a memory. He recalled a simple scene of laughing in the cafeteria with Blayne. Hysterical college stupidity and romance. He couldn't remember the joke. He could just see the milk coming out of Blayne's nose. He smiled before he opened his eyes.

"Well," Emily changed the subject brilliantly, "you certainly seemed to have saved our asses, I mean our jobs."

"So far," he said absently. "I mean, thanks for all your help."

They could hear Garret gloating from across the room. He stood at the center of attention.

"Production meeting first thing in the morning," he said. "No more waiting. Get this thing moving."

People nodded and concurred and did all the business bullshit they were supposed to. Blayne stood in the ring around his father and nodded along seriously. He looked at Ben out of the corner of his eye. He had absolutely no intention of being at that meeting in the morning.

Ben and Emily and Todd stood there and looked as professional as any of the business small talk going on around them. But they all knew there was something wrong. Despite the excitement and self-congratulatory celebration spewing from all these important people, there was tension and worry circulating in their small circle.

Ben was the only one of them who knew what it was about, and truthfully he wondered if there could be more danger bubbling under the surface. Even Emily and Todd had their faces twisted into expressions of concern. They looked so fresh and scrubbed in their fancy clothes. But under Todd's brightly parted orange hair there was a clouded scowl. And Emily's pretty face managed to look sad framed in her dark locks.

"Actually," Ben continued quieter, "I'm beginning to wonder if this is really the right career for me after all."

Neither of them laughed.

CHAPTER 20

Ben took the rest of the day off. He took himself and his fancy suit to the bank, and he took every cent out of his newly fattened savings account.

Thanks to his father's weakness, Choices, inc and Garret's dirty money, Ben had a tidy little severance package that would last years. There were more zeros there than Ben had seen in one place before.

But each of those dollars signs represented lost time. Those were years Pete Abrahms had wasted away. They were years that had been stolen from Ben and Blayne.

No amount of money could buy them back. Ben only hoped that there was enough here to buy their freedom and keep them safe. He hoped this tainted shush money could buy them time—new time for him and Blayne, a future to replace their stolen past.

By the time Ben returned to the job, it was hours past quitting time. The summer sun glowed orange and red where it sat along the horizon. And the office tower reflected the twilight like a disco ball in its darkened windows.

Ben walked into the building, past security and into the elevator without incident. Maybe things had blown over. Maybe Garret believed their little performance. Maybe everything would be all right.

There hadn't been any hired guns waiting in his apartment this afternoon. The place just seemed empty and spooky, and Ben couldn't remember if everything was where he had left it. He tried to tell himself it was just his imagination as he packed a small bag. He hadn't seemed to have accumulated anything worth saving over the past decade.

There hadn't been anyone following him when he stopped by

the travel agent and bought two one-way tickets in cash on the spur of the moment.

Ben triple-checked the location of the tickets in the backpack again as he watched the elevator lights count floors. Thirty nine. Forty.

He hoped it was all right to have rolled his expensive suit into the bag beside his spare underwear. Regardless, it was charged to the company's account. He was much more comfortable in his white tee and jeans anyway. The only thing he still wore from this morning was the manila envelope tucked into his snug jeans and under his tee-shirt.

Forty two. The elevator eased to a stopped, and Ben's stomach jumped with it. The doors opened onto darkness.

Ben saw a shadow shift on the lobby couch. Immediately he knew it was Blayne. He recognized the way he moved and the shape of his form. He must have been waiting there for quite a while. Ben only hoped he had gotten some much-needed rest while he waited. But he doubted it.

They ran into each other's arms without a word.

Blayne still wore his new suit, and Ben wrapped his arms under the jacket, along the warm cotton that covered those wide shoulders.

Blayne held onto him for dear life. He stroked his face with the back of his hand. He kissed the corner of his jaw. There was a day's growth of stubble there.

"Everything's going to be all right, isn't it?" Ben asked into the crook of Blayne's shoulder.

"Everything is going to be perfect."

They led each other into the conference room, their old office. Posters still clung to the walls. Images of their secret razor hung everywhere. No one seemed to think they needed to be protected from the 'competition' now.

"By the time they're having their production meeting and setting the assembly lines into motion, we'll be halfway across the country," Ben said.

"I hope they don't miss me in the morning."

Blayne peeled off his jacket and tossed it onto the conference table. He reached hungrily for Ben again, as if the moment it had taken to remove his coat had been another decade apart.

He kissed him deeply, running his hand along the side of his torso. He could feel the tight flesh under the light shirt. The sinew of his flat stomach. The solid breadth of his chest.

Blayne ran a finger along the circle of Ben's nipple until it poked stiffly at the white fabric. Then he put his mouth there. He kissed and chewed softly through the shirt. He felt the warmth of his mouth and the heat of Ben's skin meet through the cotton. He heard Ben's low moan, and realized he wasn't nearly close enough.

Ben pulled his shirt over his head, allowing Blayne to envelope the actual flesh with his mouth. He lapped at the hard nipple and tasted the salt and softness of Ben's body.

Blayne leaned Ben onto the conference table, cushioning him against the expensive jacket he'd just laid there. He kissed down his torso, from his nipple to the waistband of his jeans, following the dark stripe of hair that divided his stomach and dipped into his navel.

He nuzzled at that patch of fur as he unbuttoned Ben's jeans. The manila envelope fell to the floor.

Ben moaned again as Blayne's fingers released the pressure that had been building under his fly. He put his hands in Blayne's tawny hair and lifted his soft bangs so he could watch Blayne's face as he ran wide lips across the shape of Ben's erection under boxers.

Blayne kissed and caressed Ben's hardness through more cotton. He inhaled deeply the scent of soap and desire. Unlike Blayne, Ben had found time to wash the night's excitement from him.

Blayne ran his fingers along the length of boxer-covered flesh, defining its shape and size, squeezing the firmness of tonight's own unique excitement. He took the head of Ben's cock in his mouth, cloth and all, and he let his hungry wetness drool onto Ben's clean underwear.

He couldn't wait any longer. His own erection was throbbing

insistently inside his new pants. Blayne let himself fall completely to his knees, damn the wear he was causing his expensive suit.

He ran his hands along the down of Ben's legs where they dangled from the edge of the table. He let his fingers find their way under fabric, into the thicker hair where his breath had been trapped warm and moist inside boxers.

He grasped the naked flesh of Ben's rock-hard penis, and the intensified closeness of the anticipated moment drove him wild.

He ripped the boxers down, and the upward thrust of Ben's hips that allowed the underwear to be removed jabbed his long, straight cock toward Blayne's face.

Blayne took the bait. He swallowed Ben's erection as fast as he could, leaving the forgotten boxers around Ben's dangling ankles, shackling him there on the conference table.

Blayne inhaled slowly through his nose as he savored Ben's shaft. He had what he wanted, and now he could take time to enjoy it. He worked his head up and down gradually, following the trail of his own eager drool, from the head to the pool of pubes at the base. He ran his hands along Ben's thighs at the same pace, reaching higher toward his torso, stroking slowly at the trail of fur there.

His mouth continued its motion, feeling the tapered head of Ben's cock at the back of his throat and then on the tip of his tongue.

Ben arched his back, leaned into Blayne's mouth. He ran his own hands along the starched cotton sleeves that reached up his body. He found the warmth of Blayne's big hands on his flat stomach and held them there, squeezed them hard to emphasize the reality of the moment and this incredible sensation.

Slowly, Ben sat up, clenching the muscles of his stomach under their clasped hands and pulling his dripping hard-on from Blayne's lips.

Then he kicked the boxers from his ankles and wrapped his calves around the width of Blayne's back. He embraced him with his legs.

Blayne slurped his wet lips and empty mouth, and he looked up at Ben's smile above him.

"How could I ever forget that?" Ben asked him.

Ben grabbed the loosened knot of Blayne's tie and pulled him to standing. He kissed him and tasted the warm friction his of own erection on Blayne's tongue.

He bit tenderly at Blayne's neck and burrowed under the collar of his shirt. As he continued to explore, button by button, he discovered the day-old fragrance of man and night-long adventure. The musk and earthy richness excited him even more.

He tasted it on Blayne's smooth, tan nipples. He lapped it from the deep ridge between pecs.

By the time he had freed Blayne's thick shaft from his wrinkled new pants, Ben was covered in his scent and panting for a deeper taste.

He unhooked his ankles and released Blayne from the circle of his legs. Then he immediately rolled over, pressing the line of his cock into Blayne's suit coat and displaying his ass perfectly where he bent over the table. He braced his feet against the floor.

"In the backpack," he breathed eagerly.

Among the few necessities Ben had saved from his apartment, condoms and lube were on the top of the list. They were right there next to his toothbrush.

Ben closed his eyes and gripped the jacket under him in anticipation. He wrung the fabric in his hands as he felt the chill of lube trickle down from his tailbone. He pressed himself against the softness of the material and the firmness of the oak table beneath as he felt the rub of Blayne's thick shaft along his crack, spreading ass cheeks and lube and eagerness.

Ben waited. He held his breath as Blayne held his hips. He relaxed as Blayne pressed the fat head against his hole.

Ben could feel the coolness of latex stretched by Blayne's desire and enveloping his broad mushroom head. And Ben felt his own slow widening, as Blayne stretched him gently and Ben's own flesh enveloped the wide tip.

Ben exhaled. Blayne leaned forward and braced himself. He placed his hands against the table, on either side of the man under him.

In one long, restrained motion, he fed the rest of his shaft into Ben. He pressed the inflexible hilt of muscle and bone against Ben's spread ass. He held himself there, inside his lover.

Blayne waited, feeling the supple warmth within Ben and the taut ring cinched around the base of his cock. He ran his huge hands along Ben's back. He kneaded shoulders and muscles. He let his fingertips trail featherlike down the valley of spine.

Ben's whole body sighed. He felt the full size of Blayne inside him, and his every muscle shifted to accommodate it.

Then they both began to move. Suddenly the wait was over, and the entire room was full of steam and bucking hips.

Blayne leaned into Ben. He slid in and out of him eagerly, pushing into the space that had opened just for him.

Ben reached his arms out across the table. He splayed himself before Blayne, bent and vulnerable.

He was filled with ecstasy and this man. He widened his stance on the floor and raised his hips. He made his ass even more available to Blayne and welcomed the fast heat of entry, again and again.

Ben felt the bulging passion inside him, the sudden surge that spread the head of Blayne's cock even wider. He felt that moment like a shiver, when Blayne's clenched cock was at its fullest, its hardest. And it pounded into him several times before it found its destination deep inside.

And there it released all its tension. It burst its hot passion into the very core of Ben's ass.

Blayne leaned back, pressed into Ben. He poured all the passion and fear and anticipation of the past day into Ben's body.

And when his own body stopped throbbing, he grabbed Ben by the hips again. Instead of collapsing onto him in exhaustion as he should have, he raised Ben to standing and held him against his own sweaty torso.

He reached around and gripped Ben's primed cock, stroked it

slowly. He kissed the back of his neck and began to pivot his own hips again.

His motion rocked them back and forth. It shoved Ben's erection through the circle of his fingers. Blayne pushed them forward, beyond his own orgasm. He pushed Ben from behind and pulled him back by the cock.

He pushed Ben until he arched his own back and opened his mouth wide in a silent cry. Until he shot long spurts of semen out over the table, out over the fancy fabric of Blayne's new jacket.

"Sorry," Ben said as they crawled under the conference room table naked, as they covered themselves with the soiled remnants of Blayne's suit.

"I'm sure you'll find a way to make it up to me."

They cradled themselves against one another under jackets and shirts, under the conference room table and the cover of night.

They settled into exhaustion and their hiding place and waited for their last night at Mandatory to end.

Their eyes fluttered shut and their arms grew heavy around one another. Under the table it was like a childhood fort, one of those incredible places created from chairs and blankets and kitchen tables. From here they couldn't see the gaping windows of the glass tower or the city skyline. They could just see the protection of the table's underside, each other and the backs of their own eyelids.

Then their eyelids snapped open.

The night's silence was suddenly pierced by the dinging of the elevator bell. Someone was coming.

Ben and Blayne rolled between chairs and pulled on pants. Blayne stepped hastily into shoes, and Ben tucked the manila envelope holding the presentation into the back of his jeans. Over the past twenty-four hours, it had become an important accessory, like a good-luck charm or a wedding ring.

Their exhaustion and love and nakedness had cost them time. There would be no escape down the back stairs tonight.

By the time they stood and faced the door, Garret was already walking into the room. He flipped on the lights.

He stood there, still wearing his suit from the meeting. Harsh lines. Another red tie. He probably never took it off.

And although Ben and Blayne had managed to pull on most of their clothes, they still felt naked and exposed. They stood there under the fluorescent lights and looked expectantly at Garret, as if he were a real father catching them in the middle of some childhood scheme.

But he wasn't a father at all. He'd never done a single thing to support that relation. They both knew this man in front of them was the enemy.

You can't win without an enemy, Ben thought to himself silently. But you can't lose either.

"Disgraceful!" he fired his first shot at them. "After everything I've done for you."

"After everything you've done to us, you mean," Blayne said.

His voice grated with emotion. Ben stepped to his side and took his hand.

"We remember," Ben said, lacing his fingers with Blayne's.

Garret didn't budge from his post at the door. He wasn't caught off guard by the fact that he had just caught his son embracing another man naked. He didn't blink an eye at the news of their newly restored memory. His eyes were steely and cold, nearly as gray as his temples, almost as hard as his clenched jaw.

He was in control again. He may have bought their grand ruse this morning, but he had to double check their story. Every angle had to be covered. It had to be business as usual. And as usual, Garret was the boss.

"All a mistake," he barked.

For a moment, Ben thought Garret was actually trying to excuse the past ten years. As if car chases and shock therapy just happen accidentally. But the way he glared at them standing there together made it clear he felt no remorse. He had made no mistake.

"Never should have met," Garret continued with disgust in his voice. "Never should have made childish, rebellious decisions that needed to be cleaned up. Never should have made the mistake again."

There was no telling what he would do this time. What unimaginable lengths would he go to to clean up the 'mistake' this time? If his extreme measures hadn't worked before, what extremes would he go to tonight?

Blayne didn't care. It didn't matter anymore. The only thing that mattered at this moment was the truth of their relationship, the reality of love that stood in front of Garret.

"A mistake?" he scoffed. "It wasn't a mistake. It was destiny. I fell in love with Ben all over again. And even you can't control destiny."

Blayne pulled Ben even closer, slid a protective arm around his waist. Garret didn't respond. He didn't move. It was the most chilling reply he could have given. It said that Blayne was wrong. It said Garret could control absolutely anything.

"The only mistake," Blayne continued, "was having you as a father. Because you never were one. You were a boss. And a son is not a company. I am not another product you developed. Not any more. It's your company, Garret. But it's my life. You stole my life and gave me a lie."

"Gave you another chance," Garret shot back. The look in his eye was pure contempt. "That is not a life."

And by that, he meant Ben. He meant everything that should have been Blayne's life over the past decade.

"This is love," Blayne corrected. "After all those years, I finally learned to love, and you destroyed it because it didn't fit your narrow definition. But you don't even know what love is."

"Love," Garret practically spat. "Nothing but fantasy. And weakness."

"It can't be all about control," Ben said. He was terrified of the way Garret stared them down, but he couldn't remain silent. Keeping his mouth shut had never been his strong point. "You have to give something up. You have to be vulnerable. Love is a beautiful weakness. I have to give everything to this man and trust him with my life."

Ben put his hand to Blayne's chest. They stood there with a different kind of strength. Their solidity was their union. It was not the anger and hate that gave Garret his rigid stance.

"You never knew when to give up," Blayne added. "But I do. I have to know when to leave."

They took a step forward, challenged Garret's stronghold. And Garret actually stepped to the side. But his bitter expression said he wasn't taking their advice. He wasn't giving up. He was letting Blayne lose.

"Fine. Walk away. Run. Just like your mother."

Blayne stopped and faced his father, or the man who should have been one to him.

"That's right," he said. "I can't believe I ever blamed her. Can't you see? There isn't enough power and fear and money in the world to make people love you. There is nothing you can do to force people to stay."

They were out the door, pushing the elevator's down button. Blayne was never going to look back.

"You'll never see a penny of this company," Garret called after them.

And then Blayne had to look back, just to laugh.

"Keep it. Keep your secrets. Keep control," he said. "Never forget what you chose and what you've done. I can't steal your memories, and I don't want to. I want you to remember this for the rest of your life."

The elevator opened, and they stepped inside.

And that was it. After all this, Garret thought the worst thing he could do was to cut Blayne out of the family fortune. He thought taking away the company was worse than taking away memories. Mandatory meant more to Garret than anything, anyone, life itself.

Ben and Blayne squeezed their sweaty palms together. They looked at each other with a hundred exhausted emotions on their faces.

This was it. This was the beginning of their new life, their new memory. From this point on, it wasn't about reclaiming the past. Finally, it was really about building a future. Together.

The elevator stopped. But the panel above the door didn't say lobby. The number that was lit was thirty nine.

"Hello, darling."

The doors opened onto a dark floor, but there was no mistaking Jeanette's crisp, tight voice.

"What the hell?" Blayne cried out in complete bafflement.

"You didn't think it was going to be that easy, did you?" she asked as she stepped into the light of the elevator.

She looked prim and proper as usual. But somewhere under the tight bun of her hair and above the harsh pleats of her suit there was an unusual blush in her face. There was something daring there that said whatever she was doing was completely crazy.

Blayne couldn't remember her looking this worked up on their wedding day. He also couldn't think of a single thing to say. Ben just stared up at him in puzzlement.

"Think of it as my last wifely duty," Jeanette said as she hit the doors-shut button.

A moment before the elevator opened onto the lobby, Jeanette reached over and took Blayne's hand from Ben. They had no idea how to react. She smiled politely, and Ben and Blayne just stared ahead at the parting doors.

There were half a dozen men in matching black standing there. The smallest of them was Jeanette's weaselly, blonde lover. He stood at the head of the pack, chattering away on a phone in his British accent.

"Absolutely, Mr. Brandon. Not a problem," he said into the phone. "Here they come now."

Jeanette dragged Blayne from the elevator by the hand. She even managed a big, flashy smile for the crowd.

"Good news, men," she called as she strode right past the blockade to a car beyond the glass doors. "Now you can all go home to your wives."

They laughed, but there was a sound of relief between the chuckles. The weasel retrieved Ben from where he stood shell-shocked in the elevator. He placed a hand on his shoulder and patted it like an old chum.

"Mr. Abrahms and I have to go talk to a man about a severance check." the lover chortled through his accent.

Ben didn't know what to expect or what to do. He wanted to shrug that grip from his shoulder and pry Jeanette's claw from Blayne's hand. But something stopped him. He looked at the broad-shouldered thugs in black and the bulges under their coats. Those definitely weren't the kind of bulges he liked to see on men. They were slung low on hips and concealed poorly under arms and breast pockets. He decided Jeanette's plan was a safer bet than anything these men had in mind.

The blonde thing ushered Ben into a car immediately behind the one Blayne and Jeanette were climbing into.

The black, company cars were identical. However, when their engines roared to life, they headed in opposite directions.

Blayne's car took a right. Ben's car took a left. They headed down parallel blocks. A left. A right. At the next light, the cars met up again.

Ben could see the taillights of Blayne's car as Jeanette's lover matched her turn for turn. But he couldn't hear the conversation that was going on inside the front seat ahead of him.

"I owe you this," Jeanette said to Blayne. "I owe you this last chance because we never loved each other."

She drove in silence for a while. She followed the turns that Blayne pointed out. She looked straight ahead.

When she finally came to a stop in front of the windowless building, she turned to him.

"But if you love him, Blayne, you know what you have to do."

There was a tear in her eye. The Ice Queen had melted.

"I know," he said as he opened the door to leave. "Thank you."

Ben's car pulled up as Blayne closed the door on his ex-wife. They rejoined hands and stepped over the threshold.

"Two nights in a row, boys," Afterglow's bouncer said as they entered. "You're becoming regulars."

Ben laughed. He had to release all this tension somehow.

"I wouldn't get used to it," he said. "We're moving tomorrow."

Blayne squeezed his hand harder than he meant to. He tried to smile and failed.

"Too bad," the bouncer called after them. "You're an adorable couple. How long have you two been together?"

Ben and Blayne looked at each other for a moment. Their eyes locked, brown and blue. They knew each other so well. Now it was no longer a lingering feeling. It was a store of memories and crazy experiences that no other two people could ever share.

"About ten years, I guess," Blayne said.

"Wow," the bouncer remarked. "Impressive."

"It was a long-distance relationship," Ben joked.

But he didn't laugh. There was something in Blayne's expression, in the way he held Ben's hand as they stepped to the darkest corner of the bar. There was something in the tremor of his voice that kept Ben from feeling the incredible relief he should have.

"I can't," Blayne began. But he didn't continue.

He just grabbed Ben and held him close. He held him so tightly that it was frightening. And Ben held him right back. They squeezed the breath out of each other to keep the inevitable words from being spoken.

When they finally came up for air, the look on Blayne's face was even more frightening.

Tears hung to lashes and lids, brimming, waiting to fall. They were the tears that roll at the height of passion, at the moment of realization when it becomes perfectly clear that this is the only man in the world. The only one he could ever love.

They were tears meant for pillows, for caresses and soft kisses. They didn't belong here.

"I can't sacrifice you just because I love you."

Then the first tear fell.

And in the morning, Ben got on that plane alone.

CHAPTER 21

B en couldn't be as kind as Blayne. He couldn't just give up and let it all go. Even if his revenge was petty, he was going take it. It was all he had left.

The first thing he did that day when his plane landed was stop at the airport post office. He mailed an official resignation so Garret could read the postmark and know he had gone far enough away.

But he also did it to let him know where he was. If Garret wanted to come after him, Ben didn't care anymore. He may have run. But he was tired of hiding.

Before he left the post office, Ben put a manila envelope in front of the cashier. It was a little crumpled, but the address written across the front was perfectly clear. It would get to the competitor's offices without any problem.

At that very moment, Blayne was probably sitting dutifully in a production meeting halfway across the country from Ben. The entire board was making decisions and phone calls that would set factories into motion, jump start manufacturing and commit Mandatory once and for all to the production of Control. There was no turning back now.

"Keep the change," Ben said to the cashier as he walked out.

It may have been spiteful and childish, and it certainly couldn't begin to make up for the pain Garret had caused, but it was the first hint of a smile that had flashed across Ben's face since he had landed in this unfamiliar city.

**

More smiles came as the months passed. It doesn't take amnesia to distance someone from memories. They get farther and farther away all by themselves. Pain and fear dull over time, even if they can't ever be forgotten.

Love, however, is a different emotion. It hangs on for an eternity. It's like poetry or a sweet song that lives on through the ages and gets stuck in your head a hundred years after it was written. A hundred years after it got stuck in its composer's head.

Its rhythm and beat continue to whisper to you even after you lose the words. Ben had already learned that lesson. He had spent a decade chasing that familiar sound through the dark hallways of his mind.

But now his mind was dazzling with memories. As all the people around him lost memories every day, forgot in time's usual ways, he remembered more and more.

His memory came into focus slowly, like vision on a late morning after a night of even later drinking. The fuzzy images sharpened and cut their way through the fog.

His memory wasn't perfect, but it was college after all. He no longer had an entire semester lost abroad in some forgotten land.

He remembered meeting Blayne sometime around Christmas. He remembered how much easier it had been dragging him out of the closet the first time around. He remembered a million little things that had led him to this strange destination.

And now again, it was almost Christmas. What would that have been? Their eleventh or twelfth anniversary?

It was that last-minute season when every store was packed no matter what it sells. The drugstore where Ben found himself was crammed with people loading up on stocking stuffers or searching hopelessly through aisles of cosmetics and foot cream for that perfect elusive gift.

Ben had already found what he wanted. He held the plastic package in his hands and smiled down at it in disbelief.

The razor was exactly what he would have expected. It was exactly what Ben had thought the giant competitor would do to ruin the design, and he was thrilled. So were all the people who bought it.

Mass production had significantly cheapened the product. They named it 'Power' and molded its body out of grayish, slightly glittering plastic. The shape was the same. The size was similar. But its antique finish looked more like stripes of black paint. And it weighed about half as much.

Which is also how much it cost.

Mass production had allowed the competition to cut corners, lower the price, and get the razor on the shelf about a day after Mandatory launched Control.

Ben could see Control sitting behind glass, behind the drugstore's counter, next to electric razors and nose hair trimmers. It looked beautiful sitting there being dragged down by it's heavy price tag. But it also looked a lot like the bit of copycat plastic Ben held in his hand.

No matter how beautiful, no one wanted an expensive version of the poor man's razor. If they made mobile homes out of marble it wouldn't make them any more attractive to the rich and famous. Exclusivity was lost. Control was lost.

Garret Brandon would never be a poor man. But Mandatory was hurting financially from this punch in the marketing gut. It just wasn't the company it used to be.

And Ben had noticed that Mandatory was running new advertising for the old products again, hoping to rekindle their image with the classics. But they had made a few changes. Ben almost laughed the first time he heard his mutated tagline slapped on the end of an after shave commercial: "Because cool, soothing relief is Mandatory."

Somehow, it just didn't have the same ring to it. But they didn't stop while they were behind.

"Because odor protection is Mandatory," some guy insisted as he lathered up his armpits . "Because minty, fresh breath is Mandatory," another smiled.

Now that really stinks, Ben thought.

Garret had lost respect. He'd lost control. He'd lost even more than that.

Suddenly a man bumped against Ben in the crowded drugstore aisle. There was something familiar about the way that shoulder felt pressed against him.

"What the hell are you doing here?" Ben asked.

"I was just picking up your Christmas present," he answered.

Ben looked down and saw the same cheap, plastic razor in Blayne's strong hands.

Ben didn't know what to say. He couldn't believe out of all the drugstores in the world, out of all the people crammed into holiday crowds, that he and Blayne had ended up here standing next to each other.

He looked deep into those brown eyes. He noticed the playful way Blayne's sandy bangs fell across his forehead. And Ben wrinkled his nose at him. He cocked his scarred eyebrow at him in disbelief.

"I don't believe you," he said.

"Me?" Blayne feigned innocence and held up the competitor's razor. "What I can't believe is this. I can't believe we pulled this off, and Todd and Emily actually ended up working for the competition."

"You're changing the subject," Ben said. "You know Todd could finagle anything. He got her to say 'yes' didn't he?"

"Todd and Emily married," Blayne mused dreamily. "Now that's unbelievable."

"You followed me here, didn't you?" Ben returned to the initial topic.

Blayne didn't pay attention, or he pretended not to. He continued to stare off into the distance as if he were imagining what the wedding would be like or how Todd and Emily's new jobs were working out. But there was a smirk in the corner of his mouth that betrayed his guilt. He glanced quickly at Ben's condemning blue eyes and then back into space.

"I guess they didn't really have jobs to go back to," he continued his diversion. "And Garret couldn't prove anything. Todd and Emily were innocent. Besides, I'm not sure he wanted a lawsuit at that point."

"You little sneak," Ben accused.

Blayne's smirk got a little wider, but he continued to stare off innocently. He looked like a child caught peeking at presents. He stood there in his sweatshirt and jeans, a million miles away from the stodgy, starched suit Ben had encountered at the coffee shop.

Blayne swore that he was never going to wear a suit again. That morning months ago, his tie had felt like a noose, and his jacket was the only thing hiding his nervous perspiration.

He had shown up at the production meeting like a good son. He was a little late, but Garret almost allowed the relief to show on his stoic face when Blayne walked in alone and took his place at the conference table.

"We've decided to go ahead with production immediately," some bigwig had announced to him.

Blayne just nodded his head.

"So we're all in agreement on the subject," another concluded. "What's your position, Blayne?"

"My position?" Ben said to the room full of bosses and investors. "Sometimes I'm a top, sometimes a bottom. But no matter what, I'm always gay."

Then he had stood and left.

Every single person of importance in Garret's life was in that room. Every rich, uptight bastard and frigid, business bitch connected to Mandatory was left in silence around that table. And Garret just sat there.

He couldn't change the truth. He couldn't erase that moment from the memories of everyone there.

All those yeas and all that hate just to cover up one, simple truth. Having it spoken aloud so clearly, thrown out into the air without hesitation, was the last thing Garret expected.

There was no more enemy. There was nothing to fight about anymore. There was nothing left to protect. Blayne had thrown down his final weapon. He had surrendered the truth.

"I don't know what I would have done if you'd really left me," Ben said to Blayne's smiling face.

"Oh, you just would have forgotten about me all over again," Blayne said. He was trying to keep seriousness from seeping into the moment. But he couldn't help looking Ben in the eye and letting love creep into the corners of his smirk.

Ben closed his eyes to hold back emotion. He remembered that day, the day he'd left. He'd stood alone in that strange airport with his nerves standing on end. He'd sat in that terminal all day with his bag at his feet. He had watched that gate for hours, hours before the next plane was even supposed to arrive. It had been like holding his breath for a decade. Like waiting to remember his entire life. And then Blayne had finally walked through the gate.

"I hope you know," Ben said to Blayne right there in the drugstore with closed eyes, "when I close my eyes, I'm not shutting you out. I'm making a memory."

And Blayne kissed him. He held him close for several moments amid the holiday crowd. Then they both opened their eyes as they continued their kiss. This was one more moment they would never forget.

"Well now that you know about another one of your presents," Ben said, "let's go home."